
NATALIE'S WAY

A Natalie Grace Thriller

CHET BAKER

To my brother.

Tom

Love you man.

PROLOGUE

It's remarkable that I survived the day I was born. If it hadn't been for Father, who delivered me on the kitchen table right after breakfast, Mother would have probably drowned me in the sink and buried the body next to Rover and Fido under the old oak tree out back.

You see, my parents, Kendrick and Sophia, had a good thing going for themselves before my arrival on that rainy September morning. To say I was unplanned was an understatement. I dropped into their world as a gatecrashing, needy intruder landing in the middle of their comfortable, self-absorbed lives. But I never asked to be born. Nor did I get to choose who brought me into the world. Birth is a crapshoot. But destiny is different. It's based on how much hatred, paranoia, and abandonment one can take and still keep going.

Kendrick Grace lectured at one of the country's most prestigious and expensive colleges. With three doctorate degrees in physics, philosophy, and psychology, the intelligentsia showered him with honors and awards for his brilliance. But once I came into his world, he deserted his celebrity lecturing and dedicated his sole purpose in life to educating his little fireball.

I never saw the inside of a schoolroom. Kendrick home-schooled me with the fundamentals of reading, mathematics, and social sciences. Then came deep, advanced insight into philosophy and psychology. He was brilliant. And I was being called a prodigy.

Beyond academics, Dad and I were inseparable. We fished on Lake Champlain, cheered for the Reds at Fenway Park, and shot up fence posts and tin cans at the county dump. It was great fun being dad's daughter.

But teaching me the essentials of becoming a polished young woman, Father whispered tongue in cheek, were beyond his pay grade. So, he left matters of refinement, intimacy, and human reproduction to Sophia. She would be my advisor on female topics and relationship insight.

Mother was a stunning beauty. She also held a doctorate in comparative literature from Berkeley. She authored eight best-selling romance novels under a pseudonym to avoid public scrutiny of any parallels to her own life. The characters in her books were dominated by beautiful-looking people like Sophia. However, the narratives always focused on life's devious and clandestine side. As a result of writing such dark themes for decades, she had forged her mind into a pawn of hedonism with no perspective on how to advise a young girl on love, intimacy, and commitment. She couldn't teach what she had never developed in her own life—relationships built on love, dignity, and devotion.

Beyond their academic achievements, each indulged in their own peculiar ways that prompted tatty whispers from Middlebury friends and colleagues.

Kendrick moved through academic circles, quoting

Diogenes, Freud, and Jung. As a steadfast husband, he followed an unwavering moral compass for his marriage. Sophia, however, harbored darker passions. During her husband's absences, she showed up at midnight taverns, seeking pleasure in the company of sturdy, blue-collar young men.

It was no coincidence that I inherited a unique blend of their individual qualities. I grew into a rough-and-tumble tomboy with an IQ of 147. I grew tall and willowy and got mother's green eyes and black hair. Whenever I heard I inherited Mother's looks, I denied it and described myself as unrefined and culturally lacking. When boys contrasted my lanky body with Mother's curves...well... I just laughed. I thought of myself more as a twerp than a beauty queen. I was just a gawky budding teen, oblivious to the attention I increasingly drew from men, deaf to their suggestive comments and blind to their leering glances. It was Mother, in her fifties, who still stole the show with men.

In my seventeenth summer, I had the fabric of my character set for life. My identity, temperament, and mental makeup were well established. But it all came crashing down when I lost my innocence to violence in the backseat of a lawman's car. It shattered my perfect world and introduced me to an indignity beyond comprehension. Mother and Father had either overlooked teaching me how to deal with something like that or failed to understand the human spirit and skipped that lesson in my education. A piece of my sum and substance was missing. I became aware I was emotionally fragile, incapable of handling such an affront to my dignity.

Shame sealed my lips. That soul-crushing ordeal became a cross to bear as I matured. I forged an impertinent self-identity. Still, part of me was missing. Whatever it was, it sat at the intersection of intellect and something immortal, sacred perhaps? Spirituality? Was that it? Is spirituality merely a compass for the soul, a bridge between the known and unknowable, or perhaps just a control mechanism?

No matter. I had crossed the Rubicon sexually. The ordeal, however horrible it was, had opened my eyes to the power of sex. It affected me callously. I used it as a vendetta. Disempower men I thought needed it. At eighteen, I was promiscuous. Like Mother like daughter.

Two years later, I discovered the first two pages of a three-page letter hidden in Father's workshop. A woman's words hinted at intimacy. It questioned everything I had come to believe about Father. Was my birth truly unplanned? Was Kendrick the paragon of loyalty I'd always believed? The letter's revelations questioned my moral foundation and shook my sense of self-worth.

It was time to go. Leave the nest.

Kendrick had done what he could do for me. Nothing more to learn under him. I was fortunate to have a Father save me the day I was born. And educate me to be who I am. I knew my next education would come as a class in real life. Cold and scary. Out in the big world on my own.

I wondered what Father would be when I walked out that door. Thinking of him alone with Mother was frightening. But I had no choice. I needed to leave soon. Learn who I was.

As he watched me gather my belongings and prepare to leave any day, he hugged me and said,   "Cook up your destiny, Natalie. Do it your way."

When and how I left home that dark morning was a violent blur, fast, and brutal.

Sorry to leave you that way, Father. So sorry.

CHAPTER ONE

Vermont, 2018
Late September

I tear a label from an empty beer bottle and yell down the hall. "Hey. I need to go home."

No answer. I wait.

When the Oasis closed, hours ago, we wound up here to finish the flirting that I started with him at the bar. It was just innocent alcohol-laced teasing. Now with him finished with me, here I sit in this drafty old, neglected farmhouse in nothing more than this sweat-soaked t-shirt that I refused to take off for him last night.

Probably the only thing you refused him.

Empty beer bottles litter this rickety old kitchen table where his gone and forgotten grandmother used to fry him up bacon and eggs as a boy. The smell of dusty fabric and years of bacon grease frying makes me want to vomit. A breeze from an approaching storm whistles through the weathered barnwood walls, fluttering a drippy candle on the table. Then comes the sound of pit-a-pattering. Rain sprinkles on the window.

If this turns to rain the roads will get bad. Yet here you sit, waiting for him to take you back to get your car at the bar.

I grab the last empty bottle and scrape at the label, frustrated for letting myself get into this frame of mind. I pace in anger, frustration, and guilt. I've bitten my nails to nubs.

Why not just go back there and kick him out of bed? Is it your fear of men?

What a mistake coming here last night. Grief runs up my spine while that merciless mantle clock ticks off the hours until sunrise when I can get home to Mother. She's alone. At least I hope so. I need to be there before Dad returns from his business trip.

You knew better than to go out last night, Natalie.

Guilt has its claws in me for drinking and dancing at the dance hall, looking for another cowboy to screw around with. And especially for hooking up with that dreamy-eyed guitar cockroach down the hall.

"Hey," I shout, thumping knuckles on the table. "You, in the bedroom. I've got to go home. Can you hear me?"

Of course you can't. You're sleeping like a baby in that mysterious place where you guys go after female satisfaction turns you into Jello. You probably don't even remember my name.

Then I think of the letter. My gut twists into a knot. "Something bad's about to happen at home. "It has to be about that letter," I whisper, closing my eyes. "You need to be there right now." It haunts me as I get dressed and head down the hall to the bedroom.

I nudge his shoulder. "Hey, wake up."

"Whaaa?"

"Let's go please."

He lifts up, rubbing bloodshot eyes. "Huh? What's up?"

"Take me home."

"Why?"

"Cuz something bad's about to happen."

"How do you know?"

"I just feel it."

He coos, curves an arm around my waist and pulls me down. "Oh, come on baby. You're dreamin'. Nothin's wrong."

I push away. "Don't call me baby. I'm nineteen."

"Whatever." He yanks me down on him. "Just a little longer?"

I twist away. "Sorry, boy."

"C'mon. Don't be like this, girl. Be nice."

"My name is Natalie. Natalie Grace. You got that, Charlie?"

"That's not my name. It's..."

"Shut up. I don't care what your name is."

"Well, good for you, Natalie Grace."

"Look, dumb-ass. I'm serious. Let go of me."

He twines fingers through my hair. "You're not going anywhere, baby." His hand slips under my shirt.

I elbow him away, pull free and stand over him. "Get up."

"No. You're crazy. Go on, get outta here. See you around." He flops back down and buries his face in the pillow.

"Charlie, I need a ride. Please take me to get my car."

"My name's not Charlie."

"I don't care what the hell it is. And I'm not asking anymore. I'm telling you to get up and take me to get my car."

His head pops up fully awake, smirking, realizing what I said. "Ha. Oh. That's right? I brought you here, didn't I? Well then..." He grabs me. "You ain't goin' nowhere till I have ..."

I'm dressed in minutes. He's out cold, his guitar busted over his head. That's what he gets for disrespecting girls with little tolerance for stupid people. Especially a girl prone to reckless impatience. And I don't apologize for what I did.

CHAPTER TWO

The wind is strengthening, getting darker. Charlie won't be up for a while. Besides, he'll be nursing a headache and in no mood to drive me anywhere. I need to get home if it's not too late already. No time now to go for my car parked at the Oasis. I find the keys to his pickup and head to the house I've called home my entire life.

You should have listened to your gut and stayed home last night.

The truck's headlights bounce on the damp dirt road through the dark Vermont pines as I drive with the windows open. The fragrance of damp black earth, broad leaves, and pine needles I love so much can't subdue the worry I have for Mother and Dad. Especially when Dad's away and she's vulnerable to her obsessions. God, I hope I'm just being a worrywart. It scares me though. Dad's expected home early this morning. I hope she's alone.

The storm worsens, battering the pickup around in the muddy road, sliding back and forth, wipers swishing and thumping over the windshield.

What are the odds she's alone?

Almost home, rumbling over the cattle guard, through the gate, I see a vehicle parked in the weeds behind the house next to the barn by Dad's little Toyota work truck. His Honda's not around. Pulling in next to the big black SUV with its antennas and government plates turns my stomach. It's like a cutaneous melanoma sitting there.

Ugh. You were only seventeen, Natalie. Seventeen.

I park in the sticky mud. Each step toward the back porch door reminds me of the fond years of my youth. There's a soft light in the window on the second floor. Her bedroom. Panic builds and urges me to turn and leave.

You have to do this, Natalie.

I let the squeaky porch screen door slam shut after me. A signal to upstairs that I'm home. I stomp mud from my shoes on the wooden porch and clomp up the stairs.

Her bedroom door is open when I pass by. They keep going at it.

They either don't know you're here. Or don't care.

Seeing him on top of her, between her legs, is the final indignity. What he did to me in the back of that government car two years ago... *ugh.* Calling me his little sweetheart. Telling me I was pretty, making me feel like a woman. Feelings I can't scrub away. Reluctantly, I accepted what he took from me, not what he did to me. The loss was my innocence. But him with Mother in Dad's bed, I just can't accept. I slam my bedroom door.

Mother calls out, "Hey, Nat. Do you mind shutting my door? Thanks, hon."

I can't remember the last time I cried. It's hard for me to shed a tear. But here I sit on the side of the bed hugging Mister Teddy, crying until the sappy emotions dry up, and cold, unemotional thinking takes over.

The tote bag Dad bought me from Smugglers Notch years ago is overflowing with random clothes and a few accessories. Then I see the pink track team running shoes, tank top, and shorts. Running is my sanctuary, my well-being, where I go for mental health. I'll need those things more than ever now. I pull stuff out to make room in the tote, but it leaves me with only one extra pair of button-fly jeans. And fewer t-shirts. One last look around before flicking off the lights for the last time.

In the hall, I slowly pull Mother's bedroom door closed. The gentle click of the door locking rattles me.

I run downstairs with the tote flopping at my side. Father could be home any minute. If Dad finds him up there with her, it won't be pretty. Oh, he won't make a fuss. No. Sadly, he'll just go into his office, close the door, and pretend nonchalance while another piece of his heart slowly dies a mournful death. She's killing him with her two-timing. Her years of cheating in smelly roadside dives and flings with cowboys, cops, and college boys have reduced him to a life of enduring acquiescence.

I'm furious. It may be a lawman up there with her, and I may burn in hell, but right is only right. Immature impulsiveness takes over. This is it, Natalie. One last time, is this what you really want to do?

Headlights appear coming up the drive.

What happens next is not clear: mayhem, bedlam, chaos. Blurry, disturbing images. Fire erupts with a whoosh, violent hungry flames climb the walls, smoke billows into the twilight of morning. Intense heat scorches my face, and hair singed by explosions. I stumble back and watch in morbid fascination as my childhood home is devoured by the inferno.

Sunrise peaks over the trees, neighbors gather, faces illuminated by the orange glow. Father sobs at my feet. The marshal crawled out on hands and knees, coughing and puking. Sirens wail their approach. A police car slides to a stop, lights flashing, radios squawking. A fire engine arrives too late to matter.

As sunrise creeps in over the waking land, the house is a pile of charred rubble. The gas can from the barn lies empty on its side next to the chicken coop. The stone fireplace still stands, smoking like a dying cigarette in an ashtray. A gun. Yes, a gun. I am holding a gun. Head spinning. Father and the lawman both in a pool of blood. Pain pierces my soul with the notion that I'll never see Mother or Father again. The smoldering embers of this morning will cling to me for the rest of my life.

A pleasant black woman officer gently lifts me off the ground and brushes ash and dirt from my clothes. She gives me a hug of condolences and then snaps handcuffs on my wrists.

"How old are you, hon?"

Before you answer that, Nat, remember you're on your own now. Hold onto everything Dad taught you. So think before you answer her question. She can't arrest you if she doesn't know how old you are.

I look at her and bite my lip. "I need help, lady."

CHAPTER THREE

Three months later.

Downtown Denver a dollar in a bus station vending machine gets you brown water for coffee.

What did you expect, Natalie?

Fifteen minutes until my bus leaves for California. Pretty sure I'm being watched. Just about everything spooks me now. Being on the run does that to you. Like that guy pretending to read his phone either sees me as a hooker or a criminal. Or maybe just a runaway he can coax into his van. He doesn't look that dangerous. Too well-groomed in gray slacks, white button-down shirt, and navy-blue sports jacket.

Then again, so was Ted Bundy.

It's going to be a long ride. Better stretch the legs. I toss the coffee and step out of the station into the heart of the mile-high city. A beautiful crisp morning. I shield my eyes from the bright morning sun and stretch. Like all big cities, rush hour traffic is frantic. Everyone in a hurry.

At the street corner, two young women in stiletto heels and form-fitting jeans and t-shirts are hanging out, smoking, selling it.

Ah. I didn't know they work this time of the day. I'm also in jeans and a t-shirt, just like them. The only difference is I'm in running shoes. And they have a job.

I head back toward the bus station. He's still there, the stalker leaning on a streetlight pole, trying to look inconspicuous. Not doing a very good job of it either. Something on his belt flashes in the sunlight.

A cop. Shit.

I panic, wipe my nose with the back of my hand, and look around. Running is out of the question. Wouldn't know which way to run anyway.

Slow down, Natalie. Maybe he's just a vice cop thinking you're a hooker. But the FBI doesn't care about prostitutes.

Time to catch my Greyhound. He moves to the side to let me pass. I avoid eye contact.

"Excuse me, miss." He reaches out to stop me.

Oh, God.

"Mind if I ask you a few questions?"

I give my best annoyed look. "Depends."

"On what?"

"What you intend to ask."

He holds up a black wallet with credentials and a gold badge. "Special Agent Ray Waters."

Oh God, oh crap. A Fed.

"Can I ask you where you're headed, Miss?"

Even though I'm a dark brunette, I pretend the dumb blonde act. "Uh. West."

"Uh-huh. Well, okay. Can you be a little more specific?"

"Nuh-uh."

"All right then. Are you from here?"

I'm almost five ten. He's about an inch, maybe two, taller with curly blond hair and a mustache to match. It also covers up a cleft lip scar that's impossible not to fixate on.

"Nuh-uh," I repeat.

His eyes narrow into a flat stare. His way of goading me into respecting his authority.

Come on, Nat. Stay cool.

"I didn't know you boys are into screwing with hookers on street corners."

"Is that what you're doing, miss? Soliciting?"

"Yeah. Just trying to get an early start on the day, pay a few bills before meeting with my investment broker."

He pulls his lower lip.

I'm so nervous. "Sorry. I have a bus to catch, Mister Agent."

He follows. "Miss. Can you give me just a few seconds?"

I stop. "Why me and not them?" Nodding at the girls on the corner. "Is it the way I dress? Because I'm young? What is it?"

He pulls a photo. "Does this girl look familiar to you?"

It's grainy and overexposed but clean enough to recognize myself. A time I was with Dad at a Red Sox game years ago. Gooseflesh breaks out head to toe.

"No. She doesn't look familiar." I head to the bus.

He follows. "She's about your age."

"How do you know when you don't even know how old I am?"

"You ever been to Vermont, miss?"

I step up the pace. "No, sir."

He's right behind me, telling me the girl in the photo is dangerous. "We think she may be in the area."

"What did she do that makes her so dangerous, Mister FBI Man?"

"Murder."

I force myself to keep walking, blood pounding in my ears, him right behind me asking questions.

We reach the bus.

"She's about your size," he says.

The driver hasn't opened the door to board yet. This Fed is still hounding me. I fold my arms and face him head-on. "Got a name of this girl? Height, weight? Hair color? Any distinguishing marks like tattoos or birthmarks you care to share?"

Oh, you shouldn't have mentioned the ink, Nat.

I tug my jacket sleeves to cover my wrist.

"Her name is Natalie," he says. "About twenty years old. Five nine or ten. Hundred and twenty pounds at the most."

"Natalie who?"

"Don't know."

"That's all you got?"

The bus driver calls out, "All aboard."

I lift the tote over my shoulder. "Pretty name. And too pretty to be a murderer. She looks awfully young."

He moves with me in line to board the bus. "I didn't catch *your* name."

"Call me Runner."

"First or last name?"

"Call me Runner."

"Okay. Where are you from, Miss Runner?"

"I'm from nowhere, bud. Sorry. This has been a hoot. But I gotta get. Good luck."

"One last question, Miss Runner."

I stop, sigh, and drop the hick pretense. "You know it's the questions you law guys ask that tempt us to tell lies, especially when there are no good answers. So what do you want to know, Agent Ray? Or whatever your name truly is?"

He lifts his credentials again. "Ray Waters. You can call me Ray."

I blink slowly and chuckle.

He cranes his neck at me. "I'll ask again. You ever been to Vermont?"

It takes all my discipline to lie without answering in an octave three notches higher than usual. "Never been east of the Mississippi, sir."

CHAPTER FOUR

Two hours later, on a Greyhound bound for California, drowsy from the sway and the steady humming of the highway, I mumble to myself, "How did he get that old photo of me?"

"Sorry?" the girl next to me asks.

"Oh. Sorry. Just talking to myself."

"Mmm." She goes back to reading.

I try to curl up for a bit of comfort to write in my journal. But these seats are just too damn small. I'm almost five ten. But thin. You'd think I could fit comfortably. But no. I squirm and bump her, a shortish, pimply-faced, athletic girl with stringy blonde hair. "Sorry."

She smiles. "No problem. I hate these buses. I fly whenever I can."

"I don't fly. Getting on a plane scares the crap out of me."

She nods. "What's your name?"

"Call me Runner."

"I'm Dee." She leans over. "Do you drink, Runner?"

"Beer mostly."

"Ever had any of this?" A bottle of hundred-proof peppermint schnapps.

"No."

She screws off the cap, takes a sip, winces and hands it over. I study it for a second before taking a sip. Between the two of us half the bottle is gone. The conversation gets deep, and tongues loosen.

Dee's story is she got in trouble with the law. The judge gave her the option of jail or joining the Navy. So now she refers to herself as a low-grade criminal headed to San Diego. "Maybe it's best they ship me off, away from civilization." Then she points to my tattoos. "I've been thinking about getting one."

"Umm. What kind?"

"I dunno. Maybe something mean. Something sexy. Or at least startling. Like that one on your arm, there."

Tattooed Girls Are Good Fucks

I smirk. "Vulgarity always gets attention. Doesn't it?"

She nods and changes the subject. "Where you headed?"

"A little place across the bay from San Francisco. Danfield." I pull knees to my chin and hug tight. "I have to find someone there."

"Family? Friend? Lover?"

"Hardly. To be honest, I don't know who she is. I found a letter to my father from her."

"How you gonna find her?"

"I don't know."

"What kind a letter?"

"Handwritten. Personal thoughts."

"Love letter?"

"Could be. I really don't know. But it was emotionally open

with genuine feelings. Risking vulnerability. No mention of physical interaction."

"What about your mother?"

"I don't have enough time to discuss her, other than being a loving mother. She was also a decadent, licentious sex addict with a thing for bad boys in beer-smelling saloons. Her drug of choice whenever Dad was away. She never tried to hide it from him. He accepted it because he loved her more than anything despite her infidelity. It's always bothered me that he was so accepting of her ways. A disease, he called it; something she couldn't help."

"So why do you have to find this woman?"

"Why?" I look at her with deep curiosity. "Wouldn't you want to know about something like that?"

She shrugs.

I pick at a fingernail. "It's a mystery to solve. I never imagined Dad would have such feelings for another woman. And I guess I feel the need to let her know he's gone."

"Gone. You mean dead?"

"Yeah." I gaze out the window. "He and Mother died the same day."

"Crips! How?"

"I can't remember exactly." My mind drifts back as I explain. "I remember shaking, watching flames licking at the sagging roof, timbers cracking, collapsing, a man stumbling out, pants around an ankle, gun belt dragging, coughing and puking, Father crying for Sophia as the roof comes down with unbearable heat, smoke, pushing me back." I stare into Dee's wide eyes. "I'll never forget Father's blubbering and..."

Dee stares dumbstruck at the story.

I regain composure. "Dante said the darkest places in hell are reserved for those who maintain their neutrality in times of moral crisis. Well, Mother and this woman letter writer, they are my crisis. And it's moral. How can I stay neutral? How can I not want to know who the woman was that maybe was responsible for that day?"

"What about your father? You said he died that day too."

"Um, uh... yeah, that's what I said, didn't I?" I pinch my bottom lip and tap a finger against it. "He. Um... uh... Well, he asked me to..."

"Asked you to do what?"

I can only stare at her. The words about him handing me the gun are stuck in my throat. I can only mumble, "...the gun," and nothing more.

She sees the distress. "Oh, my God. You didn't."

I nod and bite a lip. "It's what he wanted."

She sips at the schnapps and goes understandably silent for not knowing how to respond to something like that.

I brush at my jeans like I'm trying to clear away the memory and make everything right in my life again. Now it's my turn on the schnapps. And I don't hold back.

Dee frowns. "Who was that man with your mom that morning?"

I glance at her. "Can I trust you, Dee?"

"Sure."

"He was a federal marshal. I'm on the run. The Feds are after me."

She turns serious with a fist to her mouth. "They'll catch you, Runner. You know that, don't you?"

"They may, but it won't be easy. You see, I'm what you call off the grid. I was home-born to unique genius parents who didn't trust the government. Dad was a professor with three doctorates. Mother a well-known author with a Ph.D. in comparative literature. I got excellent homeschooling from both of them. In spite of her arcane cheating nightlife, she had motherly instincts that I learned from. But it was mostly Father who taught me about the richness of life through books and his extraordinary experiences and wisdom. There are drawbacks though. Like who I am to get by in society. I have a set of fake documents: fraudulent Social Security number, driver's license, birth certificate. The papers required to get a checking account, buy a phone plan, and for job applications. But no credit cards. Too dangerous. No fingerprints to track me. Nothing to pin me to anything."

"How did you get them papers?"

"Long story, short answer. Met a guy in Denver when I was on the run. He found me at the end of my rope with a dead car and starving in an abandoned old tavern. He took me under his wing for a few days, no questions asked. We just hit it off. Don't ask me why. Just friends, that's all. He's a little on the wrong side of the law himself. He's a master forger."

The rest of the trip is quiet between us. She and her magazines. Me with my journal.

"Is Runner your real name?"

I take a deep breath. "It's Natalie. Natalie Grace. But Runner is who I really am. And that's all I'm saying."

An hour later we pull into the Vail Transportation Station for passengers leaving and boarding. Dee grabs a suitcase to meet her brother, who's going to drive her to San Diego. We hesitate for a second then hug.

"Well, I wish you all the best, Runner. Good luck."

I'm jealous watching through the window as she meets her brother. But I frown when a man approaches her and flashes a badge.

Hell. Christ, it can't be.

It's the curly-headed guy with the blond mustache from Denver—Agent Ray Waters. Dee turns and points at the back window where we were seated.

But I've already hustled out with departing passengers, ducked around the back of the bus with the tote. I race across the lot, downstairs into the parking garage where a young couple are loading suitcases into the back of their van with California plates. Save-the-world stickers cover the bumper.

"Hey, guys. Where you headed?"

CHAPTER FIVE

A year later.
Danfield, California

On a Friday afternoon, my last day at the hardware store where I've been stocking shelves, pretending I know the subtle differences between nails and screws, and snacking on free popcorn for breakfast, lunch and sometimes dinner. That's how broke I am.

On the way out, Mindy, the only other girl in the store who's warmed up to me, stops me in the hall. "Runner, heard you're leaving."

I hold up my final check. "See. Two hundred and seventy-eight dollars. Two hundred of this is spoken for: rent I'm behind on. I'm eating refried beans and tortillas and I'm almost out of my pills. Yeah, I'm just fine, thanks for asking, Min."

"What happened?"

I rub my neck and give the short version. "HR didn't accept

the Social Security card I gave them. It took this long before they ran the number."

"Why give them a bad Social Security card?"

"Long story."

She grabs my arm and sees me out. "You need some fun, girl. The annual Modesto Street Festival is tonight. Street bands and boys with cash to spend on us. I've got some good biker buddies. Should be fun."

"Yeah, Min. Sounds exciting. But I'm practically broke. I've only got about seventeen dollars to my name."

"That's plenty. The way you look, you won't spend a dime. Believe me. Freebies all night for you."

I'm not a big drinker, but the idea of meeting new friends interests me. The thought of happy faces, red-hot bands, and maybe a PBR and a burger from a cute guy... well, yeah, sounds good... but.

"Let loose, Runner," she urges. "Forget about serious crap for an evening. Live a little."

Nine forty-five, Modesto, main street is hopping. A ZZ Top cover band is on the main street stage. Bluegrass tunes roll out from an open-door bar down the street. A girl plays a honky-tonk fiddle in the middle of the street. In the Whiskey River Saloon, a wild dive bar on main street. Mindy introduces me around. I bury my snobby pretense and show some smiles. Genuine smiles. I am having a good time. Something other than worrying about the law grabbing me. I'm on my second beer when this motorcycle geek introduces himself. An Econ grad student by day and biker by night.

"How 'bout a ride?"

My immediate instinct says no. But I stop and give it some thought.

You owe it to yourself, girl.

He seems nice enough and gets a B+ for his looks.

Quit worrying, Natalie. Take a chance.

He buys me a Modesto Festival t-shirt. It's black to fit in with the group to wear on the ride which turns out to be thrilling. The big throbbing machine between my legs and the cool early evening wind in my face feel wonderful. The beer buzz is working. Fun, fun. An hour later, we're back at The Whiskey River. Econ Boy changes from beer to Jägermeister. The cops haul him off after starting a fight with the karaoke crowd. Mindy is nowhere in sight.

I'm stranded, standing on the tavern porch, four dollars to my name, watching the crowd dwindle. I'm nervous, wondering how to get back to Danfield. And it's getting late.

"Need a ride?"

His hair is the first thing that puts me off. A redheaded flat top. And when I say red, I mean flaming red that compliments the cinnamon freckles sprinkled across his face.

"No. No thanks."

"It's the hair, isn't it?" He grins.

"No."

"Okay. But my name's Jimmy if you're interested in that ride home later."

I give the female cold shoulder, the one I've refined perfectly. The emphatic go-away shrug.

"Too bad," he mumbles, walking away.

A half-hour later, after declining several offers by red-faced, bandanna-wearing, whisker-cheeked bikers, I'm angry at Mindy for abandoning me. It's getting late. No money. No idea how to get home. I lean on the porch railing, chewing the rim of an empty red Solo cup, refusing more drinks. I'm already in a low-grade buzz. I hate everyone right now. It's obvious I'm unapproachable, except for the red-top shrimp, who shows up again. "So how you gettin' home?"

"I'll find a way."

"Where's home?"

"Danfield."

"That's quite a walk."

"Don't worry. I'll make it."

"I'm sure you can." Out comes his hand. "I'm Jimmy, and I don't bite."

Reluctantly, I shake. "No. I don't think you're the biting type."

He's persistent. "How about I offer you that ride again?"

I look away.

"So if I don't bite, how about you swallow some pride, lighten up, and let me get you home safely?"

I toss the chewed-up cup away and fold my arms with that cold-shoulder attitude.

He buries his hands in his pockets and lowers his head with a sheepish grin. "You're warming up to me, aren't you? I can tell."

I give the slow, soft soap blink and chew at the inside of my mouth.

He nudges me. "Didn't catch your name."

"Didn't give it."

"If I ask real nice?"

"I'm Runner."

He raises an eyebrow. "That your real name? Or are you running from something?"

Go ahead, Natalie. You've had just enough alcohol in you. Tell him. He'll never believe it. See how he reacts.

"The FBI is after me."

His eyebrows lift.

"I'm serious."

"What for?"

"Murder."

He giggles. "Sure they are." He folds his arms. "Here I am about to take you home and I haven't even read your rap sheet yet. Maybe check the wanted posters in the Post Office first?"

"Very funny." I look away.

"Runner. Is that really your real name?"

"It's what I answer to."

"Okay." He nods. "So, whenever you're ready, let me know."

Decision time. Should you?

I don't cherish the thought of walking home. So... "Well, I guess so."

It's a little after midnight; I'm pouting in his dirty red car. He stops for gas and a six-pack. Finally, we pull up in front of the Sentry Arms, a charming middle-class neighborhood at the west end of Main Street in Danfield. A hundred-year-old, two-story brick with neatly trimmed landscaping, flowering bushes, and giant oaks. We drink and talk until it's that awkward sign-off time.

This isn't a date. So no kiss required.

"Runner." He gets serious. "How long have you been in California?"

"Not long."

"What kind of work do you do?"

"My work?" Pause. "My work right now is looking for a job."

"Any luck so far?"

"Only a few low-paying jobs that haven't lasted long."

"What're you looking for?"

"Something meaningful." I burp and rub my hands, anxious to get out.

He pulls out a card. "Take this. Call me when you get hard up for cash." He nods at the apartments. "This place looks nice. I know what the rent must be. It ain't cheap."

I glance at the card.

Jimmy Barone
Adult Entertainment
And Other Odd Opportunities

I gasp, "Adult entertainment?"

He pulls at his ear. "What do you think it is?"

"What else? Prostitution."

"In a manner of speaking."

"There is no manner of speaking, Jimmy. It is, or it isn't."

"There are shades of gray in most everything, Runner."

"If it's not prostitution, then what is it?"

He pulls at an eyebrow. "You'd be surprised if you knew."

I study the card. "There's no phone number."

He hands me a pencil. "Write this down."

"Why? I have no interest in what you're doing. And if what I think you're doing right now is propositioning me to have sex with men..." I laugh with a one-fingered salute and reach for the door.

"I'm not propositioning you for anything, Runner. But if you're looking to make some serious money, I'm giving you an option to consider. That's all."

I toss the pencil at him.

"Well, okay. But if you ever need to get out of a money jam and want to hear more about how I work and how much you can make, write this number down."

"I have no interest in you or what you do, Jimmy Barone."

He grabs the card back. "You probably think what I do is bad. But if you hear how I work and who I work with, you'd be surprised how much you can make. And it's not the dirty business you've heard about." He scribbles his number on the card and stuffs it in my back pocket as I'm climbing out of the car. "Good night, Runner. Look forward to hearing from you."

CHAPTER SIX

I leave Jimmy and charge into the apartment to a community room just off the entry filled with mismatched turn of the century furniture. I flop down in an antique chair next to Avril, my roomie stretched out on an overstuffed rustic ornate sofa banging away on her laptop while talking on the phone.

"What a pervert," I mumble, trying to get her attention.

She pays no attention. I want to talk girl to girl. So, I run upstairs to our apartment, grab the last two beers in the fridge, and back downstairs offering her one to get her off the phone.

Avril is a curvy, blue-eyed, blonde Texas girl with soft, wavy hair and puffy Hollywood lips. She rolls her eyes in conversation and mouths *blah, blah, blah*, pointing to the phone. I hold out the beer. She nods. Avril has never turned down anything in her life except good respectable men. Bad boys are her weakness. We have something in common.

"Gotta run," she tells the caller. "Talk later."

After a long chug, she wipes her mouth and burps. "So what'd you do today, Runner?"

I explain the festival, the Harley ride, and Jimmy the pimp. She shrugs and returns to the dating site searching for the man who's going to take her to nirvana. Avril is too impatient to find someone on line. Her relationships begin in bars. Not online. And they usually end in bed on the first date. Her boyfriends are the not-for-long variety. She closes the laptop, takes a long drink and wipes her mouth again. "Jonathan came by today looking for Ruckus."

I roll my eyes at the pet name Ruckus I've been tagged with. Jonathan Bland is a guy I see pretty regularly. He's pinned that silly name on me. I'm not a pet name kinda girl. I think he uses names like that to express affection and closeness. I don't like it but tolerate it for his sake. Truth is, I think he uses it to validate the relationship and exert subtle control over his girlfriends. He thinks I'm his girlfriend. I have a different opinion.

I take a sip. Avril is back to thumbing through men's profiles.

I ran into Avril my first day in Oakland when I got off the bus and wandered into a dirty little gas station asking where to find a room for the night. Avey was paying for a fill up. We met, and I was her roommate at the Sentry Arms in Danfield that day. I can't afford the Sentry without her contribution to the rent. She's turned into a real friend. More than just a roomie.

I finish the beer thinking of Jonathan. He is an absolute heartthrob I met a month ago at a coffee house. It got hot and heavy between us fast. Maybe that's the reason I'm pulling away, letting the relationship cool. He's become very serious. But I still have a wandering eye. He's convinced it's just a phase I'm going through.

Avril whispers, "He's crazy about you, girl," as she flips through profiles.

"Jonathan is just someone to pass the time with, Avey. Yeah, he buys me dinners and he's always ready to help if I need some-

thing. No questions asked. The only problem is he's the posses-
sive type. *Ugh.* So, for as good-looking and rich as he is, he's
beginning to wear on me." I sigh. "Jonathan Bland isn't my long-
term answer."

Avril blows her cheeks out. "When you get around to kicking
him out, send him my way. Would you? Just one night. That's all.
I want to enjoy him for at least one night."

"He's not your type, Avril. He's no bad boy. He won't hold
your attention very long. Just too nice for you."

She pinches a lip. "I know you're hard up for cash. Why don't
you just ask him for money? He'd give you anything if you just
ask. You know he adores you."

"I know. I just don't want to be indebted to him."

"You mean any more than you already are?"

"Stop it. I just let him buy me dinners. That's all."

"Hogwash, fiddlesticks. You need him. I've seen how you are
after a night with Jonathan. You're a different girl. Satisfied. He's
your rock. Lean on him, girl."

"I don't lean on any man, Avey."

"So you just like to screw em."

"Yeah. That's right. Anything wrong with that?"

She chuckles. "Oh, honey. You're askin' the wrong girl about
promiscuity. You know me." Then she changes the subject. "How
was the hardware store today?"

"I quit."

She looks up, mouth open. "Again? That didn't last long."

"Long story." I bury my face in my hands. "This isn't what I
expected being out here in California."

"But you're safe here from whatever it is you're running
from."

"I have to tell you something, Avey. I did a bad thing back in
Vermont."

"How bad?"

I pause for a second. "I killed someone."

"Yeah, right."

"I'm serious."

"Tell me this is a joke, Runner."

"Wish it were."

Her face turns sober. "My God, girl. What did you do? Who was it? Why?"

"A guy who..." I get up and pace in a circle. "He was a law man."

Her jaw drops. "You shittin' me?"

"He got me pregnant."

"You had a baby?"

"No. He took me to a butcher to get rid of it."

"But he raped you."

"It happened in the back seat of his cop car. He was Father's friend. He offered me a ride home when Dad and I were at a courthouse on business. Dad needed to stay and trusted him to take me home. The creep told me he had fallen in love with me. I fell for it. I was on top of the world having a man like his type want me."

She jumps up and hugs me. "Oh, Runner. My God. He exploited you. Violated you." Her eyes are huge. "A fucking federal marshal?" She goes from angry to curious. "What did you do to make him..."

"God, Avey, I was seventeen. What's the matter with you?" I push her away and stiffen up. "I'll forget you even asked me that."

Avril wrings her hands. "I didn't mean anything by it."

I change the subject. "I've been on the run, lying low since Vermont. But they'll eventually find me. They never give up looking for someone who kills one of their own. The FBI never quits."

"I'm sorry, Runner. So sorry."

"As the years went by I realized what he did. I had to let it go. But it wasn't what he did to me. It's what he was doing to Mother. That fateful day, Dad was out of town. I found him, that marshal having sex with Mother in her bed. Dad's bed." I stop, transfixed by the memory. "No wonder..."

Avril cocks her head. "No wonder, what?"

"Do you know why I'm in California? No. Of course you don't. There's a woman out here who meant something to my father. I'm looking for her."

"What kind of woman?"

"That's just it. I don't know anything about her. I found a letter from her hidden in Dad's work room in the barn."

"Love letter?"

"A short handwritten letter. A touching, caring, kindhearted letter that ended mid-sentence. The third page is missing. I sensed nothing physical in the writing. But it was between two people who cared deeply for each other. She referred to Father as 'my dearest'."

"How are you going to find her?"

"I don't know. All I know is the letter mentioned where she often met him."

"Where?"

"The Coffee Bean Cafe. Right here in Danfield."

She stares at me, an inquiring stare as if trying to understand something I'm holding back on. "You've mentioned Denver a couple a times. What was that about?"

"It's where I got stranded in my escape from Vermont. Dad's old Toyota broke down there." I share the rest of the story the best I remember it.

She smirks with an eyeroll. "Some man you just met in an old bar? That's hard to believe."

"I know, huh? He was a crazy man. He had to be crazy to go by the name of Peter Longer."

"Peter Longer?" Her mouth drops open. She laughs. "You gotta be kidding."

"Yeah, I know."

"What did you have to do for it?"

"Nothing. We just shared hamburgers, commiserated over relationships, teased each other since both of us accepted the fact that we were screwed up. That was about it."

CHAPTER SEVEN

A month later.

Morning, seven thirty. I'm beginning to panic that I might have made a mistake coming out here. This la la land is so dang crowded, weird, and expensive I can hardly afford anything. Maybe if I find a job that pays better than flipping burgers, stocking shelves, driving a delivery van, working for tips as a restaurant server, I just might make it. But so far, nothing's worked because minimum wage sucks and I hate being told what to do by nincompoop managers.

In the top of my bedroom closet is a cash stash. It's what's left of money given to me by my friend in Denver. Totally out of the goodness of his heart. Five grand to help me get started here.

I spread it out on the bed for a recount. It's down to a little more than nineteen hundred and change.

Damn.

This isn't going to last long if I don't find a decent job. I've been disciplined with my spending habits, not touching it except for rent and maybe cash for an emergency getaway if I feel the law closing in. But food, health, and bathroom necessities are chipping away at it. One more rent payment and I'm out on the street. I stare at Dad's letter folded with the money, reminding me I've made no progress in finding her.

Ugh.

I fold the letter and put it away with the money in a leather pouch, and hide it again behind a tote bag on the top shelf. I'm essentially broke now. The next rent will pretty much clean me out. No time to waste.

But how do you track down someone when you don't have a speck of information about them?

The only clue is her unusual handwriting. The lettering is unique. A scrawling, ornate-unbroken flow about it. And the letter mentions The Coffee Bean Cafe. I've been there dozens of times to study women coming and going wondering if one of them could be Father's secret friend. I love that place. Especially their strong black coffee.

I'm pacing again, convinced I've seen that FBI guy from Denver lurking around.

Is this just paranoia? Or can it be real?

I guess knowing that if I get desperate, Jonathan is there for me. And maybe it's one of the reasons I haven't been serious about finding a job. I hate lowering myself to crawl to him for financial help.

You don't need his money. You are not his Ruckus. You are and will always be Daddy's girl.

I curl up on the sofa and forget about money or the law after me. I blank Jonathan out and remember my time fishing with Dad. We'd wander aimlessly on Sundays along a rambling creek lined with sycamore, birch, and maple trees. The gentle song of water flowing over a little fall washes over me now, filling me with his memory.

Father has his trousers rolled up, knee deep in the chilly creek. I smell the sweet fragrance of his tobacco as he puffs on his pipe, studying life in the sand and rocks, explaining the exiguous life forms in his scholarly jargon.

But I wake with the wail of an ambulance siren racing to some emergency, bringing me back to the reality of adult life.

I have to do something I'm not proud of. Something Dad wouldn't want me to do.

But you're up against it. Running out of time.

I find my wallet, pull the card out and make a call to the number in pencil on the back.

He answers. "Jimmy Barone. How can I help you?"

CHAPTER EIGHT

Hearing Jimmy's voice startles me. I hesitate. Can't speak. Heart pounding, hands shaking.

Again, he asks, "Who's calling?"

"Jimmy, this is Runner. Remember me?"

"Runner. Runner. Oh, yeah. From Modesto. Yeah." He gets right to the point. "Hurtin' for money?"

"Something like that."

"Yeah? So you've been thinking about what I said?"

"Maybe."

"Maybe? What is this, twenty questions?"

"I'm just saying I'll listen. That's all. I don't know anything about you. You don't look like a pimp. Hell, you're almost articulate."

He chuckles. "Three years of college. Accounting major at an Ivy League school. I'd shoot myself if I knew I'd have to do that shit every day for the rest of my life. So now I run a nice business."

I laugh. "Nice business. What a crock of shit."

"Listen. I provide clean, attractive, educated women for men to meet. I don't judge what they do in private."

"These girls, what about them? Where do they come from?"

"I employ girls I can trust. Pay them upfront so they know they're getting their money. I take all the financial risks. I'm more than fair with my cut. And they come to me by word of mouth. Nurses, secretaries, business managers. Even college students who need help with school loans. Some girls only want one or two meetings to pay off a credit card or cover the rent for a month. Others, like teachers, do it for the summer. It's up to them how much or how little they work. No pressure."

"But you approached me, Jimmy. Why?"

"You have a special look about you. You're wickedly seductive. Sexy. Most men don't want to marry you. But they secretly fantasize about what it would be like to be in bed with you."

"You mean screw girls like me."

"All my clients want something different. And your sultry allure makes you very much in demand. So when I met you, I could see you had the 'it' factor in a tomboy sort of way. You're a fantasy to men and women alike."

He's pandering to you now, Natalie.

"So you interested, Runner?"

"Depends on the money."

"Well, for a beginner, a rookie like you, figure on about three hundred an hour. Four hundred tops. But for a girl who's been at it for a while and receives positive feedback from the client, her take could be as high as eight hundred. Some girls are in the thousands."

"You're kidding."

"I'm not. My clients have the money to satisfy their fantasy needs. My girls are good products to sell."

"Product? Is that what you call them?"

"My girls are chattel, objects, commodities to my clients. Like it or not, that's how men look at them. They want something they can get dressed, walk out, close the door behind them and go back to their families. They pay handsomely for that discretion and freedom."

"You disgust me."

"Oh my God, Runner. Come down off that high horse of yours. I'm just telling the truth. At least I'm honest. But that doesn't mean I don't care about my girls."

"Your girls? Your girls?"

"Where else can you make three hundred an hour without any business experience?"

I hesitate, jolted from that remark and instantly thrown into remembering my pathetic checkbook balance and rent coming due.

Make that kind of money for an hour, Natalie?

"You're saying to me right now, today, I can make three hundred dollars an hour?"

"Yeah. I take twenty-five percent. That's a much lower cut than the other escort services. And you'll make a hell of a lot more than that if you stay with it." He pauses. "How badly you hurting for cash?"

"I can go awhile. Don't have to decide right now."

"Nothin's gonna change, girl. Stupid to wait. And I think you need the money now."

It turns quiet between us. He breaks the silence. "I can get you a client this afternoon for three hundred. And whatever tip you'll earn."

"With a man?"

"Oh Christ, Runner. What did you think? A donkey?"

"Forget I said that." I pause. "I'll think about it."

"Three hundred, girl."

I hesitate. "What's this guy like?"

"He's a delivery truck driver. He called asking for a date this afternoon."

"What's he like?"

"This one? He's a regular client on the lower end of the paying spectrum. And he's not on your level of sophistication. But he's decent, harmless, does his business and leaves feeling guilty for cheating on his wife and kids."

"My level of sophistication? What does that mean?"

"They're not all Brad Pitt types. But he's a good one to see if this business is for you."

"Let me think about it."

"What's to think about? An hour's worth of work. And with this one it'll only be about fifteen minutes. Three hundred dollars."

I hold the phone, biting a fingernail.

"Runner?"

My voice cracks slightly. "I can't believe I'm about to say this."

"Good," grunts Jimmy.

An hour later, Jimmy meets me at the Westward Hotel, formerly a Best Western. The lobby is small, smelling like disinfectant and dusty plastic flowers. I sit tense, alone on a timeworn flowery sofa, waiting to meet a man who's paid to have sex with me. The registration desk clerk gives me a quick, knowing glance.

God, how embarrassing.

Jimmy shows up with the three hundred dollars. Then gives me a blonde wig. "Here, wear this. Marty likes blondes. Call me when you're finished."

Ten minutes later, Jimmy's gone, and a short man in brown

polyester slacks and a mustard-stained shirt under a blue-checked sports coat walks up. He looks me over. "You the hooker?"

My neck hair stands on end. I stand up and look down at him, feeling like I just stepped into a pile of dog shit.

"Wow, you're pretty. I'm Marty. What's your name, baby?"

I'm taller than him. But he's a hundred pounds heavier. I can't tell which bothers me more. The gut hanging over his belt or the pack of Marlboros in his threadbare company shirt pocket.

"I'm Marty." His voice has a slight quiver.

"I know. You're repeating yourself."

"Wow. You really are a pretty one."

I can't control my disdain or the eye roll. "Yes. I heard you the first time, Marty."

He stares at the tattoo on my arm. "I like it," he mumbles. "Let's go, baby. I only got an hour."

Baby? You called me baby. Twice.

I stare with repulsion, genuine and obvious, and think about yanking that table lamp and busting it over his ridiculous comb-over. What woman would ever consent to go upstairs with a toad like Marty? But here I am, needing money, about to violate any sense of morality and self-worth.

I stand frozen. *Are you really going upstairs with this creep?*

He frowns and nods. "Come on, baby."

I clench my jaw and slowly follow him toward the elevator.

God, this can't be happening.

CHAPTER NINE

I step off the bus packed with people. The diesel chugs away leaving me choking in a cloud of black smoke. My eyes go blurry in the bright sun. This heat is unbearable. The black Modesto Festival t-shirt clings to my body. My feet are baking. I toss the blonde wig away and lift my arms to air out armpit sweat.

I'm ashamed about that delivery guy, Marty. *Why did you ever agree to that?*

The walk to the apartment is a little over a mile through Danfield with its assortment of colorful storefronts, hanging plants, neatly trimmed trees, and bright restaurant canopies for outside dining.

I stop with the smell of chocolate coming out of the open door of the Chokolate House. Time for a rest on the outside bench under the awning. A little schnauzer leashed to the bench looks up at me. We greet each other with our eyes. He jumps up on the bench and settles down against my leg.

"Hey, little buddy. You a good listener? Huh?"

His eyes say he is.

"Wanna hear what I did today?"

His head cocks. *Yeah, what did you do today?*

"Okay. Well, I did something my daddy would frown on. I..."

Little buddy looks away before I can go on. He ignores me. He's more interested in the sidewalk traffic, especially that little white poodle prancing towards us.

I scratch behind his ear while I mumble. "All my life, I've been told I'm tough. Yeah, a tough little tomboy cutie. Kinda like you. But I hated being called a tomboy. Still do."

I scratch his back while feeling the need to reminisce. "My daddy's gone now. So is Mom. I miss 'em both. I got my smarts from two very smart people. And *merci beaucoup* to Mother for my looks. Her beauty was legendary. She was also an acclaimed crime novelist. But I have to say, Mother was also a tramp, like that little poodle over there."

Lil' buddy isn't paying any attention to me. He's fixated on her. I draw in a deep breath, ruffle my hair in frustration, and exhale slowly.

"I have no money, lil' buddy. And no job. And I did something today that's putting me deeper in debt."

He snaps a look at me for a second, like he understands. Then he's back drooling over the little Jezebel trotting by, swinging her hips.

You're just like all men, lil' buddy.

A gentleman appears from inside with a double scoop of vanilla. Lil' buddy gets a lick and is off to continue on with his simple life. I'm jealous.

Admit it, Natalie.

I return to my walk through the heat, flicking sweat off my chin, thinking how men like Jimmy and Jonathan and that FBI agent are so piously judgmental and self-righteous. And that mysterious letter writer, what gave her the right to fool around in Dad's life anyway?

Will you ever be a one-man kind of girl, Natalie? Does settling down with one guy sound good to you? Monogamy. Ugh!

Mother had a philosophy about sleeping with strangers. The way she put it, bedding a new man was like a splendiferous wedding night. Raw emotion, ever-lovin' unadulterated sex. So delicious until it faded out after time into the equivalent of sitting down to boiled potatoes and ham for dinner.

I kick in frustration at a weed struggling to grow out of a sidewalk crack. Life can be just like that little weed.

"Find a job, Natalie. That'll fix everything."

CHAPTER TEN

Ahead up the street, there's a guy leaning on a lamppost smoking, watching me walk his way. The closer I get, the red hair becomes more obvious. My stomach tightens. I think about crossing over the street to avoid him. But that'll just make it worse.

Jimmy flicks his cigarette in the street as I approach. "I hear it didn't go as planned."

"You could say that." I keep walking.

"Whoa. Hey, hey, wait up." He grabs my arm. "Why in such a hurry?"

I snatch away. "Get your hands off me. Don't ever do that again."

"What happened back there with Marty?"

"He was disgusting." I keep walking.

"Hang on. Wait." He leaps ahead of me. "Just stop. Tell me. What happened? Did he do something you didn't like? Tell me if he did, baby."

My fingernails dig into my palms. "I am not your baby. You

got that? And I'm not one of your girls. And furthermore, I don't want to be one of your girls. I'm not a hooker. That's what Marty called me."

Jimmy holds up a hand. "Now, wait just a second. If you don't want in this business, that's your right. I respect that you didn't want to do it with him. But maybe it was just that one time. You were nervous. It happens. But if you want out, I'll gladly wish you well. Or you can try it again with a better client. Tell me what type you won't service."

"Service," I snort. "God, it's like I'm a mare for breeding."

"Bad choice of words."

"I don't want any part of what you're selling, Jimmy. I guess I just don't have what it takes to give myself to some stranger so I can pay the rent."

"You telling me you've never had a one-nighter with a stranger?"

He's right. I gaze around, wanting get on with my walk home. There's a kid busy with a squeegee and rags cleaning the windows in the restaurant on the corner. Pretty flower boxes and vines frame nice big windows. Oakes Bar and Grill. It's where my roommate works.

I resume my walk. Jimmy follows along blabbering. "You'd be good at this, Runner. I know what I'm talking about."

"I have nothing more to say."

"How you gonna make it on cheap low-paying jobs? Hell, you can't even keep a job anyway. So tell me. What don't I understand about the glamour of living on the street? Cuz you know that's where you're headed."

"Look, Jimmy, I've given you my answer and..."

He interrupts. "Save it, Runner. You have your reasons. But you should think about it. Let me help you financially while you figure things out."

"Is this what your girls are doing while they lie back and take it from disgusting men while deciding which line of work they want for themselves?"

"For the record. Most clients are reasonable, law-abiding, prosperous men. Not disgusting creeps."

"What part of your description did Marty live up to, Jimmy?"

"Marty was..."

I hold up my hand and stare. "You are so transparent, Jimmy. Do I look stupid to you? You're sticking your nose up the wrong twat, buddy. This one will bite your nose clean off. Now get out of my way."

He concedes. "I'm sorry I set you up with Marty. But you have to return the three hundred I advanced you. Hand it over."

I keep walking. "I need it."

"You reneged on the assignment, Runner. You didn't earn it."

I begin to panic and dial down the attitude. "Give me a week, Jimmy?"

"Why? What for?"

"I may change my mind."

"You want me to believe that?"

"Yeah. I need to get my mind right about doing something like what you're explaining. It isn't on my list of career choices, but you never know."

He lights another cigarette. Scratches his chin. "You got a week, baby."

I flare up and glare with clenched fists. "Don't call me baby."

He studies me. I get the impression his offer isn't what he's really selling. Why is he giving me such leeway? Is something else going on in that pumpkin-colored head of his?

You're trouble, Jimmy Barone.

I brush sweat from my chin and notice that nice-looking restaurant bar behind him.

It's gotta be nice and cool in there.

Then I look back at Jimmy and seriously consider kicking him in his curly red sack, which I've done to a few stupid boys back home. Instead, I look back again at those restaurant doors.

Nothing to lose.

The rush of cool air inside Oakes Bar and Grill hits me like a 7-Eleven slushy. I breathe in and hold my arms out like a bird. The sweaty t-shirt turns cold against my skin immediately. I look over the place looking for who's going to hire me.

CHAPTER ELEVEN

Jimmy sits in the parking lot with the AC full blast watching through the restaurant window as Runner looks around holding out her arms. He thumps fingers on the steering wheel to "The Gambler" on the radio. The song defines his sense of himself. You have to be daring and ambitious to win at gambling. He knows bold undaunted determination is a strength of his. He has what it takes to win despite overwhelming odds.

It's also what got him booted from the FBI.

Good riddance.

But what he's facing now will be the biggest caper of his life —toppling a mob boss from power. It will take fearless moves with help from a few of the right people. He's done his homework and recruited key players. Now all it needs is the right female to kick it off. A lightning-rod provocateur to light the fuse. One who can incite trouble and mischief without even trying.

Jimmy lights up, takes a long drag and stares through the window at Runner approaching the owner.

Vance, you don't stand a chance against her.

He drives away, headed to the far end of Main Street to meet with the owner of the Sentry Arms Apartments, Cicero Chevalier LeBlanc, a French descendant from Haiti, a former lawyer in the DA's office, but now disbarred for aggressive real estate dealings. It was Cicero who called Jimmy about a girl he should look into. And that was Runner. And now that he's interacted with her, he knows what she's made of. Time to put her to the test.

Jimmy sits with Cicero, in a storage room upstairs for privacy. Cicero asks, "How's the plan coming?"

"It's coming along. But it won't be easy. It's a bit of a gamble, for sure. But one I'm willing to risk because the upside of success is so overwhelming."

"What do you need from me, Jimmy?"

"What's your opinion of her?"

"Anything in mind?"

"Well, she's the most unusual girl I've ever met. But attitude, oh brother, she has plenty of it. So, is she the one to do this?"

Cicero folds his arms. "She's reckless. Hard to manage. She does things her way. That's her shortcoming. She's a thoroughbred. It's a crapshoot if you can handle her."

"Don't dodge the question. Do you think she can do what we need her to do?"

"Of course, she can. But getting her to go along with your plan might be difficult."

"Why?"

"Her morals. High on the ethics meter. She's also one of the most intelligent people I've ever met. Even though she's young, she'll see right through your bullshit, Jimmy."

"What's her weakness?"

"She has a few. She's young. She's promiscuous. And she's hard up for money. You make the offer high enough, she might be desperate enough to overlook morality. Who knows what she'll agree to."

Jimmy gets up and paces, repeating why he thinks she's right for the job. "She's perfect for him. He likes pretty young girls. The quirkier, the better. And those gorgeous green-diamond eyes, those tattooed arms, that tall willowy body that makes t-shirts, jeans, and sandals look sexy... He'll fall for her for sure." Then he frowns. "But she told me something that could be trouble."

"What?"

"Something about being on the run from the FBI."

"Was she drunk?"

"No."

"Do you believe her?"

"Maybe something to it. Not sure."

Driving away from the Sentry Jimmy thinks back to what Runner said about a murder back in Vermont.

Not a bad idea to check out.

He dials the New York FBI field office and connects with an agent he was close friends with years ago—Angela Bickerstaff. After small talk he gets to the point. "Angela, do you know anything about a Vermont murder where a marshal might have been killed?"

"I don't know much about that, Jimmy. Here's a number. Ray Waters. He can be more help to you than me."

"Waters? Did I ever meet him when I was there?"

"Probably not."

"What does he look like?"

"About six foot, curly blond hair. A cleft pallet, hardly notice-able, hidden by a tacky mustache. He's one of a kind."

"Doesn't ring a bell. How do I get in touch with him?"

"Is this a good number to reach you, Jimmy?"

"Yeah."

"I'll have Waters get in touch with you."

CHAPTER TWELVE

With my arms still stretched out to cool off, I see the restaurant bar is larger than it looks from the outside. It's a big bright friendly grill with lots of red and white vinyl checkered tablecloths, rustic wood-paneled walls, dark planked-wood flooring, and a low coffered ceiling. Must be at least a dozen TVs.

Slouched at the end of a long, shiny bar top is a man on a stool with a half-smoked cigar stuffed in the corner of his mouth. An unusual-looking character with a thin, slicked-down comb-over and a silly pencil-thin mustache. He's humped over studying a big green ledger book. He squints up at my standing there and narrows his brow. "Help you, young lady?"

When I'm nervous I have this bad habit of going on the offensive. "Who are you?"

"Who wants to know?"

Careful, Natalie. Calm down, take it easy.

I take a deep breath. "Me." I hesitate with hands clasped behind me like a schoolgirl. "Sir. I'm looking for a job."

"You are, are you?"

"Yes, sir. Is the owner around?"

"The owner. Humph." He grunts. "I guess that'd be me. Good enough for ya?"

"Yes, sir," I say in my best sycophantic, bootlicking way. "Could I please get a drink of water?"

He pulls the cigar out of his mouth, takes a piece of tobacco from his tongue, and signals a server for a glass of water before returning to his ledger.

I drink it down in three long gulps, gasping for breath. Followed by a burp. He glances up at me with a smirk and returns to reading.

Wiping my mouth, I hesitate. "Thank you." Then remain in front of him, staring.

He opens one eye wide and studies me. "Something else?"

I'm so nervous and jittery, and I launch into stupidity. "I can clean those windows every day like crystal. Wash dishes squeaky clean. Keep that bar up to date. What's so hard about serving drinks? I've done that. Drinkers like me. I..."

"Woah," he says, looking me up and down like I'm a lobster on the Wednesday night special. "What are you doing?"

"I'm explaining to you that you should hire me."

"What's up with the tats, girl? And the dark death-like outfit. You look like a chewed-on licorice stick." He turns back to his ledger and answers his ringing phone. He nods once listening to the caller and then gives a couple "yeah, yeah" while looking me over. Then he says into the phone, "Gotta go," and hangs up. "You were saying, girl?"

I have an equally disparaging comeback crack about the way he said I look. I want to tell him about how stupid his wispy comb-over and pencil-thin mustache look, but I hold my tongue. "What's your name, sir?"

He glances up and nods at the sign behind the bar. "Oakes. I'm Vance Oakes. Head butt kicker."

"Well, Mister Oakes. I never intended to ask for a job. I came in for a drink of water. But I can see I'd like to work here. And I'm sorry for not being more respectful. That's not my style."

He rolls the cigar around in his mouth. "What is your style, girl?"

"I'm good at taking orders. I'm a hard worker. I'm whimsical, charming, and I'm charismatic. I'm smart. That's no joke. Don't take that lightly. But I'm just a real person with kindness and empathy for 'most everyone. I can be a little difficult sometimes. I know I am. But I'm also the perfect person to be a bartender because I'm a good teaser. I know when to use my assets. I also know when to stay cool. You will NOT be sorry when you hire me."

He smirks. "Already got a window cleaner. Got a so-so dishwasher. Don't need another server. Have a good, experienced bartender. So have yourself a good day, smart kid."

I nod at the windows. "You call that clean? Look at 'em; kinda like they were washed with monkey piss. And that water bowl out there on the patio for dogs. It's empty. Hell, I'd never let that happen. I..."

He holds up a hand. Taps ash into a half-empty glass of beer. "If I were to hire someone like you, a fiery shoot-from-the-hip gothic pinhead, I'd never hear the end of it from my customers."

"But what if your customers like me better than what you already have? And I'm not sayin' what you already have aren't good. I'm just saying..."

"Sayin' what? What have you got that's so different and better?"

"Our customers will fall in love with me. When I'm working

here, you'll see how I care about them. I know how to flirt. Toy with customers right up to the edge of going too far. I'll sell more drinks because of it. And I'm good at it. You'll get compliments about me. I promise they'll like me. You'll be happy you hired me."

He turns on his stool and faces me directly for a ten-second stare-down. Him with his cigar, me cringing.

"Big words for a little girl. How old are you?"

I drop down an octave to sound older. "Twenty-two."

"Bullshit."

"I look younger than I am."

"Hell. Who are you kiddin'? You don't look a day over eighteen."

I counter. "Well, you don't look like you could own this place either, Mister Oakes. Looks can be deceiving. Can't they?"

He grins. "You ever worked in a place like this?"

"Yes... I... have. A little laid-back dive on the outskirts of Middlebury. I went from cleaning the floors, emptying garbage, and keeping things neat. I learned fast. Pretty soon, I was mixing and serving when the bartender didn't show or got slammed. I learned how to close out the register and lock up when Jasper, the owner, was too drunk to do it."

"How long were you there at Jasper's?"

"I got kicked out when the town preacher wandered in and saw me mixing up a pitcher of margaritas and guys hanging over the bar telling dirty jokes with their butt cracks on full display. Fourteen months, to answer your question."

"So you can take dirty offers from drunks? Crude ribbing from jealous women? Ignore sexual innuendos from college boys? Willing to get your hands dirty cleaning toilets?"

I add, "And don't forget the concupiscent old men who want to pinch my ass."

He raises an eyebrow. "Concupiscent?"

"It means lusty feelings."

He tucks the cigar in the corner of his mouth, lifts his head back, and scrutinizes me with that one eye again.

You got his attention, Natalie. Reel him in.

I pull out a handwritten note from my roommate. "Here."

"What's this?" He chews on his cigar and mutters, reading it under his breath. "Humph." He hands it back. "Eck is a bartender here. How do you know her?"

"Avril Ecklund is my apartment roomie. She keeps telling me to come in here and ask you for a job. She talks about you, Mister Oakes."

"Oh, really. What does she say about me?"

"Nothin' I can repeat. But it ain't that bad."

He grins and swaps the cigar to the other side of his mouth. "What's your name, kid?"

"Runner."

He doesn't blink, just accepts the name. "You know what a barback is, Runner?"

"Of course."

"Well, I need one who can learn the bar business from the grubby ground floor up. Who can become a real bartender. You wanna do that?"

"Heck yeah."

"It's conditional. But you can't come in here looking like that. Fix that hair. Maybe wear something a little less Stephen Kingish. Be here at eight tomorrow with an ID. Not a fake either. I've seen 'em all. I can tell the bad ones."

Here we go again. Peter's fake documents. They're so good he'll never know.

I draw my shoulders up and make a face like a kid who just got the gold star in school.

"Four rules, Runner. There are four cardinal rules to work here."

"Okay."

"One. Don't ever be late. Two. Never, ever complain. Three. Never, never, ever get involved with the customers. Four. No matter what... you always smile."

He pulls another shred of tobacco from his tongue and repeats, "Never! Got it? Never get involved with the drinkers."

I walk out knowing there's no way I can follow those rules. Just no way.

CHAPTER THIRTEEN

After meeting Oakes, I walk tall on the way home with enough money to buy coffee and a month's supply of contraception. It feels so good to have cash that I want to scream.

But bliss doesn't last long.

I have no idea how to repay Jimmy the three hundred after reneging on my assignment with Marty. The thought of what he wanted me to do is sickening. Hell, even Mother never did it for money. Her promiscuity was for pure pleasure. God-given lust she couldn't ignore. Never confuse love with lust, she often told me. Speaking of lust, Jonathan comes to mind. I don't think we'll ever gel. Then I think about Father. For all these years I've held him in high esteem, and in my eyes he was the most moral man in the world. But now I realize I never really knew him because of finding that letter. I have to find her. Maybe I should hang out more at The Bean. That's where I'll find her.

Are you kidding yourself, Natalie? Do you really think you can find her?

. . .

Passing Happy Jack's, the corner liquor store on the edge of town, I decide to celebrate with something dark and expensive. I'm not a drinker except for beer and the occasional liquor when offered to me to get me in trouble.

I buy a cold six-pack of Mexican dark lager.

You've earned it.

Then the dark side crashes over me as I near the Sentry Arms. Logic kicks in. The bar gig will allow me to only tread water for a while. But for how long?

How close are the Feds in finding you?

At the apartment, Avril prepares for a date. It's an event just watching her get ready to go out. I open two bottles while she primps. We clink. I tell her about meeting with Oakes. She laughs, spewing suds through her nose.

"That's great. But you'll be busting your ass. It's a lot of dirty work. Fatiguing."

"Well, I'm glad to have it, Avey. Thanks for getting me in the door."

She's out the door. I'm alone now, drinking, fidgeting, chewing the inside of my cheek, knowing I've probably made another mistake by getting a job in a bar. How am I going to make enough to repay what I owe to Jimmy? And I'm not asking Jonathan for money. No way.

On TV is a blurry image of a body found in a ditch. Oh gezus, oh God, it's him. Marty Iszenski. I tremble just thinking about meeting him, and now he's dead. Did I have something to do with it?

He's of no concern of yours, Natalie. You hear? Not any of your doing.

I dial the redhead pimp. "Jimmy. Have you seen the news. That was Marty, wasn't it?"

"Yeah."

"What happened?"

"You tell me. You killed him."

"What? What did you say?"

"I asked why you killed him?"

I slam down the phone and frown into a kind of oblivion of no memories with him. My mind churns in search of anything that might connect me to something like that.

You didn't kill him, Natalie.

The phone rings, Jimmy calling back.

"What?"

"You were out of your mind, Runner. I should have never put him in front of you."

"Bullshit. You're lying to me. Why?"

Click.

I throw the phone at the sofa.

This can't be happening.

CHAPTER FOURTEEN

Two weeks later, I'm having breakfast in The Bean checking the want ads for something better. I've been doing grunt work at the bar every day. Avril had it right. It's exhausting work. The pay is pitiful. I've been busting my ass for what? I told Jimmy to give me a week to repay the three hundred. It's past that deadline. He'll be knocking on my door any day now.

Speaking of Avril, I haven't seen her in over a week.

I find a decent-looking ad for a job in a downtown office. I decide to apply for an interview. Three days later I have an interview scheduled for ten o'clock.

I hustle to get myself as business-spiffy as possible by borrowing one of Avril's button-down shirts. The trip on the bus to the office takes forty-five minutes. Ten minutes in the waiting room to meet the manager. The interview ends five minutes after I meet this priggish woman and ask what the job pays. She answers by wanting to know what I'll spend my pay on.

I feel my face heat up. I must be glowing red-faced. "You know... hon." I stand up. "I'll spend it on rent, food, transportation, medical attention, condoms, oxy, and ammo. You know, drugs, alcohol, and rock n' roll. All those necessities."

On my way out, I'm self-chastising, but okay with it.

You can't help yourself, can you, Natalie?

Back at the apartment, exhausted, I find the place ransacked, things strewn all over. Chairs overturned, drawers empty on the floor.

You've been robbed. But why? Nothing here of any value.

I call Cicero. After seeing the mess, he frowns. "Have you called the police?"

"Hell no. I don't want the police involved in this. What are they gonna do anyway? After all, it's just Avril and me. And I haven't seen her in days. Only some clothes, cosmetics, and a couple beers in the fridge.

"Anything else of importance you're missing?"

"Peace of mind."

"I'll change the locks," he says, getting up to leave. "Then lock your door."

Alone and angry at myself, and now hungry, I check the pantry. But for a half sleeve of saltines and a moldy piece of cheese, it's bare.

I whisper to myself, "For a flat-chested girl it's not good to lose any more weight. Hell, even Jonathan mentioned it."

Thank goodness I have a job in a restaurant to snack from the kitchen. I sit down to collect my thoughts. On the back of a past-due phone bill I start a list of what's bothering me.

•Trouble with a pimp
•The lurking law. Jail or a mental ward await

•What I came to California for, finding Dad's letter writer. That's faded, considering how the other issues are piling up

•Birth control pills. Almost out. *Good God, that would be your worst nightmare.*

•Fifty-seven dollars in my checking account. Thirteen in my wallet.

•Rent almost due. With my savings, I'm good for one more month.

Rent!

I look up in sudden realization.

Oh, Christ!

I jump up and race into Avril's bedroom. In the middle of the floor is my tote bag. It's fallen from the top of the closet. Contents are scattered around. The cash pouch is missing. Nineteen-hundred dollars. I scream obscenities as I go through the bag and everything again, wondering if I missed it somehow. But no. It's gone. I've been robbed. God—.

What the hell are you going to do now?

I fall on hands and knees, vomit building. I roll over and stare up at the ceiling until the urge passes. It's obvious now that drastic action is needed. Hands clenched, I bite knuckles and chew on my cheek.

Do it, Natalie. Do it. You have to. Do it.

I pull out a card I haven't seen since Denver and call the number. It rings three times. Voicemail: "Please leave a message at the tone."

"Hey, Mister Longer. It's me, Runner. Remember? Been a long time. How's Detective Redd? Just thought I'd ask. Well, I'm in trouble. Imagine that." Long pause. "I could use a little help, if you know what I mean. I just thought of you. And how you helped me out in Denver. I'm just wondering if... well, if you maybe could help me again." Pause. "Well, that's all." Then I give my phone number. "Hope you're good. Bye." Final pause. "Miss you."

I hang up, knowing nothing will come out of that call.

Should you call Jonathan?

"No," I shout. "No, no, no."

After more pacing, I slowly, and reluctantly, pull another card from the wallet.

JIMMY BARONE
Adult Entertainment
And Other Odd Opportunities

I stare at the phone number on the back. That Marty guy comes to mind. *Ugh.* I puff my cheeks and sigh. I am so hungry and so tired but can't relax. I walk around, scratching at my eyebrows, grabbing my hair.

No choice, Nat. You have no choice.

I grab the phone and stab in the numbers.

CHAPTER FIFTEEN

Jimmy answers in his typical nonchalant salesy pitch. "Looking for fun? Good. Barone speaking."

"Jimmy, it's me, Runner. Remember?"

"Remember? No. Who is this?"

"Quit the theatrics, dumbass. It's me."

"Oh. Runner. Right, yeah. Why, of course, I do. Who could forget your cheery personality? What's up?"

I pause for a couple seconds. "I'm just wondering..."

"Go on. No need to be bashful."

"Okay." I clear my throat. "What kind of money we talking about?"

"Well, first of all, it's so good to hear your voice. Now, what are you wanting to know?"

"Cut the crap, Jimmy. Get down to business."

"Okay. All right. This is good timing. I've got a special client you'd be perfect for. Nothing like Marty. Four hundred for an hour of work."

"Work. Is that what you call it?"

"You'd be smart to cut the attitude, Runner."

"Okay, okay. What do I have to do for it?"

He pauses. "All you got to do is just meet a man in the Grand Plaza Lobby Eatery downtown, Market Street, tomorrow. Be nice to him. That's all."

"Sex, you mean?"

He hesitates. "You ever had sex before, Runner?"

"What do you think?"

"Ever made money doing it in the back seat of one of those Chevys?"

"Get on with it, Jimmy."

"One hour, Runner. Just one hour is all the time you have to spend with him. Just be nice. Don't do anything you don't want to do."

"What's different with this guy?"

"Everything. He's rich. A gentleman." Jimmy pauses for effect. "I've provided girls to him before. He's a unique cat. Yes, he wants pretty young girls, of course. But more than that, he wants a challenge. No kiss-ups. He actually gets a little nervous, tongue-tied, apprehensive around pretty girls like you. But it heightens the experience for him when he's triumphant with his conquest. He may or may not invite you upstairs."

"Tomorrow, you say?"

"Yeah, noon tomorrow."

"Christ, Jimmy. I have to think this over."

"What's to think over?" He pauses. "I gotta know now, girl."

I hesitate for a second to find the strength.

Go for the fences as Father would say. Go big or go home.

"Seven fifty, Jimmy."

"What?"

"I want seven hundred and fifty dollars."

"Where'd you come up with that number?"

"Seven fifty."

"C'mon, girl. Don't do this. You already owe me three hundred for not following through with the last client."

"I don't know what that was, Jimmy. But you're not getting any of that money back. And you know it."

"Don't fuck with me over money, baby."

"Don't call me baby. Whatever you do, don't do that."

"Okay, okay."

I fold my arms. "So it's seven fifty. Not a penny less. Seven hundred and fifty smackaroos."

Jimmy's quick to reply. "Look at it this way, you—"

I interrupt. "Not a penny less. And if you continue to haggle, the price is going up. It's up to you."

A big sigh. A pause. "Right. You win. Can you get a ride downtown?"

I ignore his question and make my demand: "Up front."

"What? What do you mean up front?"

"The money. You said you paid up front."

"You want to get paid seven fifty before you go meet him?"

"Yep."

"That's not the way it works, Runner. My cut comes out first. You get the rest."

"And what's your cut of what a girl makes, Jimmy?"

"I told you earlier. Twenty-five percent."

"So if I make seven hundred and fifty dollars, that gets you a hundred eighty-seven. Right?"

He shrugs. "I round it off to two hundred."

"So your opinion of twenty-five percent is really almost twenty-seven percent then."

"Okay, something like that."

"So according to your math, if I want to get my seven fifty, and with your twenty-seven percent take, you'll have to charge the customer more than a thousand dollars. You follow the math? It's actually about a thousand thirty."

"Look, Runner. I'm not going to charge a customer a thousand dollars for a rookie. Let's just quit with the math, you egghead. I'll give you five hundred. That's it. If you really treat him right, he'll tip you."

"I don't work for tips, asshole."

"The hell you don't. You're a bartender."

I bow up and scratch the back of my neck, realizing my mistake.

He's got you there.

"Five hundred up front, you say?"

"Yeah. Five hundred."

"If I don't get it beforehand, Jimmy, I'm leaving. Won't even say hello to your client. He won't even get close enough to smell the DDT I'll be drenched in as a precaution. Do you understand?"

"You are awful. You know that, don't you?"

"Up front, Mister Barone."

"Be there fifteen minutes early. Don't be late. You'll get your money delivered in an envelope."

"You better be telling me the truth."

"Listen, Runner. I've been lenient with you. You're a good kid. But this is business. Money is sacrosanct with me. Marty didn't treat you right, and he refused to pay. You saw what happened to him. Right?"

My eyes open wide. "You... you killed..."

He ignores the insinuation but doesn't deny it. "Let's just move on. You have nothing to worry about if you do this. But if this client isn't satisfied, I'll come after you. No ands, ifs, or buts. Got it? And if, for whatever reason, you don't pay me back, you'll be very sorry. Remember Marty? And you better believe what I say is the honest-to-God truth. Suck on that before you agree."

"Why me, Jimmy? There's lots of other girls out there ready to sell themselves for a lot less than what I'm asking."

"My gut tells me you're perfect."

"What's your highest-paid girl?"

"Five grand for an overnight."

"Phew, five grand. Why so much for her?"

"She isn't the only one," he corrected. "And if you stick with it and play the game right, you'll be right up there at that level in no time."

I puff up my cheeks and blow out with a little whistle.

"You're right for this guy, Runner. That's why you're worth pursuing. So what do you think? Want to earn some real money?"

"If he wants a rebel, independent, smart ass, I know the part."

"You sure do, honey."

I remember my checkbook balance and my stolen emergency fund. "Yeah, I'm sure."

"Okay. You will meet him at the Grand Plaza Hotel downtown, on Market Street. His name is Henry Denny. His father is a billionaire who owns a conglomerate of industrial businesses, international shipping, real estate, and government contracts. He's a powerhouse. His son, Henry, is a spoiled kid with a lot of money who wants more than money. He wants to be God. His weakness is young women. You'll fit the bill."

"How will I know it's him?"

"He'll be impeccably dressed with a rosebud in the lapel."

I hang up and head to the shower to try and cleanse my soul.

CHAPTER SIXTEEN

Avril showed up last night, like nothing had happened for the time she was AWOL. No reason for her absence. I didn't ask; none of my business. And this morning she offered to drive me to the Grand Plaza for my meeting with Peter's customer.

Traffic is terrible in this city. She drives like an old, retired drill sergeant, honking and flipping off cars. She's a terror when things don't go her way. But sweet as sugar otherwise. She pulls up at the curb on Market Street in front of the Grand Plaza Hotel.

"Get your ass out, girl," she says, looking over her shoulder at the traffic building up behind us. "Get out before that cop comes over."

"I am. I am."

She's giddy for what I'm about to do. "What a la-de-da place to get your first paycheck for screwing some dude," she shouts over the downtown noise. "Be ready to run if he's the creature from the black lagoon. I want full details of everything. Okay?"

"Sure, yeah."

Then she looks at me seriously. "Be careful. You hear?"

I lean in through the window, pinch her nose, and thank her for the ride. "Get outta here, Avey. See you tonight."

She pulls away, honking and waving in the rearview, almost clipping a jaywalker.

It's eleven forty-five, lunchtime. I take a seat at a little round cocktail table and tug at the sleeve of Avril's white button-down Oxford shirt. I borrowed it to cover the ink butterfly on my wrist. But the sleeves are too short for my long arms and there's a wine stain on one of the sleeves from a party a week ago. I glance around, thinking I'm probably pissing off the rich snobs eying me for infringing on their view of one another. I don't give a rip. I am what I am.

Oh well.

I wait for Jimmy's client to show. This place is so ostentatious it's embarrassing. It's meant for the privileged class to munch on mousse pâté baguettes, lobster bisques, and chestnut salads and sip on their addictions. I've experienced these so-called delicacies many times with Father at his fancy banquets honoring him for his numerous scholarly achievements. But this isn't my style. Give me PBRs, chicken wings, and shelled peanuts in a barnwood-walled beer hall and I'm a happy girl.

Still time to get up and walk out, Nat.

A short server appears like a penguin in an ill-fitting black and white uniform. "Get you something, hon?"

Hon? He called you hon. Is that what he calls other women here? Let it go. Just... let... it... go.

The leather-bound wine list didn't have me in mind when they listed the prices. "Wow," I whisper.

The server holds back a grin.

So what do I do? I order the most expensive-sounding bottle of red wine listed. If he doesn't show, I skip out into a dead run. They won't catch me.

The wine arrives on a silver platter. Beside it is an envelope. Inside are five crisp one-hundred dollar bills with a note. **Be nice.**

The server grins.

I drop the envelope into the threadbare Smugglers Notch tote hanging over the back of my chair. Then I take a sip of the overpriced wine.

"Honestly, Wilbert, this isn't very good."

"Oh, I'm so sorry, miss. My name is not Wilbert. But would you like something else? Thunderbird, perhaps?"

"You know, Wilbert. I think you're screwin' with me."

"Now, miss. Why would I do something like that?"

"Well, maybe you know why I'm here. And my tip will probably be larger than yours. You're just jealous."

"Touché," he whispers.

"Look, whatever your name is, I gotta tell you the sweet reds Dad and I drank fishing off a Lake Champlain dock were much better than this." I tap the label. "I've never been a wine kind of girl, so this expensive glass of Chateau de Hoojamaflip is wasted on me. What I'd really like is a basket of greasy fries with a half-dozen packets of catsup. The greasier the fries the better. Just like your personality. And how about a couple cold PBRs to wash 'em down? Can you get that for me, Wilbert?"

"My, my. You are a little stinker, aren't you?"

I wink. "Don't take it personally. Maybe the greasy-character crack was uncalled for. I'm just nervous, and you caught my road rage. Accept my apologies."

"Apologies accepted."

"So, what's your real name, then?"

He looks around before whispering, "Gilbert. What's yours, hon?"

I ignore his question and wiggle a finger at him. "Don't call me that. I'm not your hon."

He nods.

"And Gil. I have to tell you. You look ridiculous in that penguin suit. You can do better than that."

He nods good-naturedly and steps back. "Good luck to you also, Miss Runner."

He knows who you are. What else does he know?

I look away, down half the glass of wine in two gulps and wince, hoping to make this meeting easier. I recheck the text message of how to identify this guy.

Look for a rose in his lapel.

The big ornate clock on the wall chimes noon. A hangnail becomes the object of my attention. I fiddle with my hair.

Come on. Let's get this over with. Show your face, man.

A tall man arrives at the entryway in an expensive-looking suit. And there's the rose.

It's him.

He slips through tables elegantly, trying to look inconspicuous. He's nervous, hoping to avoid a reporter or eyes from one of his social circles. It's now five after twelve. He's wasting precious minutes standing around. I have to do something or risk him walking away and me losing Jimmy's money. I'm not about to lose any more money.

The man's attention settles on me for a second. I'm underdressed for this place. And I'm the only unattached female. He immediately dismisses me, probably because I look like a hotel staffer, janitor, maid, or grunge groupie waiting for Kurt Cobain to rise from the dead and meet for tea.

He strolls around. After a couple minutes, he steps to the

side to check his phone. He glances my way for a second before he begins his last loop through the tables to find what he's paid for. He comes close, passing by only a few feet away, not giving me the time of day until I whisper, "Looking for me?"

He stops and looks down with a raised eyebrow. "Runner?"

I stretch up and whisper, "Maybe."

He does a quick inspection around the eatery before reaching out to shake. "Hello. My name's Michael."

Liar.

CHAPTER SEVENTEEN

He's very formal but stiff. He stands almost at attention. His hand is warm and mushy when we shake.

"Have a seat, Mike." I wave at the chair opposite me and wipe his hand sweat on my jeans as I take my seat.

He takes another quick look around before sitting. He can't help himself. Another scan around the crowd is necessary before he settles in to give me his attention.

Be nice, Natalie. This is his show. Let him drive.

He's finally comfortable enough to notice me. To see what he's paid for. According to Jimmy, I'm exactly what gets this guy off. And the danger of meeting me in public makes the conquest that much better. His wife, kids, and his reputation are at stake. He has more to lose than me if this goes bad. But I have to say, these types of men interest me in a ludicrous, absurd sort of way.

"Runner," he whispers. "Is that your working name?"

I lick my lips and blink with utter contempt for who he thinks I am. Gilbert reappears. "What would you like, Mister... uh..."

"I'll have a Sazerac. One ice cube."

"Coming right up, sir."

Mikey returns to me with the same question. "Is Runner your real name? Or is who you really are a secret?"

"I'm Runner. All you need to know."

He half nods. It's clear what he wants and it isn't small talk. But he doesn't know how to go about this.

I play along, coy, flirtatious. It's a delicious cat-and-mouse game we girls play with men. He tries to keep up with his stale, stilted retorts. He's dull as gray clay. I'm getting the better of him, and he knows it. His eyes change instantly from light-hearted and supplicating to irritable. He's ready to get up and leave.

Remember what Jimmy said about being on the hook for repaying him if this doesn't go well.

I can't afford to have this go bad. And right now this whole setup is headed downhill. I have to throw Mikey a rope. Can't afford to have a pimp chasing me down for money that I don't have.

Ugh.

"I'm sorry, Mike. Just my nature to be difficult before performing. I hope you understand. Probably why I'm in such demand. I'll make it good and exciting for you. But only if you want."

He blushes. A touch of sweat beads on the top lip of his nervous grin. God, how maddening he is. He doesn't know how to close the deal.

Ask for it, Mister Henry Denny. Let's get this over with.

But no, he just sits there like a bump on a pickle and squirms.

Come on, go for the close, Mikey.

I have to get this going. So, I reach under the little table and touch the inside of his knee and massage it gently. His voice jumps two octaves. He should be about ready to let loose in his tighty whities. But he just sits there, frozen. I lean over close. Almost choking on the bouquet of English Leather.

"Come 'ere, Mikey." My finger beckons.

He hesitates before leaning in slightly, eyes wide like a frightened poodle.

I pull him closer by the tie. "Come on, Mikey. Come closer, big guy."

Now we're nose-to-nose. I have him. His heart beats like a war drum. I get up, go around the table, yank his coat lapels, pull him close, throw my leg over his, and am in his lap. I plant a big ole' Frenchie smack dab on his open mouth, throw my arms around his neck, and go slobbering on his ears.

What happens next stuns me. This camera guy runs in, a strobe light firing like a machine gun, *click, click, click* dozens of times, before a bodyguard comes out of nowhere, pulling me off Mikey, the camera still *clickety, clicking* away.

I slap at the big galoot pulling on me. He slaps me back harder. Oh yeah, a lot harder. All this caught by the beautiful people gawking and the camera still snapping away.

So what's a girl to do?

I grab that wine bottle and smash it over the bodyguard's head. I slip and fall, bounce up and run out through the revolving door up the street looking for a dark place to hide from what I just.

CHAPTER EIGHTEEN

I run three blocks from the Grand Plaza before stopping to catch my breath and look back for any pursuit. It's clear.

I push into a side-street coffee shop. The Illegal Grounds, lawyers coming and going in their conservative tailored suits with their tanned leather briefcases.

It's busy, all tables taken. I gesture to a man on his phone at a two-top if I might share his table. He's a nice-looking, approachable man in an open-collared shirt and a smart navy blazer. He waves at the seat across from him without speaking.

I nod, smile, and take a seat on the edge of the chair, trying to calm down. He completes his call, acknowledges me and sips on his coffee.

I can't stop my hands from shaking while I call Avril. I get voicemail.

"Hey, Avey. It's almost one o'clock. Can you pick me up? It didn't work out... ugh. He had a bodyguard. I broke a wine bottle over his head. I'm not right for this kind of work; should have never left Vermont. When can you be here? Call me. So sorry to be so much trouble. Get back to me ASAP. Or maybe you can schedule an Uber for me. Call me either way. I'm in this coffee shop on..."

I look around, clueless as to where I am.

The man across from me leans over. "Sutter Street. The Illegal Grounds Coffee Shop."

I nod, lip him a thank you and repeat it to Avril and hang up, embarrassed. He's sipping his coffee and watching me while I try to appear over my chaotic arrival.

"Thank you again," I whisper.

"No problem."

We sit in silence. I'm nervous and jittery. I gather up my tote bag and start to leave.

"Hey," he says. "Where are you going in such a flurry?"

"I..."

"Sit for a minute. Take a breath. What are you drinking?"

"Oh. I have to go. I'm in a hurry."

"I'm not one to eavesdrop, but... I am sitting right here and couldn't miss the anxiety in your voice. I recognize distress when I hear it. And it sounds like you have time to kill before your ride arrives. You must have time for a cup of coffee. So what would you like?"

I run fingers through my hair and hesitate before looking into his cool blue eyes. "Well, maybe."

"It's on me. What can I get you?"

"A cappuccino, maybe."

He signals a barista. "Judy, can you bring us a cappuccino?"

"Sure thing, Bobby."

I interrupt with a raised finger to her. "Please. Can you please make it a double, Judy? Thank you." Then to Bobby. "This is nice of you."

The cappuccino comes nice and warm, creamy and frothy. I hold it out to him. "Cheers."

He reciprocates. Mugs clink. I wipe froth from my mouth. "I'm Runner. It's a nickname."

"So, you're a jogger."

"Yeah. But that's not why I go by Runner. Long story. Better leave it at that."

"Bob Simms. My friends call me Bobby. So can you."

"You a lawyer, Bobby?"

"No. Oh no, no, no. I'm a reporter. What do *you* do, Runner?"

I take a sip and pause. "I'm a prostitute."

His brows lift. A table of three men behind him do the same.

"Nice try," he says. "Not buying it."

"Yeah. I really am."

"How's business?"

"Booming."

He sips. "How long you been... uh... in your line of work?"

"About a half hour."

Bobby smirks. "You must work fast."

I tuck hair strands behind my ears and fold my arms. "My first and last client didn't work out. I'm a better bartender than hooker, I guess." Then I toss it back to him. "So what kind of stuff do you write about, Bobby?"

"Investigative stuff now," he explains. "I'm always on the lookout for an interesting story. Always political stuff to sniff out. Working on some white-collar crime things right now."

I nod. Then notice the beautiful head of thick silver hair. "You don't look old enough for all the stuff you've done."

"I'm younger than I look."

"You look great. You should be on TV."

"I'm flattered, but writing is my life. How about you, Runner? Where do you bartend?"

"Danfield. And I'm not a full bartender yet. Just learning."

"Pardon me for saying this, but... you don't look old enough to be a bartender."

"I've heard that before." Then I throw it back at him. "And you don't look tough enough to look a politician in the eye and ask if he's had his hand in the cookie jar."

He laughs. "I did that once to an FBI agent. That was fun. I learned a lot about the Feds."

My heart misses a beat at the mention of Feds. I grab at the coffee and drink it straight down, staring at him over the rim of the cup. He's very observant to my distress.

We engage in light conversation, shallow stuff. He orders me another cappuccino. "Why did you say you were a prostitute?"

"I have a mental health condition. A desire to be noticed. That's what a state-sponsored psychiatrist diagnosed me with."

He leans in. "Why?"

"Why what?"

"Why were you in front of a shrink?"

"They seemed to think I killed someone."

"They. Who was they?"

"Long story. Something I don't want to talk about."

He nods. "But were you guilty?"

I fidget. *This is a complete stranger you're talking to, Natalie. Wake up.*

He grabs my shaking hand to calm me. "There's a little bar right up the street. How about we take this conversation up there to finish over a drink?"

I glance at the time. A little past two.

Should you?

Bobby stares. Waiting for an answer.

I text Avril.

Avey, forget about that ride. Have other plans.

CHAPTER NINETEEN

Jimmy sits quietly on a sofa in a high-rise office overlooking Market Street while Henry Denny paces the floor waiting for one of his men, Orin Barlow, to arrive. Denny is red-faced, spitting-mad, bite marks on his ear, hair in a mess, and covered in wine stains. He goes from rage to bewilderment in a finger snap. He swallows the last of his scotch, ice and all, and then stares into the bottom of the empty glass.

Barlow walks in wondering why he's been called in. He studies the redheaded guy on the sofa. Never seen him before. Then he looks to Henry and asks a sarcastic question. "Something to do with a woman, Henry?"

Henry Denny's stare never leaves the empty glass.

Barlow flops in a chair, folds his arms, and taps a finger with impatience. "Is this another one of your hush-hush, clandestine pedophilic episodes, Henry? Does some strange little bohemian guttersnipe have you in a spot? Threatening blackmail or something worse?"

"I don't need this today, Orin. So I'd appreciate you just listening."

"Listening about what, Henry?"

"I want you to find the bitch who just made a fool of me."

"Made a fool of you? How?"

"Set me up."

"Set you up?"

"Yeah. In the Grand Plaza. Attacked me." Denny gives an account of the incident. "She made a fool of me. All caught by a photographer. We need to find who's responsible for this and destroy those fucking pictures before they get to the press. We need to pay off a blackmail ransom, whatever it will be, and catch the bastards."

"How did you come about being with this girl you say attacked you?"

"None of your business."

"What do you mean, 'None of my business'? It's my business to know who you're hanging out with. That's what your father hired me for."

"This girl was different, Barlow. Tall, thin, provocative with tattoos. A dark-eyed spitfire."

"How old?"

"What difference does it make?"

"So, she was young."

"Yeah. Eighteen, nineteen, maybe twenty something."

"What was she like?"

"What do you mean?"

"Her personality. I need to know as much as I can to do my job."

"She's enigmatic, precocious, and clever, and she knows it. Got a mouth on her. She never had any intention of going upstairs with me."

"You had a service find her?"

Jimmy raises a hand. "I found her for him."

"You're the pimp. So it's your fault."

"It's as much a surprise to me as it is for Henry."

"What's your name?"

"Jimmy Barone." He produces his card.

Barlow knocks it away. "I hate pimps. Scum of the earth."

Denny comes to Jimmy's defense. "I've used Jimmy before. Never had any problems with his girls. They're first class."

Barlow tells Henry, "You're a good lawyer. Not many times has anyone gotten the best of you. And now this teenager lays you out like a dusty rug. I've known you since you graduated from law school. Watched you build your business under the watchful eye of your father. He's getting tired of your dirty promiscuity like I am. Rescuing you from these women is wearing me out."

Denny glares. "Look at me. You lame-brain goon. You don't get paid to pass judgment on me. And you don't really know how I treat those girls. That's my business."

Barlow stands his ground. "Listen to me, Henry. I'm not a miracle worker. The day will come when you're in too deep for me to pull you out of the shit hole you've dug yourself into."

"I want you to just do your job, Orin. Whatever I tell you to do, you do it. Understand?"

"My loyalty is to your father. Not you." With that said, Barlow turns to leave.

"Where you going?"

"I've got to get started on this. I'll begin at the Grand Plaza. I have to meet this girl. Did you even get her name?"

Jimmy answers. "She calls herself Runner. No doubt a working name."

Barlow asks, "Any idea where she lives or hangs out?"

"I found her in Modesto. Other than that, I have no idea where to find her."

Barlow scratches his head. "Something tells me we've got to tread carefully with this one."

"Bullshit," says Denny, pouring himself another drink. "Just drag her ass in here. I want that girl in front of me by tomorrow. She's got something coming. And, of course, I want to know who's behind the photos. No time to waste on this. Got it?"

Barlow and Jimmy share glances.

"Well?" Denny waves at the door. "Get the hell out of here and find that little bitch."

CHAPTER TWENTY

Weeks later, I've cleaned restrooms, washed windows, emptied the garbage, and even written the restaurant chalkboard specials. I hum a tune while going through my routine. With Avril's help, I'm learning the bar business fast. She lets me mix drinks and push orders out when it's busy. The list of drinks I've learned to make gets longer by the day. How I handle customers and even help Avril close out the register at night gives me more confidence to think I just might like this business. It's not rocket science. Oakes notices me taking on more responsibility with a good attitude and tells me, "You may actually make it as a bartender someday."

High praise from one who isn't known for handing out compliments.

Connor O'Grady is the full-time, big-cheese head bartender, a big, sandy-headed gay from Belfast. I do my best to keep the bar up to date, clean, and refreshed for him. But he treats me like a child. Doesn't give me an ounce of support or encouragement. He only bitches over how I do things. Okay, so we don't get along. But when he tells Oakes to fire me, it gets serious. Oakes doesn't of course. But lying about my work standards, that's when I decide to do things my way. Show him who I really am and what I'm capable of.

In the restroom, I splash water on my face and stare into the mirror. My eyes go slitty. I whisper to the she-devil, staring back. "He doesn't know who he's dealing with."

With the help of one of the bar's most loyal regulars, Jay, who happens to have a crush on me, we come up with a plan to get O'Grady in trouble. It's known the Irishman has a short fuse and a wicked temper.

Jay suggests we goad him into starting a fight.

So, I interrupt O'Grady who's in a conversation with a customer at the bar. He glares at me. "I'm talking to Mister Barlow right now, Runner. Go clean a toilet or whack off or something. Don't bother me again."

The man who O'Grady is in deep conversation with stares at me. More than just a pervert's leer. He turns to me like he wants to know me better.

"So your name's Runner. Is that right?"

"Yep."

Why do..."

But Jay shoves him out of the way before he can finish and shouts to O'Grady. "Don't talk to her that way, you fucking fairy."

Soon, four cops are breaking up fights. Tables and chairs tossed around. I'm in a corner, arms folded, watching it all when a detective comes over.

"How did this get started?"

"O'Grady threw the first punch."

While he takes my statement, O'Grady handcuffed and yelling obscenities at me. "Watch your back, bitch. The shit you pulled on Henry Denny. Ha. He's gonna have your skinny ass. You better hope the cops get to you first. Cuz if Denny gets his hands on you, you'll wish you were dead, you cunt."

The detective frowns. "What's he talking about?"

Gulp. *Change the subject, Nat.*

I shrug, reach over, and brush a piece of ash from the kitchen fire off the detective's shoulder. It's a flirt. He recognizes it. Questioning over. Order restored.

I call Mister Oakes, who is out of town. "The cops just arrested O'Grady. They're hauling him off." I give brief details. For almost a minute, all I hear are long draws off a cigar.

"What have you done, Runner?"

"Sir?"

"I said, what have you done to handle things?"

"Oh. I called the police. They handled the fight. Settled everyone down. There was some water cleanup, a few broken glasses, and a shattered chair. Nothing too bad. I called Avril. She was on a date but showed up to help restore order. With things under control, she left. Just me now. The customers are buzzing with excitement. O'Grady had a loaded gun in his backpack and some drugs. The customers are all in a good mood. Laughing over the excitement."

"Well, okay. Good." His next words surprise me. "Can you handle it?"

"Handle what?"

"Run the bar until I get a replacement."

I freeze. "Why not Avril?"

"She's a good bartender but a little unreliable. And she has her own shifts. So... you ready to step up and take care of things until I find a replacement?"

"Uh..." I glance around at the guys at the bar watching me. "When will that be?"

"I don't know. Does it matter?"

"Yeah. It kinda does."

"Runner." He pauses. "Can you handle it for now?"

"Oh. I don't know."

He draws my name out in two long syllables. "Run...ner?"

"Huh..."

"Did you hear me? I asked if you can handle the bar by yourself now?"

"I. I... uh.'

"Run...ner?"

"I guess so, Mister Oakes."

"Gezus, call me Vance. Okay? Listen. Tomorrow I'll try to be there for the big party. But if I'm not, just be yourself. Work with Avril. Be the best you can. Got it?"

I clear my voice. "What if I'm not ready?"

"Quit saying that."

I hesitate, realizing how I must sound. "Okay, okay. Yes, sir."

"Now take a big deep breath. Show me what you're made of, baby."

My skin prickles. "Don't call me baby. Don't ever call me baby... sir."

I hear him chuckle. I'm pissed.

"Runner?"

I blurt out with a smidgen of contempt. "What?"

"Those customers, they still there?"

"Yeah. What about them?"

"Buy 'em a round. On the house."

My hands shake. I hang up and turn around to the small group of regulars led by Jay with a welt under his eye. They're waiting to hear what Vance told me. With hands on hips, I frown, take a deep breath, and shout. "Drinks on the house."

. . .

At the apartment I'm still shaking from the mayhem in the bar and wondering how O'Grady knew about Denny. Avril's not here to talk with. So, I make a call to an old friend for advice. Same guy I met in Denver. Someone like me, crazy. I get his voicemail on a bad connection.

Lea...ve a mes...sage at the s...und o...the...ep.

"It's me, Runner. Remember me, Peter? Seems like forever since we shared burgers and fries in that old, abandoned tavern. I don't know if this number I'm calling is still good. If it is, will you call me?" I give my number and then my address. "I need your advice." I pause. "Okay, what I really need is your help. What's new, right? Well, thanks. This is my second call. Hope to hear from you."

I hang up, wondering if I will ever hear from him again.

CHAPTER TWENTY-ONE

Denver, Colorado.

Richard Redd, retired Denver Police Detective, is making chili in his kitchen at home. A call comes in from somewhere in the 505 area code. "Hello, Rich."

"Who's this?"

"It's me, Peter."

Redd breaks out in a smile. "Well, well, outlaw. Where you been hiding out these days?"

"Oh, somewhere that doesn't make a difference to anyone. How the hell are you, detective? All recovered from those wounds?"

"Almost. But I expect I'll never get back to a hundred percent. Doin' fine though. Except when you call to interrupt my cookin'."

"You still making that famous blazing hot chili a yours?"

"You know it. What's up? Why am I so lucky to get this call?"

Peter chuckles. "I got a call from our little friend, Runner. She's in trouble out in California."

Redd straightens up. "What kinda trouble?"

"Well, I don't know. I never answered her. She just left a message. Sounded stressed."

"So what's this call about, Pete?"

"A favor, maybe."

"What kind?"

"Would you be up for a little visit to California, Rich?"

"Maybe."

"It's a lot to ask, I know, but..."

"I understand. Pete, I owe you one huge favor. What can I do to help?"

"We've got to know how bad it is for her. The trouble she's talking about. You know how she can find trouble wherever it is. This sounds like something serious for her to call me. After all, we haven't spoken since Denver. Now, out of the blue, she reaches out."

"I got it. You have an address for her?"

"Yeah. But the connection was bad. The address she gave was 743 West Main Street. Danfield, California. Her phone number broke up. Bad connection. So I don't have a number to give you."

Redd scratches the back of his neck. "You know I'm a retired cop." He pauses. "Make that a crippled cop at that. But I'll see what I can do. See what kind of trouble she's gotten herself into."

"Yeah. Let me know what she's up to. Thanks, Rich."

CHAPTER TWENTY-TWO

Morning comes early after a stormy night of dreaming that O'Grady escaped prison and came after me. Maybe I feel a little guilty for getting him fired. Almost! He was a jerk. And how did he know about me and Denny? Is he connected to Denny somehow? Does he have friends itching to get even with me?

You've stirred something up, Natalie.

Paranoia kicking in. Schizophrenia, maybe? I'm beginning to wonder.

Stop it, Natalie.

Concentrate on the big party scheduled for the grill this evening. Being paired with Avril makes it better. She knows the bar business so well the night will come off without a problem. Maybe Jonathan will show. I'd feel safer with him there watching over me.

My shift doesn't begin until four. Time to visit The Coffee Bean and linger around, hoping to find a clue to the letter writer. Why do I have this crazy notion she'll simply walk up and announce herself as my father's lover?

It's a nice three-block walk to The Bean. Before reaching it, I run into Joey, the homeless kid who pushes around on a wheeled platform. His loyal dog, Clipper always at his side. Joey's legs were lost in a car accident years ago. He and his dog hang here on this corner most days for handouts. I give him a five from my tips and sit on the curb for a chat.

"Thank you, Miss Runner."

He tells knock-knock jokes. We laugh at how terrible they are. I scratch Clipper's head. "So how are things, Joey?"

"We just fine, mam. Such a lovely mornin'. How 'bout you?"

I'm chatting with this sweet guy with no legs. He never complains. He wears this infectious smile with his lovable dog at his side. He begs for food. He doesn't have much. Neither do I. But look at the difference between us. His smile is genuine and sincere. No put-on fake poor-me attitudes. But me... I'm the queen of bad attitudes and the leader of poor-me club.

"I wish I had a dog, Joey."

"Didn't you have one growing up?"

"Never. Mom and Dad were too busy and didn't want another distraction."

"Oh, that's too bad. A dog can be your best friend in the whole wide world."

"My best friend was a stuffed teddy bear I slept with."

"Well, that's something. Teddy bears don't poop."

I chuckle. "Maybe if I had a dog, I'd be more happy."

"Aren't you happy now, Miss Runner?"

I grin back, squeeze his arm, and scruffle Clipper's fur. "I'm fine, Joey. Just fine."

I wish that were true.

The Bean's after-lunch crowd has gone now. I linger over a grilled cheese, chips, and lemonade. Lorraine, The Bean's owner is deciding what items to advertise on the chalkboard. A girl about my age, daughter Sunshine, is adding the menu items in yellow, green, and red chalk with a kitschy, ornate-cursive font style.

Sunshine is a clone of her mother. Rich auburn hair and green eyes. Lorraine tells her, "Let's add rhubarb muffins for three dollars."

I watch the letters go on the board, smooth, careful, with meticulous care taken to look good. Everything about this cafe is eccentric, cool, and cozy. I compliment Sunshine on her work. "Beautiful."

"Thanks."

"Is Sunshine your real name?"

"Yep," she says, carefully chalking the price in red without looking up.

I'm about to leave when I notice an older, attractive woman alone at a table watching me, tapping a pencil to her lips. She's thoughtful, staring intently at me.

Go ask her if she's Father's mysterious lover. Go. Go now.

My phone rings. A woman's voice in a foreign dialect. She starts in unemotionally.

"Listen carefully, Miss Grace. You're in danger."

"Who is this?"

Ignoring my question, she continues. "Your friend, Peter Longer is..."

I interrupt, jumping up at hearing the name. My heart racing. "Peter?"

She continues. "I calling on behalf of Mister Peter Longer. Please carefully listen. Do not interrupt. There is a cargo vessel to dock in Port of Oakland very soon. You have paid-for passage to French Polynesia. It not a passenger cruise liner, so no luxury treatment, okay? Just cabin. Look for confirmation from maritime shipping company Almarani. They will forward to you confirmation when is expected to arrive. Tell no one of this ship or your passage on it. You will not be listed on manifest. Do you understand this?"

"I guess, but..."

"Once aboard, you are on your own. No recognition by captain of your presence as a passenger. If asked by port authorities in Tahiti, you say you are crew member. Understood?"

"Tahiti? Yes, but..."

"No more voice contact. Look for text confirmation. Goodbye."

Click.

The evening behind the bar goes well with Avril and I working together. Maybe because I'm deliriously happy with the news of a boat coming to take me away to Tahiti. The happiest I've been since leaving Vermont. Jonathan pulls up a stool at the far end of the bar. I lay a napkin in front of him with a grin. "What'll it be, mister?"

"You look good tonight, Ruckus."

I roll my eyes. "You too, handsome."

The rest of the hectic evening he sips on two drafts while watching me work. He's here because I told him I need a ride home after closing. His reward will be me spending the night at his outrageously opulent home with a pool, tennis courts and a four-car garage for his expensive cars. What I like best of all is the king bed swathed in sumptuous, cool, crisp percale sheets and luxurious goose-down pillows to get lost in. To be honest, the bed experience is better than him. I could be persuaded to live with him just for that bed. But that's not going to happen.

You have a ship to catch.

CHAPTER TWENTY-THREE

It's been over a week since hearing from Almarani. Nothing so far about the boat's arrival. I'm losing faith that it's even real.

Stress comes with life, Natalie. Deal with it.

It's my day off today. Three-thirty in the afternoon. Avril and I decide to do something we've not done yet: find somewhere to hang out and turn loose from the worries plaguing us. Have a few drinks, commiserate, validate each others' feelings and disparage the men in our lives.

We stroll into Elmers. A rustic, beer-soaked tavern on the outskirts of Blackhawk. Nothing more than a barnwood, hole-in-the-wall with a small dusty dance floor, wobbly tables and license plates nailed to the walls. Two guitars, a drum set, and a mic stand are ready for the evening gig.

I'm not due back at Oakes for my shift until tomorrow. Avey has to be back late this evening.

After a few drinks, we're at it, laughing like schoolgirls at the antics of men. After about the third drink, the conversation slowly turns melancholy and then drifts to the point of gravity. She clutches my hand, grasping for something, desperation in her eyes. Regrets spill out. A litany of woe, as she kneads my hands with fingers trembling like autumn leaves, mumbling missteps and indiscretions she's made all her life.

"You know..." Her voice trails off as if lifted by a soft breeze of uncertainty, but headed to the edge of confession. "You know, if I could make a wish, I'd go back and..." She trails off into a reverie, unable to finish the thought.

My brow furrowed. "Go back? Go back and do what, Avey?"

"I'd go back and learn to stand tall, be strong like you, Natalie. I'd make friends and be responsible and upstanding."

"But we can't go back, can we, Avey? The cake is baked, its flavors set. The flowers have bloomed, their petals unfurled to the sun. We are who we are, shaped by the hands that raised us."

"So, what does that mean? Are we to be like we are for the rest of our days?"

I linger in thought, sifting through memories of my childhood and what it means for my future. While she waits for my answer, her gaze wanders, studying each man entering the bar. However I answer, I know it will be but a vanishing echo to her as her lustful desires take charge. She's already lost in want, beholding her choices for tonight.

"Avey, you still with me?"

She turns to me. "Uh, uh-huh." Her face serious. "Life is about choices, isn't it, Nat? So many I've made I still regret."

"Well, as Einstein famously said, 'Learn from yesterday, live for today, hope for tomorrow.'"

She drops my hands and leans back, reminiscing over her childhood days. "Running from commitment started early for me, Natalie. Family, school, religion, and my little brother. I abandoned them all." She fingers her glass in thought. "When I was young, I was a straight A student living in a comfortable home. I was in need of nothing or no one." Her eyes begin to glass over with tears.

"A little brother arrived; his name was Toby. He grew into the son Mom and Dad always wanted." She sniffs. "After his death, they were left with me. The wild child who never accepted their virtuous, incorruptible lifestyle. Church on Sunday, Bible studies on Tuesday and Wednesday. Toby had adopted their faith totally. He was only ten. Drunk driver."

"Oh, Avey. I'm so sorry."

"Well..." She sighs. "That's when I left responsibility, integrity and morality behind. Cancer of the soul won me over."

I stiffen at the mention of the word cancer.

She waves her hand. "Look around at this place, Natalie. This is my life now. Places like this with a different guy every night but dancing to the same old song. These places attract me." She twirls a curl around her finger. "You're not the type to abandon a friend, are you, Natalie?"

My chin rests in the palm of my hand as I stare at her thinking how wrong she has me pegged. She doesn't know I'm hightailing it out of here as soon as that boat hits the pier.

"No, Avey. I'd never abandon you."

She wipes a tear from her chin. "I want to be like you, Natalie. You're in control."

I avoid the flattery. She's drunk and rambling, not knowing what she's talking about. Doesn't realize how out of control I am. How terrified I feel if I'm caught by Denny or worse captured by the law and sent to some mental institution.

Avril mumbles on. "I think of all the men I could have had a loving, lasting, relationship with. But no. Here I sit now, waiting for that same old song to play again. The same faces." She finishes with a smack of the lips and goes back to studying the men giving her the eye.

Avril is on the carousel of grief with no way off, and she knows it. Making love for the fun of it is just a placebo to ease the pain. I get up and go to her side of the table and hold her. I feel the warmth of tears on my neck.

She pushes away and holds me at length. "You would never abandon me, would you Natalie?" She sobs and hugs me again, shaking like a leaf.

"No, Avril. Never."

We lean over the table grinning with wet faces and share genuine affection in this dusty old tavern as the band begins its warm up.

"What about you, Nat? When are you gonna find your man?"

"Are you familiar with the term ignis fatuus?"

"What?"

"It's Latin for false hope, will-o'-wisp, paramnesia—fact versus fiction. So, I don't know if I'll ever find love."

She relaxes, wipes tears, and laughs. "You're a brain box, Nat. Where did you learn all that stuff you toss around?"

"Father."

She wipes her chin and stares. "You look on edge, girl. It scares me to think of you so uptight. Is it the law that's after you? Is that it?"

I chew on a stir stick before answering. "I've been told I'm schizophrenic, Avey. It's common for schizophrenics to be on edge with delusional thoughts, paranoia, hearing voices, and hallucinations."

"Bullshit. You're not schizophrenic."

"Listen," I say to her, "I got hauled into a psychiatrist's office after the fire for evaluation of my mental competency before they could complete an arrest for suspicion of arson resulting in death. The substitute shrink on staff that day spit-balled his diagnosis. Not much thought went into his prognosis. I escaped when he excused himself from the office for a minute. I just got up and walked out the front door without anyone stopping me. Been on the run since."

Elmers is filling up. The little band begins. Avey walks over to a cowboy for a dance. I check for phone messages, expecting to hear from Almarani. Nothing.

Avril's back with a beer. "What are you doing on that damn phone, girl? We're supposed to be havin' fun."

I want to tell her what I'm waiting for. But I hesitate, remembering I am to tell no one of the boat voyage. But this is Avril.

I lean into her. "Avril, I'm..."

"You're what?" She frowns.

"I'm..."

"What are you trying to say?"

"I'm leaving."

She touches my nose as a broad-shouldered cowboy tugs at her to get up and dance. "I already have mine picked out for the night," she says, strutting onto the dance floor. "I'll be leaving before you tonighht. No worries."

The little dirt band belts out red-blooded rock, country, and bluegrass. Avey and I dance nonstop with all kinds: old men, skinny boys, thick-legged rodeo types and biker dudes. We slide across the worn hardwood, dipping, purling to the beat, head flying back, slinking, belly-to-belly. Locking onto their eyes, selling it hard.

I lose track of time. Haven't seen Avril since the first few dances. The last I saw of her was leaving with some guy in bike leather. No matter, I find my own entertainment. The next three hours are a brazen collision of lust and mindless, carefree freedom in a tall ranch-hand's camper trailer.

Seems like my issues are similar to Avril's. But I know I'm different.

It's your Mother's blood running through your veins fighting with your father's morals.

But the results seem to be the same.

CHAPTER TWENTY-FOUR

Jimmy arrives at Oakes' Bar for a meeting with Vance to take a call from Denny. Jimmy's sure the call will be an ass-chewing for not having already found Runner hog-tied and lying in front of him.

Vance asks, "What the hell are we doing still working with this crazy son-of-a-bitch rich kid without a lick of common sense?"

"Because he pays well. I can't afford to lose that pile a money he throws at me every month. Same with you."

Vance pulls the cigar from his teeth. "He trusts us. You find him girls. I coordinate those Almarani cargo ships."

"I do a lot more for him than just girls, Vance. You know that. And his daddy's ships make a lot more than what you make selling beer and burgers."

Vance snuffs the cigar out. "But beer and burgers are a lot safer." He shrugs. "I've made up my mind to get out of that export racket. That's Federal time if things go wrong. I have one more shipment coming in. After that I'm telling Henry I'm finished."

"When will that be?"

"Should be here in a few days. You can never tell about tramp steamers. Always late. Other times ahead of schedule."

"What kind a contraband are you shipping out this time?"

"Guns."

"Where to?"

"French Polynesia."

Jimmy nods, then orders a cup of coffee from the server. "By the way, how's our girl working out?"

"Which girl? Here or at the titty bar?"

"Don't play dumb. Here. Runner, of course."

"If she wasn't one of your plants, I would a fired her by now. But she's a good worker. I just hate her smart-ass mouth. But the regulars like her. They like her flirting. She's good at it. They'll miss her when she's gone. So, when do you plan on getting rid of her?"

"Not sure exactly. We might use her again. We can keep an eye on her if she's working here. But it should be soon."

"I don't like this, Jimmy. A lot can go wrong. My life is invested in my establishments. I don't want to fuck up what I've worked for. I'm just wondering if this is something I'll regret."

"Old man Denny is who we need to be careful with. Don't want to piss him off. Henry Denny is where he is because of his father, Gerald. All my life, I've wanted to be someone. Be respected. Feared. Show all the fuckers who considered me nothing more than a cockroach how wrong they were. I want to climb to the top. Be in control."

"Climb to the top of what, Jimmy?"

The phone rings.

They stare at each other. Vance answers, on speaker. "Yeah."

Denny doesn't mince his words. "You fuckers found her yet?"

Jimmy answers. "No. Not yet."

"Well, as of now, both of you are on my shit list. Find that bitch and bring her in here. And Jimmy, find me a new girl now. You hear me? I need some stress relief."

"Yeah, boss. I've got one in mind. Have her to you soon."

On the way out, Jimmy asks Vance, "Where's that tramp steamer headed after leaving here, the one soon to dock in Oakland?"

"French Polynesia. Why?"

"Who knows? I just might need a getaway one of these days."

It's blazing hot in the car in Oakes parking lot. But Jimmy's hotter for the way Henry Denny treats him. He starts the car and turns on the AC and sits considering something.

Maybe it's time for a change of plans.

Instead of softballing a plan to blackmail Henry, it isn't strong enough to hope he just walks away from his organization in embarrassment.

Take the motherfucker out, Jimmy. Make it look like Henry was the victim of his own indiscretions—one of his victims kills him, a young girl who came after him for revenge for what he did to her. But what happens if Henry kills her?

Jimmy lights a cigarette and scratches at an eyebrow.

In that case, make sure the cops are close by to witness the killing, regardless of who dies. The girl or Henry.

He knows there will be many personalities to contend with. He can handle most of them easily. Except Henry's father, Mister Gerald Denny.

Mister Denny loves his stupid son—but has finally gotten fed up with his criminal activity. Henry has grown into a liability for the Denny name. And to make matters worse, other crime bosses are talking. This means that if Mister Henry doesn't remove his son from what he's doing, the other mobsters will take Henry out.

Jimmy starts the car and heads out, still deep in thought.

Gerald Denny hired Barlow to be a cleaner. Clean up after his son's misdeeds. Barlow does his job but only tolerates Henry. Barlow is loyal to the old man, not Henry.

So, Barlow may be an issue if Henry is killed and the old man is distraught at his son's murder. He may employ Barlow to put together a team to find those involved with Henry's death. Barlow might come after me.

Barlow is a smart, formidable man to deal with.

Jimmy turns on the radio loud enough to be heard and sing along with Jimmy Buffet over the open windows.

Jimmy anointed you to save his son from being killed. And he's going to appoint you to run the vacant leadership of Henry's operation. So do this right.

Suddenly, a dark cloud comes over him. He closes the windows and frowns.

The only question, the only issue, to worry over is Runner.

She's the wildcard, the little brat.

CHAPTER TWENTY-FIVE

Midnight comes and goes. My cowboy drops me off at Oakes to see if Avril made it in. The bar is almost empty except for one couple at a table. She's chatting with the same biker guy from Elmers and asks me to watch the bar while she walks him out.

I'm alone washing glasses when in walks an odd scraggly man who takes a stool across from me. A construction type in a ragged ball cap. A front tooth missing.

I'm fried, tired, cranky, and want to go home. "Sorry, mister. We're closing."

He grimaces. "I apologize for being late. Could I at least get a drink of water?"

"Sure."

He drinks it down, all of it, larynx bobbing with each swallow. "Thank you, Natalie."

Stunned, I frown. "My name is Runner."

"You're a hard one to find, Natalie."

"Who are you?"

"No one to be afraid of."

"Why would I be afraid of you?"

"Never mind that. You're awfully stressed. You're losing weight, having trouble sleeping, and you're withdrawing socially."

"Well, if you knew me, you'd understand."

"That's just it. I do know you."

"What?"

"You're still carrying around the guilt of that fire." He sniffs at a runny nose. "It's that fire that's burning away at your soul, isn't it?"

"Okay. Now you can leave. Get out of here."

Avril returns. "Who you talking to?"

I nod at an empty stool. "He..." I glance around. "Where'd he go?" There's a glass of water on the bar.

Avril takes my shaking hands. "Come on. Let's close up. Get you to bed."

Avril drops me off and leaves to spend the night with her date. I slip into my cozy pastel Snoopy t-shirt and crawl into bed, dog-tired, wondering about my state of mind.

Ding, ding. A text comes in on my phone.

ALMARANI MARITIME SHIPPING, KSA LLC

NOTICE OF TRANSPORT ARRIVAL

(Bonnie Lynne-Vessel/Cargo)

PIER—TBD

ARRIVAL TIME

(UNCERTAIN) HOLDING PATTERN,

ORIGINAL ETA DELAYED

3 DAYS FROM ORIG. ETA.

BALANCE DUE: $3125.00 USD

UPDATES TO FOLLOW

Gezus, it's real. Really happening.

I sit up, neck hair standing on end. But what was the original ETA? I still don't know. And about that balance due...? I crawl out of bed and begin pacing. I grab the phone for another look.

Are you dreaming?

I thumb through the messages. Nope. Not dreaming. There it is.

ALMARANI MARITIME SHIPPING, KSA LLC letting me know I'm about to be on my way to Tahiti.

CHAPTER TWENTY-SIX

Four days later.

I'm preparing the bar for another big company bash tonight. It'll be hectic, for sure. Just how I like it. Should be good tips tonight.

It's been more than a month since I took over O'Grady's shifts. I'm doing okay. Couldn't have done it without Vance and Avril's support schooling me on the subtleties of bartending. Even though confidence is building, I'm still a little nervous as the crowd builds.

Avril is late.

I'm running up and down the bar with customers waving money for my attention. It's overwhelming. But guess who arrives euphoric, energetic, talkative, mentally alert, and hypersensitive to everything? Yeah, Avey made it with a trace of dust on her nose. She dives right in, mixing and serving. Oh my, she can really work a bar. I breathe easier and even get a little cocky. Tips are piling up as the evening races on. The fabric of Avril is splotchy. Sometimes reliably unreliable, other times solid as a rock. She'll do anything for me if I need a helping hand. It's why I've fallen in love with her.

Coming up on midnight, the crowd begins to thin. I'm cashing out a couple at the bar when I notice a loudmouth in a back booth dominating a young woman with drunken misogynistic enthusiasm, kissing, hugging, acting out his manhood against her bashful personality. I remember seeing the guy before. Always obnoxious. He's married. His ring is missing. I notice things like that.

He heads off to the men's room.

I poke Avril. "Cover for me." Then I slip over to their table and pass a note to the distressed girl.

HE'S MARRIED!

I wink at her and return to the bar.

An argument breaks out when he returns. She slaps him, shouts something, gathers her things, and hurries to the door. On her way by she gives me a fist bump which he sees. He points a finger at me while he follows her out. "Bitch."

Closing time. Avril has already picked out her guy for the night. A bushy-headed roughneck with a scruffy beard. She mouths from across the room—*I'm leaving, his place.* She blows me a kiss. Which means I get the apartment all to myself tonight.

Jonathan is gone. He left sometime after watching me like a jealous husband all night. I know he'll be sulking in his car, waiting for me outside the Sentry, expecting an invitation to come up. The idea of him tonight bums me out.

While counting cash for the register close out, a young guy

comes in and takes a stool. I lay a cocktail napkin down and lean over. "Last call, fella."

His eyes get big with a too-quick smile. "I'm probably going to get kicked out for saying this. But you scare the hell out of me."

"I do, do I? Why?"

"Well. I'm a grad student. I've been here a few times. And when I'm here, I can't take my eyes off you. I—"

I interrupt. "What's your name?"

"Hayden."

"Well, hi, Hayden. You have a last name?"

"Hogan. Hayden Harold Hogan."

"You're kidding, right?" I try to hide the smirk. "Wow. The first person I've ever met with an alliteration for a name."

He smiles. "Your name is Runner. Is that right?"

I lean over the bar within inches of his smile. "You drinking tonight or just hunting up a bed partner?"

"What's your best whiskey? And it has to be cheap."

"Jack. Jack Daniels."

His first sip brings on an ugly grimace. Tears flowing, face turning bright red. He looks at me through watery eyes. "Whew."

Is this cute hayseed for real?

He crosses me.

I study him. "So what's the rest of the night have in store for you, Mister Hogan?"

"Sharing it with someone?"

"With me?"

"That's fantasy plan A."

"Meaning?"

"Grab a coffee somewhere, maybe?"

I laugh. "Coffee at two in the morning? You gotta be kidding."

"A drink then?"

I roll my "you-can't-be-serious" eyes. "I've been dealing liquor all night. You want to take me to a bar?"

"Breakfast then?"

"Now you're talking."

So begins begin the ritual of meaningless small talk. "So what are you studying as a grad student, Hayden?"

"Law."

OMG, you're so adorable.

Four thirty am, my bed. Hayden sleeps soundly after satisfaction has him lost in the abyss where boys go afterwards. I pull on my Snoopy t-shirt, crawl into bed, and spoon into his backside dog-tired and wondering if that boat is for real. Not some delusion I've talked myself into. I snuggle closer to this warm, gentle kid.

Why can't life always be like this? Uncomplicated, warm, safe, and comfortable with someone you love?

I sit up and stare down at him. Using the word "love" is like a dagger through my heart. I've never been able to give my heart or love to anyone.

Will you ever?

CHAPTER TWENTY-SEVEN

It's almost sunrise. A gentle finger brushes over my shoulder. I open an eye, nose buried into something soft and warm. The scent of a man. Fingers graze over my neck. My eyes flutter open to morning sun casting over a kid-like smile, chin stubble, and puppy dog eyes.

The bedside clock reads seven fifty-one.

A whisper. "Morning, beautiful."

I lurch up. "Who the hell are you? Get your hands off me." I kick at him. "Get out. Get away from me."

He sits up, surprised, confused, and pulls back in shock. "I'm... I'm sorry." He rolls over, bare-assed on his side of the bed. "I'm sorry. So sorry. If..."

"Christ. Just shut up. Quit saying that. Get out of here."

He stares, stunned, and throws his legs over the side, mumbling.

"Wait." I grab his arm. "Just wait. Let me... let me think."

He's perplexed and resists my hold on his arm. I pull harder. "Wait, I said. God, just a second. Don't be in such a hurry."

He shrugs away. With both hands, I grab him again and pull. He gives in and slowly reclines back against me.

An hour later, he's showered, fresh and clean, standing at the door buttoning his shirt, looking satisfied and content, staring, shaking his head at me still in bed yawning in a full-body stretch.

I get the one-finger wiggle-wave, code for goodbye-it-was-fun-see-ya-around gesture.

"Will I see you again?"

Stupid question.

He smiles and blows a kiss. "I'll call you."

Yeah, right.

He pulls the door closed.

I sit up, hug my knees, and look out the window. Low clouds are rolling in. It looks sketchy for the week. Weatherman says a big storm is gaining strength in the Pacific. Heavy gray weather like this gives me a low-grade headache. I roll over and cover my head with the pillow. Twenty minutes later the headache is gone. Now I'm hungry.

The crowd at The Coffee Bean is bustling. I stand in line, wondering if the letter writer is here watching me. Does she know who I am?

Should you know her? Will you know her if you run into her?

At the counter, I ask Lorraine. "What, no rhubarb muffins today?"

"Only on special days."

I order my typical two-shot cappuccino and sit at a table that opens up to enjoy the morning buzz of lively conversations, the smell of roasting beans, and cups clinking in plastic tubs. A blond man in a ball cap takes a tiny table next to me with his coffee and a book. He senses me watching and smiles.

I look away quickly and notice a tough-looking guy with a bent nose watching me. I pretend to thumb through my phone, not wishing to make eye contact. He comes over, grabs an empty chair from my neighbor's table, turns it around backward, and sits studying me with a stupid smile. I give a look of annoyance. He scratches his fuzz-ball head. "Morning."

I frown at the creep. "Something interests you? Mister."

He nods with a smile.

Fight or flight, Natalie?

I give my best glare. "What are you looking at?"

He has no coffee, no drink, no food. His only interest in being here is me, for some reason.

"You bartend at Oakes Bar and Grill, don't you?"

I force back a swallow. "Do I know you?"

"Met you at the grill briefly when I was chatting with O'Grady, the bartender. You interrupted us that day. There was a fight. Remember?"

"What do you want, mister?"

"You're Runner, right?"

"Who are you?"

"Barlow. Orin Barlow." He nods with a hand out to shake. "Runner, that *is* your name, right?"

I ignore the hand. "You got the wrong girl."

"I don't think so."

"Should I be afraid of you? Should I run? Call the cops? Buy a gun?"

"Can't tell you what to do."

"You're bothering me. Go away."

"Sorry." He shows his hands. "See. I'm no harm to anyone. I

only want to ask you a few questions. Simple questions. Do you mind?"

"Yes."

He nods at the two empty chairs at my table. "Mind if I come over there? Easier to talk. Promise I'll be the perfect gentleman."

"You can be the perfect gentleman right where you are now."

My table neighbor starts to say something in my defense. I wave him off, then study this Barlow creature, an interesting-looking thing. His ears protrude with bulbous deformities, like those wrestlers or rugby players. His deep-set eyes smolder a shade of gray.

Be careful with this guy, Natalie.

"Who are you, mister?"

"Let me apologize for interrupting your breakfast. I just want a few minutes of your time."

"Go away."

"Two minutes is all I want. Two questions?"

"I said, go away."

He leans in. "I work for a man who met you recently. A wealthy man."

"I meet a lot of rich men. So what?"

"Your meeting with him went badly. He was expecting a different type of girl. You mistreated him." Barlow rattles on, describing how his boss suffered humiliation. "That scene wasn't something you dreamed up yourself, was it?"

"I don't dream up scenes. I don't know your boss, and I don't know what you're talking about."

"You're not a prostitute, are you?"

"What do you think?"

"I don't know."

"Well." Agitation growing. "I'm an astronaut in training. I plan to be the first hooker on the moon?"

Stone-faced, he asks, "Would you be willing to meet with my boss again?"

My answer is a slow sip of coffee.

"Who put you up to it, Runner? Who paid you to set him up like that?"

I stare at him. *He's trouble. This is the blowback you've been expecting from that Grand Plaza debacle. Blowback from Jimmy's stupid idea.*

I'm in too deep with Jimmy the pimp already. I can't give him up. "Sorry. Don't know what you're talking about."

"This could get ugly, young lady." Barlow pauses, looks around, bends forward, and slightly slides his chair closer. "What is important though is to—"

Before he can finish, a voice interrupts us. "Hello, hello, hello." Avril waltzes up to the table with a skinny kid in Wranglers and boots. They pull up chairs and flop down. She's buzzed. Her interruption is boorish. "I'm starved," she whines, pins back her hair and pats the young cowboy on the knee. Ain't he a beauty?" Then she recognizes Barlow's presence with a wave. "Hi, I'm Avril. I'm her roommate. Have I met you before?"

I glare at her when she leans close and whispers, "Who is this man?"

Barlow gives her a fierce stare. Then, after a minute, he stands up without saying anything and leaves.

"Who was that odd guy, Natalie?"

"I don't know. He couldn't finish because you interrupted what he had to say."

"Well, la de da. A little sensitive, wouldn't you say?"

After Avey and her boy toy leave, the man in the ball cap,

next table over, clears his throat. "I couldn't help but hear that guy pestering you. Are you okay?"

I see something about him I didn't notice before. A wispy blond mustache. "Yeah. I'm totally fine, thanks for asking."

"Have we met before?"

"No." I answer quickly and am out the door walking fast thinking. *They've found you, Natalie. The FBI is here.*

I get home, race up the stairs to pack, and run into Cicero.

"Whoa. What's the hurry, girl?"

I stop long enough to tell him I have to leave. "Something I've done."

"Calm down; tell me. What happened?"

"No time."

CHAPTER TWENTY-EIGHT

Jimmy stirs his coffee in the apartment community room, sitting with Cicero. He gives an update on details of his plan to do away with Henry Denny. Cicero's body language is detached and defensive. He mumbles, "You're full of shit, Jimmy. You don't have any idea what you're doing. I only offered to help with logistics. That's all. I do not support what I'm hearing. This has gone too far."

"Well, okay. But I'm looking for Runner. Do you know where she is?"

"No."

"When's the last time you saw her. Talked to her?"

"Couple hours ago."

"What was she like?"

"Scared out of her mind."

"What did you tell her?"

"Telling her something is like pissing in the wind. You know that. She's going to do whatever *she* decides to do."

"But what did you tell her?"

"Not much."

Jimmy looked up at the doors upstairs. "Is she still here?"

"No. Not now. She comes and goes. Never know when she's gonna be here."

A stranger enters the room. A smartly dressed black man casually approaching. "Excuse me, gentlemen. I'm looking for a girl who goes by the name of Runner."

Jimmy looks up. "Who are you?"

"Redd. Richard Redd. A friend of hers."

Cicero leans back. "What do you want with her?"

"Like I said, I'm a friend, from Denver. I'd like to see her."

Cicero folds his hands. "Well, she doesn't live here anymore."

Redd purses his lips. "Erm... I heard from her just the other day. She gave this as her address."

Jimmy reacts. "Well, like my friend said, she's not here anymore."

"Anymore? So she has lived here?"

Jimmy and Cicero exchange glances.

The man continues. "Do you know where she is now?"

Jimmy is emphatic. "No."

Redd frowns. "Do you know where she works?"

Jimmy sighs. "We don't know anything about her. And we're in a conversation here. So good luck in finding her. If we see her, we'll tell her you were asking about her. What's your name again?"

"Richard Redd."

Jimmy and Cicero share another look.

Redd picks up on it.

Cicero folds his arms. "What am I missing here? Something I should know. Is she in some kind of trouble, detective?"

"That's what I want to know. She seemed upset when she called."

Cicero stands. "Can you call her back?"

"No." He looks at both of them. "I don't have her number."

Cicero and Jimmy both shrug. "Neither do we."

Redd nods. "Okay. Thank you."

Cicero leads Redd out onto the front porch. "Do you have a number where she can reach you, detective?"

"Sure." He offers a card.

Cicero looks back at Jimmy inside the apartment, then whispers, "She needs help, detective." He gives a quick brief on her involvement with Denny. Then he finishes it off with a warning. "There's a hitman involved. A man named Mauldin. Need I say more?"

Jimmy sees the exchange between them. He can't hear the conversation but senses Cicero is spilling what he knows about Runner being in trouble.

So, Jimmy calls Denny. "It's time to get rid of the old apartment landlord, boss."

Denny pauses. "You're talking about Cicero. Why?"

"He's unreliable. I think he's the one who had the girl set you up for those photos."

Henry mumbles, "Goddamnit. Are you sure?"

"Ninety percent sure, boss."

Henry pauses for a minute. Under his breath, he expresses disappointment. "Not what I expected of him. I need to think about this."

"Think about what?"

"About some house cleaning."

Jimmy frowns. "What do you mean house cleaning?"

"Get rid of a few bad apples."

"How you gonna do that?"

"Mauldin. I've had him work for me before."

. . .

In his car, he lights a cigarette. He knows of the house cleaner Henry was talking about—Anton Mauldin.

He's a train wreck, a murderer.

Jimmy being an ex-FBI agent knows of him by reputation. He makes a call to an old friend. Another ex-FBI agent. "Hey, it's me. Jimmy Barone. Remember when we worked on a case involving that murdering asshole in Columbia? Anton Mauldin? Did we have contact data on him?"

"Yeah, we did."

Next he calls Vance Oakes.

"Yeah."

"You know that boat you mentioned coming in pretty soon? Gonna take your contraband to Tahiti?"

"Yeah, what about it?"

"What's the name of it?"

"The Bonnie Lynne. Why?"

"Just wondering. Thanks."

CHAPTER TWENTY-NINE

Three days later, I get a text.

ALMARANI MARITIME SHIPPING,
URGENT NOTICE: DELAYED
Delay Bonnie Lynne-Vessel/Cargo)
ARRIVAL TIME INDEFINITE
UPDATES TO FOLLOW

I stare at it. "Delayed. Indefinite." What does this mean? Something tells me I'm not going to Tahiti. More like across the border to Tijuana more like it.

It means I need to be here another month at least. And I haven't seen or heard from Avril. This isn't the first time she's taken off on a fling before crawling home weeks later embarrassed. Her reputation for rash, promiscuous encounters with boys is well known. But I'm worried about her safety. And we split the rent fifty-fifty. I can't afford to lose her half. Cicero is less optimistic about her return. He says he can get me another roommate. I reluctantly agree since I don't cherish the idea of breaking in a new roommate.

"I do better with guys, Cicero."

He wastes no time. After lunch, he shows up with a young girl—Holly. A bubblegum-chewing Pebbles ponytail-swinging brat. Something right out of the Flintstones. Imagine an overly developed high school senior in kaleidoscopic leggings under a paisley mini skirt, and about to fall out of the red, full-bust corset with black floral lace overlay. This girl is a boy tease. A child dressing to drive testosterone-sodden boys into wetting their jeans. I mean... come on... She's wearing high-top hiking boots. But there's no denying she's a pretty girl with her straight, silky blonde hair. I tag her with the name—Hangloose. Holly Hangloose. Avril will find that name funny. But the personality doesn't fit the Bourbon Street attire. She doesn't give off a giggly, cutesy vibe. No. Holly Hangloose exudes a stealthy confidence: cool and calculated.

An hour later two men are toting boxes into her room.

I leave her to move in by herself. I don't know if I'll ever accept this little tramp.

Meow.

The bar is extra busy tonight. With Avril gone, Vance calls in an extra bartender. The tips are good. The regulars are whooping it up, watching the games on the big screens. Jonathan's here, and damn, he looks extra good. Maybe it's because I'm just extra frisky tonight. But I don't have much time to spend talking to him. The crowd is running me ragged. So he gives up and leaves.

Damn. You're impatient, Jon. Ugh.

After locking up, I cross the street under dim streetlights, past the old Majestic Playhouse Theatre, past Happy Jacks Liquors where a taco food truck sits on the corner. Sitting on a wood-frame picnic table and benches under a yellow-hued street light are four obnoxious boys lounging around smoking, drinking, and bullshitting. Parked on the curb is a cherry-red Camaro. It's the Cheater's car, the asshole I saved a shy girl from at the bar. I lower my head and walk on by without comment.

Cheater sees me. "Hey, boys. Look who it is. The bartender bitch at Oakes."

Keep walking, Natalie. Ignore him.

I cross the street with Cheater following, rattling off all the misogynistic insults he can think of.

You've been called worse, Nat. Just let it go. Keep walking.

But I can't. I turn with a one-fingered salute. "Chew on this."

He's surprised at my fearless comeback. "Hey cunt, show us those little titties a yours."

"What did you say?"

He's laughing when I march back toward him. "What did you call me?"

He turns serious.

"I said, what did you call me?"

He's a little over six feet and grins down at me. His buddies sit on the table, excited at the confrontation. I get nose-to-nose with him. Without looking at them, I tell the boys, "You know he beats his kids, right? And he's been with your girlfriends behind your back. Guess what they've been doing when you guys are whacking off together around a case of Bud? I know cuz I've seen 'em together in the bar."

Mouths collectively open, brows furrow.

Then back to Cheater. "What did you call me, you gob of spit?"

"You don't know who you're dealing with, whore."

"I recognize a contagious disease when I see one. My guess is eosinophilic gastroenteritis."

The boys laugh and hoot. One calls out, "What's that?"

"Bad diarrhea."

They slap thighs, giggle, and crow at him. "Floyd," one of them shouts, "she got you, man. We gonna call you bad diarrhea from now on."

He's furious. "Shut the fuck up." He lurches at me. "Who do you see here, bitch? Who's gonna help you outta what you've wormed yourself into?"

"What are you getting at? Huh? You going to hurt me, tough stuff? Huh?"

"I can hurt you real bad."

"Is that a promise? Or just one of your brainless threats?"

He glances at his boys. "You guys know I can kill her right now. Or should I wait and slip up on her tomorrow? Or next week. My choice. Right?"

I walk a circle around him. "Ever killed anyone, Cheater? Huh? Ever watched those eyes fade away right in front of you? Or will I be your first? Huh?"

He licks his lips.

"Well, well. Sounds like you don't really know how to kill someone. Doesn't it?"

"What you know about killin', bitch?"

I poke him in the chest. "You won't be my first, buddy."

He takes a step back. I poke him again. "Go screw yourself, Floyd." Then I turn and head to the Sentry.

His boys whistle, laugh, and jeer. "Come on, man," one yells. "Show her who's boss."

Now they're trailing behind me like I'm the Pied Piper. Cheater and his idiot boys. I have to admit, I'm scared as we leave lighted streets. The rest of the way is mostly dark. A little neighborhood park is just ahead. I hear whispering behind me.

Have you gone too far, Natalie? Did you succumb to your brassy audacity?

Out of nowhere, a police cruiser slowly pulls up alongside. A window comes down. "Everything okay here, miss?"

I yell back, "Yeah, everything's just fine."

"Need a ride, ma'am?"

I snap a look over at the two cops. "NO."

I get home angry and edgy. Not ready for bed. At least not alone anyway. I change into a clean t-shirt. There's an all-night club on the outskirts of town.

Why not?

CHAPTER THIRTY

The next day I wake alone, in my own bed. Whoever he was has escaped like a wimp, afraid to face the music.

In the living room is an empty pint of Jägermeister on its side. Beer cans on the coffee table. I'm so hungover I fall back to sleep.

Bad idea. I wake two hours later. Too late to make my shift on time.

I hurry in for my bar shift five minutes late. That's all it takes, five minutes. Vance waits for me with his cigar chewed down to a disgusting stub of mush in the corner of his mouth.

"You're late, fuckhead."

"Well, hello to you, sunshine."

He grunts and leads me back into a restroom, locks the door behind us and points a finger in my face. He yanks the cigar out and spits a strand of tobacco. "I never give second chances, girl. Never." Then he stops and gives what he's about to say some thought. "It pisses me off what you've done." He puts the cigar in his front teeth. The next words come from the side of his mouth. "First of all, you are late. I can't have that from my bartenders. You know that, don't you? What's worse though..." He spits into the toilet and gets almost nose to nose with me. "You started an argument between a customer and his date the other night. What do you think a that?"

"Uh... it hurts."

"Damn right, it hurts."

"No. You're standing on my foot. It hurts."

He steps back, red-faced. "Don't play dumb with me, you little shit."

"I'm taller than you. So you can't call me little."

He seethes. Veins bulge in quiet rage. There's indignation in his eyes. With much discipline, he lowers his voice and pronounces every syllable verwy, verwy slowly. "We do not interfere with customers' personal lives. *Runner*! We are not counselors. We are not psychologists. We are *not* preachers or the law." He spits the cigar in the toilet and stares at me through snake eyes, hands on his hips. He curls his nostrils and sniffs back outrage. "We sell a vibe here. This is where cats come to let loose, socialize, tell lies, laugh with friends and enemies. We don't judge how they do that. We take their money and push booze across that bar out there with a smile. We don't care who they fuck or suck, their wife or a feline bimbo cruising bars looking to screw up some man's home life. It's not our business. You got that?"

"Yeseree, I shore nuff do."

He bites his lower lip, brandishing yellow teeth, and leans back against the wall, arms crossed, perplexed. "I don't know why I'm about to say this." He grits his teeth. "I'm making an exception for you. I normally don't believe in second chances. So why am I giving you one? Huh, Ann Landers? Please illuminate me."

"I think you mean elucidate? Illuminate literally means to shine a light on something while elucidate is an absolute meaning to make clear, to clarify. You can use illuminate, but it sounds pretentious. And I don't think you mean for me to shine a light on you, do you?" I wait for him to say something. It's hard not to laugh. "Okay, Mister Oakes. You're giving me a second chance, right?"

The silence in the bathroom is deafening except for the drip dripping from the washbasin faucet. The atmosphere is dense with the smell of urine and contempt. "So the real answer to your illuminate question is objectification. I'm something to you other than just me. You're stuck with me. And now I ask... why? According to your rules, I've broken several. I'm an insubordinate. So why aren't you firing me?"

He sniffs back anger. "Listen to me, Runner, or whatever your fucking real name really is. I'm giving you this second chance because..." He stops, pulls out a new cigar and rolls it around slick lips. "Now get out there and do your job. Another bad decision in this establishment, and you're gone. Got it?"

I roll my eyes. "You finished?"

"Yeah. Go out there and do your job."

The rest of the night, I go about mixing and serving like a robot. That ass-chewing from Vance did it for me.

After tonight, you're out of work, girl. God, I hope that boat to paradise is for real. And nothing goes wrong with me getting on it.

The night slows to a trickle. I whisper to the barback girl, "I'm quitting." And I say why. "This is my last night."

She's not surprised and tells me good luck.

The bar is almost empty now except for a couple of dirt-under-their-fingernails guys—Tony Rigatoni and Leo the Lion. Caterpillar drivers. Big teddy bears. Kick-ass guys you don't want to mess with if you piss 'em off. A couple of my favorite regulars. They introduce me to a friend, Eric.

Wow! Eric.

What a beautiful, rugged smile, blue-eyed, cheek dimple in a five-o'clock-shadow kind of guy he is. His black military cut with a speck of gray at the temple is perfect.

The four of us enjoy great conversation and good laughs until closing time. Sorry to see them leave.

I close out the register. Lower the lights. Jonathan has yet to show up to drive me home. He's pouting. The taxi I called hasn't shown up. Neither has Uber. Not the first time. It's two forty-five. I'll walk despite the wet weather about to hit anytime.

A walk will do you good.

By the time I lock the doors, a thin drizzle has set in. Despite the chilly, wet night, leaving Oakes for the last time gives me a good feeling.

Two blocks from the Sentry, a car slowly pulls up behind me, creeping along fifty yards back. I pick up the pace, and the car maintains the same fifty yards distance.

Who is this? And is he going to run you over? Or will it be a gunshot to the back of the head? Rape maybe?

I break into a run.

He maintains the same distance. I run faster, drizzle turning to rain. The lights of the Sentry are visible now. The car almost on my butt now. I'm in a sprint. Gasping, I continue at this clip.

This is it.

I stop, turn, and stumble back to confront my killer.

Down comes the window. "Hello, Runner. Need a ride?"

"Eric!"

CHAPTER THIRTY-ONE

Somewhere a rooster crows, waking me out of a deep sleep. Nine forty-eight when I jerk up, naked in a cold sweat, shivering, disoriented from the cock-a-doodle-do. I was dreaming of dancing with an FBI agent. That Ray Waters guy, both of us in handcuffs in a Mexican jail. I shake my head to chase that vision out.

I squint around in this small bedroom with flowery wallpaper. It smells of alcohol, baby powder, and sex. Eric snores lightly with his back to me. I hear a woman's voice.

Oh no. Wife? Girlfriend?

I don't want to get up and face that.

No choice.

She's at a kitchen stool drinking coffee and playing with a baby cooing in a highchair when she notices me standing in the doorway. "Ready for coffee?"

This is embarrassing.

She sees the look on my face. "Oh, don't worry. I'm the ex. But we still live together. We're friends and parents, and we respect each other's freedom. And it's cheaper living together."

I take a seat at the table next to the beautiful little girl in her highchair. Her blue eyes, dimples, and sweet smile caked with oatmeal awakens a warm sense of compassion and tenderness I thought had ceased to exist within me. "What's her name?"

"Angel."

Angel takes my finger, looks into my eyes, purrs and burbles. A lump in my throat grows and catches.

Were you ever like this, Natalie? A sweet little baby girl who showed love just by holding a finger?

Back at the Sentry in a steaming hot shower, fears of who I'm becoming are sinking in. I wish we could pull a cord and start life all over again. If we could, I'd want to be Angel.

I flop in my cool bed, not feeling too good. Mouth parchment dry. I drag the blanket up and bury my face in the pillow before dialing Jonathan from under the covers.

He answers. "Mornin', sunshine."

It's maddening how he's so damn cheery every morning. It must be what it's like to grow up in a Dallas mansion with a perfect billionaire family, loving parents, two older sisters, a younger brother he adores, and an English Cocker Spaniel. I'm a study in contrast. Defective merchandise, the outcome of an unplanned pregnancy. Me, a mistake for a child.

"Where were you last night, boyfriend?" I ask. "I could have used a ride home."

"Oh. I thought you had a ride picked out."

"What does that mean?"

"Well... uh... like I've always said, I'm willing to share until you realize I'm the one for you. So last night, I gave you your space. I just thou—"

I interrupt. "Who was it you saw last night that you think I wanted to go home with?" Before he can answer, I hang up and slide under the covers and fall asleep for another hour. When I wake, I'm more tired than before. I roll out, looking for Snoopy, my bedtime t-shirt.

Where are you, you loveable little pink doggie?

I pass by the bathroom mirror. Do a double-take, stop, and go back to stare at someone's face I don't recognize. She's staring back with a down-dog face, no color, and bed hair that no one should be subjected to in the morning.

"Geeezo Christ, you look bad, girl."

The cold washcloth I hope to reduce the puffiness and dark circles feels good against my face and neck. It's either my imagination or is there actually a wrinkle there?

Crap. Not at this age.

Mother had early wrinkles, crow's feet, and glossy, silver hair in her early thirties. It didn't deter guys from salivating over her natural beauty.

I pat Clinique around the eyes and chat with Mother like she's right there in front of me, cigarette smoke rolling up into her hazel-green eyes.

Was there ever any romance in those dusty-booted cowboys you entertained, Mom? Those hookups? The one-nighters? Was there, huh, Mother? What made you treat Dad with such disrespect? Did you ever really love him, Mom? Did you, huh?

I pad out of the bathroom and into the kitchen, turn on the radio, and hear cold and rainy weather on the way. The biggest storm in years.

Snoopy is wadded up on the floor next to the fridge. Undies

in the living room next to the sofa. I'm too tired to retrieve them. I pull Snoopy on and nuke a mug of water for coffee.

Two microwave dings, add a couple heaping teaspoons of instant, stir and hug the warm mug to my chest and enjoy the first sip with a sigh. On the second sip, I turn around and gasp. "Christallmightywhattha..." I plunge below the counter, sloshing coffee down the front of Snoopy.

CHAPTER THIRTY-TWO

I'm in a crouch hiding behind the kitchen counter from what I think I saw. A man in the hallway looking through the half-open door. I'm bare-assed, naked from the waist down. And I've soaked Snoopy with sloshed coffee from my quick collapse to the floor. I listen for footsteps. Not hearing any, I inch up and peek over the counter. The door is partially open. And yes, it is a man. A real man. Not my imagination. And he's still there watching me.

He smiles an awkward simper. "Whoops. Didn't mean to startle you." He slowly pushes the door open with a finger. "I'm Barlow. Remember me? Orin Barlow. We met at The Coffee Bean."

I rise up slightly. Hesitant. Frowning. "Yeah, I remember you." I slam the coffee cup down on the counter. Coffee splashing everywhere. "What the hell?" I grab a three-inch paring knife, maybe sharp enough to get through butter and hold it out at him, quivering.

"Runner, that is your name, right?"

"Get out. Right now."

"You *are* Runner, correct?"

"Out," I shout.

He takes a couple halting steps inside. "You always sleep this late?"

"Get the hell out now."

"Wait, let me exp—"

"Out," I shout and grab my phone, fumbling, shaking like a leaf, and misdial 911 twice.

He's in the living room now. Closer to the counter between us. Close enough to reach over and grab the phone from my hand. I flail with the knife, catching his wrist. He drops the phone on the counter to examine the bleeding. "You don't really want to call the police, do you?"

"Why the hell not?"

"Well, you'll have to explain why a guy like me is in your apartment bleeding. And it'll lead to how you pulled off some extortion stunt at the Grand Plaza. Blackmail photos. Remember?"

"Get the ever lovin' hell out. Now." I grab the phone and try 911 again.

"Where's your roommate? Avril. That's her name, isn't it? Avril?"

"I'm calling the cops right now."

"I'll go in a minute. But first, just listen to me. You need to hear this. You're in danger."

"Danger?" My finger hovers over the phone. "You probably have a gun or something, so I'm calling for help. Really, I am."

"You're right about a gun. I'll admit it. But first, watch this." He slowly pulls back his jacket. Delicately lifts a gun from a shoulder holster with two fingers and gently lays it on the counter. With one finger, he slides it over to me and steps back.

His hands held high over his head. "You take it. It's loaded. Five rounds. Be careful. Now go ahead, call the cops. But you'll be sorry."

I stare at a small, short-barrel, blue gun with a pearl handle and brass trigger.

"Go ahead, take it," he says. "If you're unfamiliar with guns, that one is a double action .38. Just pull the trigger. Bang, five shots rapid fire. But it's not that accurate. If you really want to hit something, just pull back the hammer, take dead aim, and pull the trigger. One shot at a time. You'll hit what you're aiming at. Your choice."

Is this a joke? Does he really want you to take it?

Memories of plinking with Dad and his .22 pistol come racing back. Shooting up boxes of ammo. I got pretty good with that little gun.

"You must think I'm stupid, mister. I know what a single action is."

He laughs and sucks on the bleeding wrist. "I don't like instant coffee. But considering our circumstances here, I'd take a cup now. Just to be social. One spoonful of sugar, please."

"Circumstances?" I shout. "Circumstances?" The gun is only inches away. Easy enough to grab?

In seconds, you can blow a hole in him or punch in 911. Decision time.

I reach for the phone.

Barlow smiles. "Your battery's dead."

I snap a look.

Crap.

He's right. So, I grab up the gun and point it at his face.

His hands go up again. "Okay." He nods. "Now, maybe we can have a little chat. I'll stay on this side. You stay over there with the gun." He slowly lowers his hands and sucks at the blood trickling down his wrist.

I tear off a paper towel, wad it, and toss it at him.

"Thanks."

"Don't get the wrong idea. I don't care if you bleed to death. I don't want blood everywhere. Nothing more than that."

"Okay."

"Listen, Mister Barlow. Only two things I want to know as I stand here bare-assed. Why are you so interested in me? And when are you going to leave?"

He nods at my undies on the living room floor. "Want me to get them for you?"

"Don't you dare touch those."

"How about you go put something on, then?"

"I'm not moving from here, and I'm not making you coffee. And I'm not going to have any conversation with you this morning. Do you understand all that?"

"Listen. I have to ask you something. I hope you give me what I need to know because—"

I interrupt. "You listen to me. I have nothing to say to you."

He's quick to respond. "I may have a chance to save you from—"

"Shut up."

But he continues. "Save you from blowback from what you did. It's serious. And friends around you may be in danger also."

I jerk the barrel up at his face. "What are you talking about?"

He shows no fear. "I'm just saying things might get bad for you and your friends."

"I know how to use this thing, mister." With steady hands now, I cock the hammer back—*click*.

"Whoa, hang on there, sport. That trigger's touchy."

All of a sudden a voice comes from the hallway. "Everything okay in there?" It's Cicero coming down the hall.

I yank the gun behind my back before he appears in the

doorway. "Yeah. Everything's fine," I say. "This insurance guy picked the wrong time for a sales pitch. He's leaving now."

Barlow grins at the fabrication. He chews at his cheek and starts for the door. "I tried to warn you."

"What do you mean?"

He walks away, saying, "You'll find out soon enough. And it will be soon."

CHAPTER THIRTY-THREE

Cicero gives me a stare as Barlow walks away.

I take a deep breath and lay the gun down. I have no use of a gun. Not even a pretty one. But it's a curiosity, so different from the little .22 pistol I shot at tin cans with on weekends with Dad. I'm tempted to toss it in the trash. Instead, I drop it in the Smugglers Notch tote bag hanging behind the closet door.

Later, with Snoopy in the wash and a fresh cup of coffee, I brood over Barlow's warning. What was he trying to say? And what did he mean, "you'll find out"?

I flop down on the sofa and turn on TV to see a breaking news story, a chaotic scene in the Grand Plaza Hotel.

Local Respected Youth Community Pioneer Cheating?

A pillar of distinction in the San Francisco community, Henry Denny, appears to be cavorting with a recognized prostitute. Three photos of a young woman with Denny in the exclusive hotel.

"Oh, no. Oh, oh... Christ, no. Oh shit."

They called you a known prostitute.

Panic erupts. I fall back on the sofa and pull my knees up in a hug.

This is what Barlow was getting at? Trying to warn you. Is there more to this? Of course there is. Be prepared, Natalie.

I dial Jimmy. It rings. I pause to reflect.

Why are you calling him?

Before he answers, I hang up. Within seconds, the phone rings.

"Yo," says Jimmy. "You called. What's up, ding dong?"

"Nothing. Sorry I bothered you." I hang up.

What have you gotten yourself into, Natalie? You're not a prostitute. The nerve of that news story, calling you that.

Two days later and I haven't left the apartment since Barlow's warnings. And Avril is missing again. I could use her friendship now.

I stare outside at a depressing day. Low-hanging, concrete-colored clouds. The day-old coffee is weak. I'm almost out of birth control and losing weight. Heck, even Jonathan mentioned how flat-chested I am. I've spent almost all of Jimmy's money. This is what broke feels like: twenty-four dollars in my checking account, and fourteen in my wallet with no prospect of improving on it. I'm a fugitive, wanted by the FBI, the big kahuna. This old world is too big for me.

I pull out the calendar to count the days I've been here. But I never get to count. "Oh my God," I sputter. "Father's birthday, today." Instantly he appears on his knees, no words, just his smile, holding his gun. Not the .22. No he's holding the blue .38, Barlow's gun. He's holding it out to me. He grabs my hand and wraps my fingers around it. All eyes on me from the crowd waiting for it. But what is it?

I run for a glass of water to quench my parched throat. Mother hands me the glass of water.

I lean against the wall and tear at my hair. Facing all this is too much.

You need someone to lean on.

Isn't it obvious who that should be?

I grab the phone.

Jonathan. Call him. Don't be so stubborn. Let him take you away from all this.

"Yes, okay." I call his number. After four rings, a voice answers I don't recognize.

"Hallo."

"Who's this? Where's Jonathan?"

The line goes dead. I call back, no answer. Again. No answer.

I beg a ride to Jonathan's house from one of the apartment residents. Two cars are parked on the curb when I get there. One is an old beater pickup with a ladder on the roof. It's Dad's. How did it get here?

Jonathan's doorbell plays "Wanted Dead Or Alive" twice. After banging on the door, I go over the stucco wall in the side yard and race through a side door to the garage. All his cars are accounted for, but the Harley is missing. I run through the house searching and slip on the polished marble floor, crashing head-first into a wall.

Ouch.

But he's nowhere, not in the gym or his office.

Jonathan, where are you?

In a panic, I run outside into a great and sudden disaster, the day turned turbulent, dramatic, the sky, a raging tempest, vicious wind howling, umbrellas flying off, chairs tossed around, thunder and lightning. Strange, unemotional men at the pool watching me scream and yell, "Where's Jonathan?"

A gold-toothed wretch reaches out, touches my breast. *Honey, put on your party dress.* I hesitate at his demand, and can't stop his clammy groping hands all over me. He pulls my body to his. I'm listless; no resistance to his needs. He hits me. Staggering back, I fall into the pool. The water is cold, blood red. A hand grabs my foot. I kick at it, whatever it is. I see clearly now. A body. A body rolling in the deep.

"Jonathan?" I dive down, lungs burning.

Oh God, don't... Oh, don't let it be. No, no, no. I struggle with him to the shallow end. "No, God. Please, let this be a bad dream."

Hours pass, calm returns. I hold his head to my breasts, combing fingers through his luscious hair. At least his face—his beautiful face remains exquisite and unspoiled. We sway together in the later afternoon as the day sinks into the Pacific.

I whisper in his ear. "I am so sorry, honey. The way I treated you. You've been so kind. I've been so mean. This stain of regret will live with me forever. I'll come to join you wherever you are. I have to go, my lover."

Then I find the keys to his Range Rover. Before his house is out of sight, I look back to see Jonathan and a woman. Mother. I do a double-take. Yes, Mother with Jimmy drinking side-by-side at the pool.

Your mind is playing tricks on you, Natalie. Keep the lid on, honey. Never give up, says Dad in the rearview mirror.

CHAPTER THIRTY-FOUR

Getting into Jonathan's Range Rover, I wipe my eyes and lay my forehead on the steering wheel to have a talk with myself. "You're over it already, Natalie. You knew him for only a short time. We slept together. That's about it. I'm sorry but no more woebegone sulking anymore. You're an adult. Act like one."

I start the car in an ugly, hostile mood. I beat on the dashboard. Why? Why did this have to happen? Am I to blame somehow? Who did this?

I pull into Happy Jacks for something to kill the pain. Outside sits a payphone covered in graffiti. I stagger over to it and dial 911. A casual voice answers.

What's your emergency?

Yeah, my boyfriend has been murdered.

Murdered, you say.

"Yes."

You killed him?

No. Not directly, anyway.

You said you did. I heard you.

"No, I didn't. I didn't kill anyone."

But you say you did. Was it your husband?

"What? Whose husband? I don't have a husband."

The person you killed. Was it your boyfriend?

"My boyfriend. Yeah, he's dead. But no, I didn't kill him."

Why did you kill your boyfriend? What did he do? Was he mean to you? Did he beat you? Was it your fault?

"Just shut up and listen to me."

Don't talk to me like that, you brat. Where are you now?

"I... I'm..."

Where did you kill him? In Vermont?

"How do you know about Vermont?"

We know all about you, Natalie. You escaped from the hospital. You're a psycho. We've been looking for you. You need to come in and see us. Give yourself up. We can help you. Fix you so you don't kill nobody no more.

"No. Wait. I didn't kill him. You've got it all wrong. I'm..." I hold the phone out and stare at the receiver as a different voice comes through.

"Hello? Hello?" A calm woman's voice. "Hello. This is the 911 emergency call operator. What's your emergency?"

"I..."

"Ma'am? What's your emergency?"

"I want to report... I..."

"Report what, ma'am? Are you all right?"

"Yes. But there's been... been..."

"Been what, ma'am?

"A murder."

"Murder or murders? Would you repeat that, please?"

"A murder. Yes. A person was murdered. How many times do I have to say it?"

"Where? Where did this murder take place?"

"At... at." I'm confused. "743 West Main Street," I tell her.

"Are you at this location now, Natalie?"

How do you know my name?

I slam down the receiver and crawl into the Rover.

Who can you count on now? Avril's gone, Jonathan's dead.

I've slept with a few men that I could call. But how stupid would that be? Cicero maybe. He's been like an uncle to me. I don't trust myself with anything right now. I think back to Barlow's warning. This is what he was talking about.

But you didn't listen, did you? No. Too headstrong and sophomoric. You're an impulsive, underdeveloped, stupid brat.

I've got a bottle of Jack Daniels all to myself.

Streetlights begin to flicker on. Headlights crawl up and down the streets like processionary caterpillars in slow motion. Everything feels strange, devoid of life, lonely, dismal and dire. I pull into an alley, leave the keys in the front seat and walk home through downtown Danfield, glancing over my shoulder in fear of anything that moves. There's a toy store on a corner with a pink storefront. I pause and stand at the window, gazing at a stuffed teddy bear. A lump grows in my throat. Oh, to be back in Vermont now.

Home, bedtime, lights out, Dad kissing me on the forehead. Snuggling with Mister Teddy.

My nose fills with snot, and my eyes tear when I walk away from the store window and talk to myself. "I'll find thirty-eight dollars to buy you, Teddy. I'll be back. I promise."

At the apartment, the first thing to do is make a call. I get voicemail.

"Mister Longer, it's me, Runner. I don't know if you got my earlier message. I'm kinda desperate here. For your information, my address here in Danfield is 743 West Main Street. Hope to hear from you, Peter, as soon as you can. It's important. Really important."

Now, find Uncle Cicero.

CHAPTER THIRTY-FIVE

I find Cicero messing around in an upstairs storage room. "Jonathan's dead," I blurt out.

"What?" His face freezes in disbelief. "How? When? What happened?"

I flounder through a dizzying memory of pulling Jonathan through the water to save him. "But he was dead, Cicero."

Cicero hugs me. "Calm down. Just calm down. You need to think more clearly. If you say he's gone, then he's gone. Nothing more you can do." He takes my hand. "Are you okay?"

"Does it look like I'm okay?"

"Did you call the police?"

"No. I called 911 on a pay phone."

"A pay phone? Which one?"

"Outside Happy Jacks."

"That phone's been out of order for a year." He scratches his chin. "Who else knows?"

"Just you. And the ones who did it."

"How many of them were there?"

"I don't remember. Three, maybe."

Cicero gently touches my swollen eye. "Oh my." Then, he picks up his paintbrush and returns to painting. "The police will put two-and-two together if you've ever been in his house. Have you?"

"Yes. Of course."

"They'll find your fingerprints. They'll be knocking on your door in no time."

"But fingerprints will be of no use to them. I've never been fingerprinted."

He frowns at that disbelievingly but continues to paint without further questioning. His casual regard doesn't seem right. But what do I know?

"What should I do? Where can I go?"

He continues to paint without looking back. "Stay here for now. Hunker down. Don't go anywhere. We'll figure this out. Go back to your room. Get some rest. You look awful."

Back at my place, I stand at the open window and unhook my bra, pull it through the t-shirt armhole, and drop it on the floor. Sweat beads on my cheeks and snakes down my face, my neck, down through the canyon of my breasts. A gust of wind lifts the curtains. It begins to sprinkle. Then I check for a message on the cargo ship's arrival.

Still waiting.

I crawl into bed under the covers and hope for sleep to come peacefully.

Impossible.

Cicero walks in without knocking and sits on the edge of the bed. "I have an idea. There's a place you can go to hide until you figure out what to do. No one will find you in this place. It's a little iffy, but one or two nights should be okay."

"Where?"

"I'm pretty sure the cops will never find you there."

"Where? Where?" Then I stop. "What do you mean iffy?"

"It's an old, dilapidated building on Main Street. The Majestic Theatre. A one-time great playhouse decades ago. A rich guy owns it now. We all thought it would turn into something good. Last year, it was an informal shelter for itinerants. The owner has pretty much cleared them out. There's a one-eyed caretaker, Norman, who sees the building isn't vandalized inside. So, as long as there's no real trouble, the cops leave it alone. It's scheduled for demolition soon."

"I've been by it. Lots of graffiti, right? It looks all closed up."

"It is. But in the back, you can get through a boarded-up walk-in door."

"It doesn't sound safe."

"You'll no doubt run into Norman. Tell him you're only temporary and won't cause any trouble. If you're nice and respectful, he'll probably let you stay in one of the dressing rooms behind the stage for one or two nights. He looks scary, and he'll use harsh language, but he's harmless." Cicero gets up. "Gotta run. Let me know what you decide."

"What is it with me, Cicero? Why am I like this?"

"You're a rule breaker, Natalie. A rebel always on the lookout for something or someone to mess with. Sex is your tool to wreck lives. Gets you what you want. But it'll get you what you deserve in the long run."

"So I'm a psycho bitch. Is that what you're saying?"

"Let's put it like this: you're young with over-the-top smarts, bumping around criticizing the world for its impotence. Until you come down from that ivory tower, you'll be continually running, searching for nirvana and a unicorn soulmate."

After he leaves me deflated, I turn the lights off, crawl into bed, under the covers with the pint of Jack, and curl up, knees to chin.

"Happy Birthday, Dad."

I screw off the top and drink, shudder, and sing Happy Birthday over and over to the man who made me who I am.

Then I think of Tahiti.

CHAPTER THIRTY-SIX

Next morning.

Cicero pounds on my door. "Oh, geez." I jump out of bed rubbing my eyes. The sun is up, almost ten o'clock. He's anxious; upset about something.

"No time for coffee, girl." Cicero tells me the police will show up any minute. "You gotta get. Now. Hurry."

"Where will I go?"

"That's up to you. But just get out of here. Call me later; I'll explain." Then he turns and trots out.

As I pack up, I check the parking lot for any cars I don't recognize. I have to go immediately, but how? I don't have a car.

Find a ride, Natalie.

One name pops out at me. Bobby Simms. I get his voicemail. "Bobby, it's me, Runner. Call me, please." I hang up, heart racing.

So, who else?

There's one. But this one is a little touchy, though. It was only a one-night sleep over. Once. But he was different from the rest. Genuine. Comfortable. I make the call.

He answers.

"Hi, Hayden. It's me. Runner."

"Oh. Oh, yeah, wow. What's going on?"

"I need your help." Hesitation. "Can you give me a ride?"

"Sure. When? Where to?"

"I'll tell you when you get here."

"Where are you?"

"I'll be at The Coffee Bean in Danfield. You know where that is?"

"Yeah."

"I'll be there waiting."

"When?"

"As soon as you can get there."

"Where do you need a ride to?"

"I don't know yet, Hayden. Just come and get me." I hang up, realizing how desperate I probably sounded. I wanted to ask him for a night at his place.

Who are you to think you mean something to him?

I have the tote bag filled with what I have time to pack over my shoulder on the stairs when Cicero stops me and wants to know where I'm going.

I frown. "Not sure."

"You got any money?"

"No."

"Here." He pulls two twenties from his wallet. "This might hold you for a day. Call me when you get to where you're going."

"How do you know about the police coming here?"

"No time for that now. I'll explain later."

. . .

The Bean is busy. I devour a piece of toast and coffee and wait for Hayden. Lorraine and Sunshine are collaborating on changing the chalkboard menu again. It's intriguing how good Sunshine is with her lettering. I wander over to the counter for a better view. Her writing style is unique, so interesting. Where have I seen that style before?

Oh! No. It can't be. Oh my God. Can it be? Holy crap. It is.

The comparison hits me like a truck. I take the journal from the tote and pull out the letter.

Oh, my. Some of the lettering is so similar that it's got to be the same writer.

I start shaking and whisper to myself, "Oh, oh, Christ, Sunshine. You're the... you're the letter writer, aren't you?"

I'm so excited, I can't help myself. "Lorraine, Sunshine."

Stunned, they stop what they're doing and stare.

"Look," I say, holding out the letter. "Here, look at this."

They glance at each other cautiously before Lorraine slowly takes it with a frown.

I'm so anxious my voice shakes. "Does this... does this look familiar to you?" I bounce with excitement. She carefully reads it. I hold my breath, fearing what I might be about to discover.

Lorraine looks up at me, then at her daughter, and back at me again. "Where did you get this?"

"It's my dad's. I found it hidden in his desk."

"Your father?" she says, repeating while scanning over it again. "Your father," she repeats. Then she studies me carefully, searching for something in my face. "Who are you?"

"My name is Natalie Grace. Kendrick Grace was my father."

Lorraine holds on to the cabinet to steady herself, then drops into a chair, mouth open, spellbound lost for words. She can only stare at me. Sunshine continues to write on the board without looking back. "Told you, Mom."

Lorraine and I connect. We are sharing personal, unimaginable feelings with our eyes. No words, nothing other than unspoken compassion, adoration for a man we both loved. No question in my mind the bond he shared with this beautiful woman was deep and meaningful. I only wish I knew more.

I look over at Sunshine. "So you wrote the letter."

She continues designing the menu on the chalkboard without looking back. "Yeah."

"Why. Why you?"

"Because someone needed to. Mom gave up, thinking the relationship had ended. And it hurt her too much to continue writing letters to him when there was no possibility of ever seeing him again. She had closed her book on Kendrick."

"Why did *you* continue writing though?"

She steps down from the stool and wipes chalky hands on her apron. "Because I knew someone would come with news of him. I just had a feeling. And here you are."

I kneel in front of Lorraine. Tears glisten on her cheeks. I take her hand. "I need to know."

She smiles and touches my cheek. "Natalie? That's your name?"

I nod.

She squeezes my hand. "We met in college, dear. He was so handsome. And kind. And smart and ambitious. He put me up on a pedestal. I was his Eve. Destiny was our choice; we were certain of it. But destiny, we learned, isn't a choice. Chance determines destiny, doesn't it?"

"What happened?"

Fresh tears trickled down her face. "Tragedy."

"What happened, Lorraine?"

"Nathan happened. Our God-given little bundle of love, as pure an angel as ever was bestowed on any two people."

I frown.

"God giveth. God taketh," she whispers. "At two months." She sniffs. "I never recovered. It tore us apart. On an early summer Sunday morning, Kenny said goodbye. Never again did we meet. Only the letters we shared keep the embers warm. That was it until I gave up."

While we stare at one another, I notice movement in the parking lot.

A tall man with curly blond hair parking outside the door.

Oh, no.

I race to the restroom and lock the door, still in shock at discovering the source of the letter writers. My mind races to visualize Dad with her. But not for long. I hear the bell over the front door jingle.

It's him. The FBI.

I puff cheeks out and hold my breath, remembering I left the tote bag on the table. *And Hayden will show up any minute. And what about money? Can't get far when you're broke.*

If I get out of this pickle I'm in now, I must find money for a getaway somewhere, somehow. It doesn't take long to know where to find some. Vance keeps his under-the-table cash safe in his office at the restaurant. I've seen plenty in there. I quickly dismiss the idea as being too dangerous.

Right now, I need to figure out how to get out of this potty room without being nabbed.

CHAPTER THIRTY-SEVEN

It's midnight. Jimmy sits with Denny in his high-rise office, waiting for Barlow to arrive. Denny is red-eyed and looking tired, and dejected. "Do you think the girl will tell us who came up with the blackmail scheme, Jimmy?"

"I don't know her well enough to answer that. She's stubborn. That I do know. Independent and headstrong."

"But you seemed to get through to her. Talked her into considering the wonderful world of prostitution. Didn't you?"

"She never really accepted the idea. But she was desperate for money. Despite her rash behavior, she has this stupid sense of morality."

In walks Barlow, looking agitated.

Denny wastes no time. "Okay, where are we with this girl?"

"I met up with her in her apartment."

"And?"

"I tried to get her to talk. Find out who she's working with and see about getting those photos. I got nowhere. The more I tried the more obstinate she got. Before I could explain what would happen if she didn't cooperate, we were interrupted by her landlord."

Denny frowns. "Cicero?"

"Yeah."

Denny scratches his chin. "You know Cicero works for me, right?"

"No, I didn't. I'm not into all the things you have a hand in, Henry. I'm just a cleaner. I clean up after you when you dig yourself into trouble."

Denny ignores the reminder. "Cicero is like a partner of mine."

"What's he do for you?"

"Real estate issues and some legal matters. He's a former attorney. Worked in the DA's office some time ago."

Barlow shrugs.

Denny turns serious. "What did Cicero do when he walked in on you two?"

"Nothing. Just wanted to know what was going on."

Denny goes over to the window in thought. "This isn't what I like to hear."

"What do you mean?"

"Never mind. But I'm thinking about how to handle this. And it might take some outside help."

Barlow looks curious. "Outside help? Like who?"

"A guy I've used before to keep order and respect from troublemakers. And I think I have a couple of them to worry about."

"Who you talkin' about? Who's making trouble, Henry?"

"I'll not say just yet."

"Don't hold out on me, Henry. I have to know these things. It's my job."

Henry hesitates. "A guy, who goes by one name, Mauldin."

"Mauldin?"

Jimmy cuts in, "I know who he is. A hit man. A lunatic motherfucker. Certifiably crazy."

Barlow frowns at Jimmy and then at Henry. "Is he right, Henry? Why would you hire a guy like that? Sounds like trouble. Do we need someone like that?"

"Never mind, I have my reasons." Henry pours a drink and changes the subject. "The girl's going to run. We have to get her before she slips away. Find out who she's close to. Friends, employees where she works, boyfriends."

Barlow confirms, "She has a boyfriend. A rich guy. He's gaga over her. From what I hear from someone she works with. She plays hard to get with him."

Henry tells him, "Let's get serious about this. What's this girl like?"

"What do you mean?"

"Her personality. I need to know as much about her as possible."

"She's a very independent young lady. She resists men controlling her. Resists authority of any kind, especially church and government institutions. A rebel. She's capricious, fickle, and unashamedly promiscuous. That's all I hear from my source."

Barlow holds up a bandaged wrist. "She's a tough one. Not a hooker like you hinted at, Henry. She's smart. Clever. Slippery."

Barlow changes the subject. "Henry, has your wife seen the photos of what happened at the Grand Plaza?"

Denny snaps, "I know how to handle my wife. I've told her I'm a victim of political jealousy, that I've been framed, so don't worry about her." He pulls at his ear. "Keep her out of this, okay?"

Jimmy stands to leave. "So we still don't know who's behind this, how they intend to use the photos or their intentions."

"No. Not yet. But we will," says Barlow.

Denny shows impatience. "So go find her. Bring her to me."

Barlow asks with a too-quick fake smile. "What if I just get the names of the ones who paid her to do this? Deal with them and leave her out of it?"

Denny shouts, "This is different, Barlow. We're dealing with blackmail here. This will be front page if we don't find the fuckers in time. And blackmail isn't the only thing that has me outraged. This girl, she's personal to me. No one does what she did to me and doesn't get what's coming to them. I owe her something. You bring her in or I'll have my hired guy do it."

As soon as Jimmy gets to his car, he calls Cicero. He knows the old landlord never sleeps.

"Cicero, listen. Things are heating up. Denny has that crazy look in his eyes again. I just left him. He's hiring someone we need to be aware of. A hit man. Goes by the name of Mauldin. This changes everything." He hangs up and makes another call to the East coast and leaves a message: "I have a job for you."

CHAPTER THIRTY-EIGHT

In his hotel room, Richard Redd finishes purchasing an online airline ticket back to Denver. He gets a call.

"Detective Redd, this is Cicero LeBlanc. We met the other day at my apartment."

"Yes, I remember."

"I just want you to know Runner has gotten herself involved in something big. Something dangerous."

"Go on."

Cicero briefly summarizes Runner's situation. "A guy is going to show up. A hit man. A very bad man with a reputation as a psychotic woman hater. Apparently, he served time years ago after a woman testified against him for something. So all women are on his shit list now. Rumors are he has a nasty habit of raping his female victims, cutting out their tongues, then telling them to plead for their lives before killing them. And Runner is right in the middle of this mess. No doubt she'll be on this guy's list."

"Where is Runner now?"

"I don't know. You might want to try Oakes Bar and Grill.

She works there. Vance Oakes is the owner. He may know where she is.”

“This hit man have a name?”

“Mauldin. Anton Mauldin.”

“You have any idea of where Runner might be?”

“I have no idea. Like I said, talk with Vance Oakes.”

Redd hesitates for a second. “How do you know about all this?”

Cicero’s turn for hesitancy. “I made a mistake.”

“Mistake?”

“Yes. I got involved with Henry Denny. And now with Jimmy Barone.” He summarizes how his life is now in danger. “I’m about to pay for my misjudgment. I don’t want the same thing for Runner.”

On his way to the airport, Redd stops at Oakes Bar and Grill to speak with Vance Oakes.

“Yes, detective,” says Vance. “She used to work here as a bartender. But she quit after a short time. She learned the bartender business pretty good for the short time she was here. But couldn’t keep her fucking nose out of other people’s business.”

“Do you know where she is?”

“No. I don’t know where she is. And I could care less.”

“Anything else, Mister Oakes?”

“No. Now I got things to do instead of talking about that girl.” He lights a cigar in thought and leans back. “She’s a head-scratcher, detective. A tough nut to crack. But you can’t help but like her in a strange sort of way. I just wish things would have worked differently with her.”

“Mister Oakes?”

"What?"

"Are you involved with Jimmy Barone and Henry Denny?"

At the airport, Redd calls Peter. "I found her. Well, I didn't meet up with her, but I discovered she's made quite a splash out here."

"Doesn't surprise me. What kind of trouble is she in?"

"She got involved with a blackmail scheme with some bad guys. The blackmail went bad. That turned into a bigger mess with a mob power struggle. The picture is turning worse, Pete. A hitman is being brought in to weed out the problem makers. And Runner started this all by crippling the ego of the organization's boss. Emasculating his self-esteem and questioning his hold over his organization. What she did sent ripples through this criminal group. Now I understand the hitman's number one target is Runner. He's a killer, Pete. Runner is right in the middle of all this."

"Runner, Runner, Runner," Peter utters under his breath. "How do you get yourself into these jams?" He pauses. "I need to get her out of there, Rich."

"One more thing, Pete. She's a fugitive. Feds are after her."

"Why?"

"Something to do with what happened back in Vermont."

Peter clicks his teeth. "Something serious if the Feds are after her."

"She just attracts trouble, Pete. Like bees to honey."

"I've been working on a way to get her out of the country."

"How?"

"I booked passage for her on a cargo ship that won't put her name on the manifest. She just needs to make it to the ship on time and get on board. How difficult can that be?"

A long pause between the two is the unspoken answer.

"Gotta catch my flight, Pete. Adios, outlaw. Keep your head down."

CHAPTER THIRTY-NINE

Peeking out from inside The Coffee Bean's restroom, I take a deep breath when I see Hayden standing with hands in his pockets, waiting to see me. The tall blond man has his coffee and takes a table nearby. Studying him carefully I see he's much older than Agent Waters. I relax, exhale, and walk out. When Haden sees me he's like a Labrador puppy, tail wagging, expecting a treat. "Hey."

"Hey, yourself."

I go over to Lorraine and Sunshine and pull them off to the side. "Listen. I have so much to ask you. But I don't have time right now. I gotta go. Promise I'll be back." I hug each of them and leave them standing open-mouthed. "I promise, promise I'll be back."

Hayden's pickup truck is an old, frightful sight, oxidized red with primer patches with two faded bumper stickers: a Jesus fish and a HONK IF YOU LOVE JESUS.

I toss the stuffed tote behind the bench seat and slide over next to him.

"What the hell's going on, Runner?"

I pull on my ball cap. "Let's go."

He notices the red under my eye and tries to touch it. "This have something to do with the trouble you're in?"

I slap his hand away. Then grab it back, press it to my cheek, and close my eyes in a display of practiced affection with a shallow apology.

"What is it?" he says. "What's happened?"

"I'll tell you later, cowboy. Let's go."

He frowns while trying to start the problematic engine. It chugs once and stops.

"Where to?" he asks, still trying to start the truck.

I ignore his question with one of my own. "What are you doing right now?"

"Trying to get this damn motor started. It needs a real mechanic before it dies on me completely." He waits, sighs, and pleads, "Come on, baby, start for me."

"No. I mean today. What are you doing today, Hayden?"

He ignores me and cusses under his breath while continuously stomping on the accelerator.

"Hayden." I tug on his arm. "You got any free time today?"

"Not much. I've got a big exam tomorrow morning. Just cramming. Why?"

I hold back in a pout. He's oblivious to my theatrics. The rest of the ride is quiet between us. Just country music on the radio interrupted by a weather alert of severe weather, heavy rain, and high winds on the way. Flooding expected.

We pull up at his place, an unremarkable little house down the street from his school and park. Probably a rental house mostly used by grad students. A police car sits parked on the curb in front.

Inside, everything is neat and tidy, albeit furnished with time-worn furniture. No dishes in the sink. No clothes strewn around. No food crumbs on the floor.

"You live here alone?"

"One roommate."

"He must be tidy. The place is clean and doesn't smell like a guy's locker room."

He throws the pickup keys on the kitchen counter. "Yeah, she's clean and tidy."

"She? Is that what you said? She."

He nods and leans on the counter. "Who is it you're running from, Runner?"

"Some guys I got cross with."

"How serious?"

"Pretty serious."

"That eye," he nods at it, "that kind of seriousness?"

I ignore the question and look around his little place. There's a black vest on a shelf next to the hall closet with POLICE stenciled on the front. "What's that?"

"That's her tactical vest. She's a cop."

"Oh."

"So what's going on, Runner?"

"Got kicked out of my apartment. I'm leaving the country."

"Why'd you get kicked out?"

"Can't afford the rent."

"Where you headed?"

"Maybe Costa Rica. Panama. Chile. Vietnam. Anywhere out of the country." I pull him close, belly to belly, nose to nose. "Hey. Let's go together. We can live a good life." I grab his hand with both of mine. "Come on. Let's do it."

He folds me in his arms. "Runner, Runner, Runner. How about a weekend getaway to San Diego after my test?"

"I'm serious, Hayden."

"So am I." He releases me and leans back on the counter. "What's wrong?"

"I'm tired of California. One big blur. I want a laid-back beach town somewhere. Doesn't that sound terrific?"

"Yeah. But not for me yet."

"How important is this exam tomorrow?"

"Damn important if I'm gonna be a lawyer."

"I want you to take me away, Hayden."

"Away?"

"Yeah, away."

"When?"

"Now."

He sighs. Runs a hand through his hair. "I'm going downstairs to study."

I give him a playful poke in the ribs.

He takes my hand. "Grow up, Runner. Do something with your life. You're impressive, off-the-charts intelligent, but you're tilting at windmills."

"Oh, so you're quoting *Don Quixote* now. How shrewd of you, Mister Hogan. Should I kiss your feet?"

"Is everything a challenge for you, Runner?"

"Oh. I see now. You're all grown up, I guess. Tell me, farm boy, you ever enjoyed a second of your life? Laid on your back, studied the stars, moon, and clouds racing by? Let me tell you what's going to happen, nerd boy. You'll make a ton of money and have two kids, clones of you and Elizabeth, Mary or Margaret, whatever her name will be. You'll probably have a yellow Labrador, a kidney-shaped swimming pool and fancy cars in your four-car garage. But in the end, will you ever be able to say you've been happy? I mean really happy? Enjoyed life to the fullest? Huh? Will you?" I stab a finger at him. "So tell me, Hayden. When was the last time you really enjoyed yourself?"

Stone-faced and wide-eyed, he pokes me in the chest. "With you."

That answer stops me cold. I pause and almost choke up as he trots down the stairs.

I call down to him, "Well, good for you, buddy."

No answer back. I flop down on the sofa in a pout when my phone buzzes with an incoming text.

ALMARANI MARITIME SHIPPING

UPDATE:

Bonnie Lynne, loose cargo, passenger passage—ETA unreliable.

Passengers check phones for boarding, possibly tomorrow.

Tomorrow? Christ. When exactly? What about money, Nat?

Crisis! This is a hell of a sudden crisis.

Emergency, pack a bag, how to know where to go. Oh, God.

I walk in circles biting fingernails. Money! I need cash and fast. Where? Where can I find some real money?

Jimmy! Let Jimmy hire you.

I'll do anything to make enough to get on the boat. Even that. How much will it take? I can make enough in two days to—

Before I can finish Father is next to me smoking his pipe. *Is that what you're going to do? Lower yourself to that level?*

"Dad, I have to. My life is over if I don't get on that boat."

Your life will be over if you do what you are thinking.

"But—" Before I can explain how desperate I am he's gone. And I'm on to other ridiculous thoughts. Rob a bank. Break into one of those rich homes for jewelry to hock. Beg on the street. I want to cry.

Then it hits me.

Oakes.

Vance Oakes always has cash in his restaurant office safe. I've seen it. The idea of raiding it is not a good idea either. But the only one I can think of. I grab the truck keys off the counter and whisper, "Bye-bye, Hayden. Good luck with that test."

CHAPTER FORTY

Hayden's pickup rattles and shakes heading to Oakes Bar and Grill. I pass by the toy store with the teddy bear in the window and feel emotion swelling up in me. I swallow away the lump in my throat and put it out of my mind.

Think about how you're going to rob a safe.

Sprinkles turn to rain. The wipers are old and smear dirty streaks across the windshield making it difficult to see clearly. The exhaust-smoking, red trash heap begins to stutter.

You're out of gas.

I barely make it rolling into an all-night diner's parking lot. Rain falling harder, wind picking up. I watch people through the window eating. I feel weak and nervous. I realize how hungry I am. I grab the tote and run inside, and slide into a window booth.

Without any money to pay, I wolf down a cheeseburger, fries, and milkshake. Diners stare at my eating behavior. When finished, I wipe my mouth and give them a WTF look.

Now what?

The waitress, a young, pimply-faced, baby-fat, sweet girl, looks to be a high schooler. She lays the check on the table. "Whenever you're ready, no rush." I stare at her and want to say the truth.

Sorry, I can't pay. I have no money. I really am sorry.

Instead, put a call in to Bobby. Leave another voicemail.

"Please, Bobby. Please don't leave me hanging. Call me back ASAP. If I don't hear from you—" I start to say when a police cruiser pulls up next to Hayden's pickup. I hang up and casually pull the ball cap bill down low over my face.

Two uniforms walk in and take a booth next to me to study the menu. One is tall with stripes on his sleeve and the other is younger, shorter, the grumpy-drawers type.

I stare at the check on the table.

Have to go to plan B. Supplication.

I pretend to rummage around in the tote looking for my wallet. Barlow's gun appears. I quickly cover it.

"Miss," I say to the server. "I'm so embarrassed to say this, but I've forgotten my wallet. Can I leave you an IOU?" I fidget around, acting nervous like I need a pen and paper. "I'll go get my wallet and come right back."

At that moment, the gun topples out of the tote and into my lap. I cover it, but too late. She sees it. Her eyes get big. She looks over at the cops and back at me. She walks over to them, chewing gum nonchalantly. "Hey Frank..."

I can't believe she's going to squeal on me.

"Frank," she says. "This chick says she's forgotten her wallet. Wants to give me an IOU. What should I do?"

"I'm not your boss, Vicky. How should I know?"

The server looks at the bill. "It's twelve thirty-seven."

I interrupt. "I'll give you twenty when I get my wallet, Vicky. Promise."

Frank, a big man in his mid-forties with a touch of gray in his military buzz cut and stripes on his sleeve, reads the menu, trying to decide. His radio chirps.

"APB—Caucasian female, blonde, roughly five foot ten inches, hundred twenty pounds, seen driving a model Range Rover. Suspect armed and dangerous."

Grumpy cop looks at his sergeant. "Hear that, Frank?"

Frank looks up at Vicky and then at Grumpy, concern etched on his face. "God dammit," he says, staring at me.

"What?" Vicky asks.

"I hate it when this happens."

"What?"

He shakes his head and looks back at me. "What's your name, miss?"

I swallow. "Runner."

He looks up at Vicky. "I hate to do what I gotta do." He frowns at me. I feel my face turning red and my throat tightening. I'm about to hyperventilate.

Vicky looks at me with big eyes and then at the tote. I'm ready to jump up and run for it.

You can outrun them, Nat. Go. Go. Go.

Frank looks at me. "Tell me, Miss Runner, what should I do?"

"I..."

He holds up his hands in frustration. "Sometimes I can't decide what to eat when I'm on a diet." He rubs his chin. "So what do you think I should get? Salad or cheeseburger?"

I stutter, "I, uh, uh. Well. I. I think..."

"What?"

"Get the salad," I say.

"Great." He orders a Cobb salad. Grumpy wastes no time and orders a double cheeseburger, fries, a slice of pie, and a Coke.

My heart races, hands tremble. Frank cracks a joke about his partner's body shape. Grumpy trash talks back. They go at it, good-naturedly jabbing and insulting each other while Vicky and I stare. Frank asks, "Which one of us would you rather go out with? Me or this tub-a-guts sitting here about to stuff his face?"

"I... I..."

Frank waves a dismissive hand. "Just teasing."

Vicky breaks in. "Frank?"

"What?"

"She doesn't have enough to pay for her meal."

"How much is it again?"

"Twelve thirty-seven."

Frank gives me a long look. "Forgot your wallet, you say?"

"Yeah. Yes, sir. I'm so sorry."

"You good for it?"

"Yes, sir. I promise."

Frank thinks for a second, then pulls out his wallet for a twenty. "Promise?" he asks again, holding it suspended in the air.

I nod. "Promise."

Vicky snaps it up, gives me a long, detached stare, and walks away.

They continue trash talking while I sit contemplating how to get out of this diner. Vicky shows up with their orders. Grumpy asks Frank, "Did you get that APB? The five foot ten girl, armed and dangerous?"

Frank digs into his salad. "Yeah."

Petulance is rooted in Vicky's face.

Time to get out of here, Natalie.

I scoot out of the booth and stand at their table, hands folded behind me. I notice Frank's name badge. "Thank you, Sergeant Battaglia. I really appreciate it. Can I mail you the twenty?"

Grumpy grins at Frank. "He's just hoping to get in your pants, honey."

"Don't believe a thing this fatty-ass says."

"How can I mail you the twenty, sergeant?"

He pulls out a card. "It's Frank to you." Then he writes a phone number on the back and hands it to me. "If you ever need help, call me."

"Thank you, thank you."

Grumpy asks me, "Have I seen you before?"

"Probably not. No."

"You're a tall one."

Frank asks, "What's your name again? So I'll know who you are if you call."

"Runner."

Grumpy laughs at that. "Runner. Ha. That's not your real name." Then asks, "How tall are you, anyway?"

"About average."

Grumpy turns to Frank. "Did you hear that APB about a tall girl?"

Franks looks at me differently. Studying me. My scalp prickles, and I'm sweating. Grumpy stops chewing, staring hard at me. Frank's phone rings; he waves me along while listening to the call.

I turn to Vicky, eye-to-eye, pleading for her silence. No response, nothing but a deadpan look in her eyes.

My walk to the door feels like forever, expecting a big hairy-knuckled hand to grab my neck any second. But serendipitous fate must be on my side for the time being. I make it out, trying to look casual, walking down the street, disappearing into a dark rain until I break into a run, the tote bouncing on my hip, headed to Oakes Bar and Grill.

My phone buzzes a text.

ALMARANI MARITIME SHIPPING
Bonnie Lynn PASSENGER BOARDING UPDATE
TOMORROW
BERTH 57—0630 hour
Oh, God. Make this quick, Natalie. You've got to get to that boat.

CHAPTER FORTY-ONE

I'm not sure if Vance will be there when I make it to the restaurant's back door. He scares me. I hesitate to go in. He hates me.

No love lost between us.

The back door is always open for ventilation and to keep the flies out. I peek in. The cooks are occupied preparing dinners. I can't trust any of them since I got O'Grady fired. The kitchen staff liked him. They'll be a problem if they see me. Maybe the new barback girl won't be like them.

If you're gonna go, better get after it. Time's a wastin'.

Unnoticed, I creep past them all and slip into Vance's office, closing the door behind me. I take a seat at his desk to rest and dry off. There's a stack of pink "to do" notes on the desk. One note connects Vance to Henry Denny's organization.

So Oakes and Denny are in something together.

Then I stare at the safe.

Wonder if the combination I know is still good. The one he gave me to pay contractors in cash under the table when I was along working the bar and he was not around.

I remember it started with a 1 and had a 67 in the combination. There were multiple fives. I know that for a fact. At least I think so.

I try—1 5 5 5 6 7.

Beep. No good.

Again. Maybe with two fives. So... 1 5 5 6 7.

Beep. Nope.

Again. 1 5 6 7.

Beep.

1 5 6 7 5 5.

Click.

"Ha!"

Inside, on the top shelf, is a short sawed-off shotgun with a pistol grip. Below it, on the middle shelf, are two small cash stacks of mixed denominations—a few hundred altogether. On the bottom, at the back, is a metal cash box. Inside are hundreds in rubber-banded stacks. After a quick count, I whisper, "Forty thousand dollars. Forty friggin' thousand dollars!"

Christ almighty, Natalie. You just may make it yet.

I open the tote and drag everything out. Then, I stuff the hundreds in a ZipLoc bag from a supply cabinet and lay them on the bottom under running shoes, a bra, and the .38. Everything else goes back in on top, with t-shirts lying over the short shotgun.

Now, let's get to that boat.

The Oakes delivery van is parked at the far end of the lot. I crack open the office door and peek out. The young barback is rinsing rags at the utility sink.

"Pssst."

She glances around.

I give her the "come 'ere" finger wriggle.

Her eyes get big and anxious. She sneaks over. "Runner. What are you doing in there?"

"Shushhh. Can you get me the keys to the catering van off the wall over there?"

She shrugs, turns back, looks over her shoulder, and heads to the utility sink.

Nope. She's afraid. Not going to do it.

But soon, she's back with the keys and a wink. "Good luck with whatever you're up to."

I almost make it out the back door before one of the cooks sees me. He yells half in Hungarian to Leo, the bouncer.

I reach the far end of the parking lot and jump in the old Dodge. The tote spills over the floor including the shotgun in full view. I fumble with the key. The starter only whines. I try again. It catches and comes to life before quitting. I try again. It starts and rumbles. I pump the accelerator. It jerks once and stops. I crank it again. *Whirr, whir.* No start. Leo, the bouncer, is outside the kitchen trying to understand the babbling cook waving and shouting something.

Oh, oh, here he comes.

Thank God he's a heavy bouncer, big and lumbering, not a runner.

The starter whirrs again. The motor chugs a couple times, stops and dies.

I try again. It jumps to life, then sputters. I drop it in gear. It leaps forward only to die a few feet ahead. Leo is at the van now, opening the sliding door, pulling himself in. I grab the shotgun off the floor and swing it at him. There's a cracking noise from his nose. He falls back and out, hitting the asphalt like a watermelon busting open. I try the starter again. The motor catches, running rough. Leo stumbles up, dazed, holding his nose, blood flowing through his fingers. He lurches at the door again. I drop it in gear. It jerks forward. Leo's eyes are wild, blood down the front of his shirt. He's gripping the inside of the door frame again. This time I aim the shotgun butt at his hand. There's a sharp cracking sound. He falls away. The old Dodge pulls out. I see Leo in the side mirror rolling on the pavement. I toss the shotgun out the door and hit the accelerator.

Sorry. You're not a bad guy, Leo. So sorry.

On Main Street I give a quick glance at the gas gauge. "Oh, Christ." It's on empty.

You'll not even make it up the street. Why do you steal vehicles without gas, Natalie?

I look around for somewhere to leave this thing.

CHAPTER FORTY-TWO

This van is a gaudy, egg-yolk yellow with giant images of burnt barbecue ribs on the side. Not a good look when trying to be inconspicuous. By now, I'm sure calls have been placed to the cops from Oakes to be on the lookout for a crazy girl in a dumpy old pickup truck or possibly driving around in a tacky yellow restaurant catering van.

The van sputters once, letting me know it's getting low.

Panic.

I turn into an empty, weed-infested parking lot behind a big graffiti-covered building on the corner.

Can this be the Majestic Theatre Cicero was talking about? It looks worse than what Cicero said. The walls look like prison walls with big patches of plaster missing, faded gray paint, graffiti, and weeds crawling up from the dirt.

I kill the engine and sit eying the walk-in back door. Maybe I'll leave the van here, get inside, and wait for Bobby.

Are you really going in there?

The rain is steady. A flash of light and thunder rolls. I grab the tote and hold it to my chest before stepping out.

Call Bobby first.

I dial, he answers.

"I'm in trouble, Bobby. I hate to ask this of you, but I need your help. Can you come get me?"

"Runner?"

"Yes. Oh, sorry, it's me, yeah."

"What's the matter?"

"My battery is running out, and I don't have time to explain, but believe me. I need a ride. Can you come? Please."

"Where are you?"

"Danfield. I know it's late, and I'm sorry. But dang, I really need you."

"Where in Danfield?"

"Behind an old theatre on Main Street. The Majestic Playhouse Theatre. There's a big empty parking lot in the back full of weeds. There's a walk-in door in the back. Looks like it's been boarded up. That's where you get in. I'll be inside waiting. Honk when you get here. Thank you, thank you so much. Please come as soon as you—"

I stop mid-sentence. Headlights up the street. A police cruiser. It's coming slowly, scanning the streets with a spotlight.

"Wait, Bobby," I shout. "Hang on for a second." I squint. "Oh, my God. He's about to turn in here. He'll see the van."

"Who?" he asks. "Who's coming? What's going on?"

I shout into the phone, "Change of plans, Bobby. There's a 7-Eleven up the street a few blocks away. Meet me there."

Click.

I start the van and slowly head up the alley turning onto Main Street. After a block, the engine sputters and jerks. I turn off onto a residential street and roll to a stop on the curb. No sign of the cop car.

I jump out in a crouch and scurry like a cockroach, heading to the 7-Eleven. I make it there, breathing hard, and collapse, huddled down next to the ice machine. Red and blue flashing lights race by on Main Street, sirens screaming. Vicky must have told Frank about me and the gun.

Oh, boy. Don't let me down, Bobby.

I slip inside, use the restroom, grab a bottle of water and a Hostess Twinkie, and wait for Bobby to show up.

Across the street, a bank tower clock tells me I can still easily reach the boat on time. But no time to waste. For only a few precious seconds, I allow myself the thought of being in Tahiti. Paradise. Sandy beaches and crystal-clear waters. I hug the tote and begin to shiver. The rain has strengthened and turned bitter. I blow into cold hands.

"Come on, Bobby."

CHAPTER FORTY-THREE

Jimmy parks behind the Majestic. He slips through the back door into darkness and down the hall to a small room that used to be a dressing room. He greets the caretaker, Norma. He looks over at Avril. She's disheveled, clothes tattered, busted lip, blood on a leg. "This isn't what you promised, Jimmy."

"Come on. Let's go. Guided by the light of his cell phone, they walk up the aisle past the audience seating area, through the lobby, and up a curved staircase to a green door. Inside to the lavishly appointed long room. He pours two drinks from a small but well-stocked bar. Then takes her back to a bedroom. "Okay, take a seat and finish your drink."

She's thirsty and downs it so fast she has to grab deep breaths between gulps.

"You hungry?"

"No. I just want to get out of here."

"He'll be back soon. Just relax. You know the drill. Don't resist or you'll be sorry. Like before."

Jimmy hands her a phone. "I'm sorry about this. Here, make a call."

She snatches it and questions Jimmy with her eyes. "Is this a trick?"

"You're free to go. But call Runner first. Tell her where you are and ask her to come and get you. She'll be happy to hear you."

Avril gives a dubious look before dialing. It goes to voicemail. Avril leaves a shaky message. "Hey, girl, it's me. I'm in that old theatre. We've passed it before. You know where it is." She breaks into an uncontrollable sob. "The Majestic Theatre. I'm... I'm upstairs. Come in through the back door from the parking lot. Please hurry."

Jimmy smiles and slowly takes the phone back. "See, now. That wasn't so hard, was it? You'll see your friend pretty soon."

"Where's Henry? I want out of here before he comes back."

"He'll be here soon."

"Can I get some water?"

"Sure. Come out to the bar. Take a seat, Avril." He pours her a glass of water. She drinks it down just as fast at the other drink and wipes her mouth with the back of her hand.

Henry has entered the room. He's obviously been drinking. He walks slowly, robotically to Avril with a foolish grin.

"Henry, you should have your girl here pretty soon."

Henry pulls a stool close to Avril and sits with his hand on her back. "Hi, again, honey." He pauses. "Why don't you make us a drink? Get us in a party mood like before. I'll have a vodka tonic. You make whatever you want. Sound okay?"

She nods meekly.

Henry turns to Jimmy. "How do you know she's gonna be here?"

"We put a call into her." He nods at Avril. "Runner will either come sneaking in on her own to find her friend. Or my men will find her."

Henry takes her hand. "Let's go back to our little comfortable room before our friend arrives."

She resists. He pulls her along. She knows she has no options other than to obey.

Jimmy holds the door. "Okay when you guys are finished I'll get Norman to come and get you, honey. Okay?" He closes and locks the door. "I got some business to take care of. Let me know when you're finished in there."

Jimmy runs through the rain to his car at the far end of the parking lot and makes a call to Mauldin.

"Yeah."

"Where are you?"

"Almost there, where you told me to meet you."

"Good, I'll be waiting."

It was a half hour before Jimmy got the call from Henry.

"I'm finished with her. Send Norman for her."

CHAPTER FORTY-FOUR

I've been waiting for Bobby too long. It's getting later and colder by the minute. I blow into my hands, teeth chattering. The wind and rain getting stronger, a flash in the sky, a loud clap close by. God, I'm so tired. I grab the phone from the tote. The battery is critically low.

Try Bobby one more time.

He answers but with a bad connection. "Bobby. It's me again. Listen. I have to—"

"Hello? Hello?" says Bobby. "Who is this? Runner? Can you hear me?"

The connection fails. I try twice more. Unsuccessful.

Oh, God.

He must be getting close. I redial and get him.

"Bobby. How long will it take you to get here?"

He sounds frustrated. "Hello. Runner? Hello?"

Two patrol cars pull into the 7-Eleven and park. I pull a sweatshirt from the tote and hang it over my head like I'm just another guttersnipe hanging out. They disregard me.

Oh Lord, let them take their pisses, get their donuts, and leave.

Ten minutes later, they're still dogging it at the convenience store. Standing around shooting the shit, as Dad would say. Bobby won't be able to get me as long as these guys are here.

I crawl to the corner of the building next to the ice machine, then run to the backside of the store, to the other side, away from the cops and cross Main Street. I'll try to thumb a ride to the docks.

But who's gonna stop and pick up a drowned rat girl in this storm at this time of night?

After three cars pass, a delivery truck pulls over. The door flies open. "What the hell are you doing out in this weather, girl?"

"I need to get to the docks. In a hurry. Can you take me there?"

He breaks out in this crazy half-smile while squeezing a chin pimple. "Sure. Sure thing, honey. Jump in."

At the first red light, he stops, lays his hand on my thigh.

I ignore it.

A ding comes in on my phone.

"Hey, girl, it's me. I'm in that old theatre. The Majestic Theatre. I'm... I'm upstairs. Come in through the back door from the parking lot. Please hurry. Can't wait to see you."

Oh my God, Avril. It's you. And something's wrong. You're scared.

I slap the driver's hand off me. He backhands me. When the light turns green, I kick the door open, roll out into a puddle, get up with the tote and run back through the downpour toward the Majestic.

She's in that theatre. Upstairs? Something doesn't sound right.

The rain stings my face. I feel someone running alongside me. It's Dad.

Come on, Natalie. This is like your track meets, remember? You were

"The one friend I have out here is in trouble. I can't just leave her without seeing what I can do to help."

Alone and running down Main Street isn't smart. The cops will be driving by looking for me. Can't be this exposed. I turn off Main Street and head for the alley behind the stores with the Majestic at the far end. It's the safest way to get to the theatre without being seen.

What are you going to do when you get there?

CHAPTER FORTY-FIVE

I slow to a fast walk to catch my breath. The tote is sopping wet and heavy, the alley terrifyingly dark except for random overhead security lights bathing a few loading doors in yellow halos.

It's so cold my fingers are turning blue.

Another flash overhead with rolling thunder. Two stores up the alley is an overhang for a little shelter from the rain. I stop and dial Bobby. No answer. *I've probably lost all credibility with him.*

Another flash overhead with the crack of thunder.

I try Bobby again. Get voicemail. "Bobby. Listen, meet me at the Majestic Theatre I told you about. I know this might sound confusing but I have to go back in there for something important. Sorry for this. Hope you're still coming. I really need you. I owe you. Thanks. My life depends on you. Thanks. Thank you again."

After a big breath, I pick up the pace and pass through the light of one of the flood lamps. Something moves. In the shadows. A flash overhead reveals the alley in eerie, brilliance for a millisecond, two men in sudden intensity.

Yikes.

I stop.

They are under a bit of extended roof and cooking on a propane grill. One is tall and skinny, the other is a little rat-face punk.

"Yo, Danny girl," the tall one shouts. "How you doin' baby cakes? You look cold. How 'bout we warm you up? Come over here and put your hands over this. We got some chili cookin'." They chuckle and come out into a halo of one of the security lights. The little one circles me, mumbling, "Well sweet cakes? Wanna make a few quick bucks, sweetie? Easy money, mi pequeña perra."

"No thanks, boys."

They laugh and fall in behind me as I hurry along. "I ain't foolin', muchacha. Looker like you." The tall one whistles and reaches out to touch the tote. "Whatcha got here, mamacita?"

I spin around and jerk back. "Keep your filthy hands off me."

"Wow," he says. "I'm Germaine, baby. Remember that name." He struts around me, holding his crotch. "Little toughie we got us here, Clarence. Bring some good scratch. I'm thinkin'."

"Yeah, baby. Fosho," Clarence mutters. "You sell it. You make ya self a sweet G-note, mamma. Easy peasy. But we gotta squeeze it a little ourselves before we sell it. So... how 'bout it? Step ova here an—"

"Screw yourselves, boys."

Clarence jumps ahead. "Now, why you be so mean, mamacita?"

I slip past them. They follow. Shorty holds out a little baggie. "Got somthin' here you ought to try. Make you feel oh-so-good, bonita."

I pick up the pace. They follow close, slinging pebbles and

yelling obscenities. We pass under another security light. Germaine grabs my ass. Clarence has his hands on me when I twist around and swing at the tall one, miss, and fall. The tote falls, spilling stuff out. I jump up. Clarence grabs me and punches me in the mouth. I stumble to my knees—Barlow's .38 is lying right under my nose. Clarence never sees it coming. I lift up with the gun and crack him hard across his nose. Blood and snot fly through the brilliance of the security light. He falls on his back. Germaine's hand is inside his jacket. But he freezes at the sight of the .38 in his face.

"Go ahead, Germaine. Let us see how much sense you have in that pea brain of yours."

He holds steady, hand in his jacket, trying to decide.

I wiggle the gun in his face.

Clarence is on his back, wailing, holding his nose.

I touch my lip and wipe blood away. Then calmly, I say, "Did you know, Germaine, that the human brain is made up of gray and white matter. Forty percent gray, sixty percent white. It's the gray matter that carries ninety-four percent of the total oxygen." I step closer, the gun within inches of his nose. "The white-lab-coat folks say that the larger percentage of intracranial gray matter generally means greater intelligence. Should we find out what percentage of gray matter you have, Germaine?"

Clarence is on his knees now, holding his nose, dripping blood onto the wet pavement.

"What d'ya think, Clarence? Wanna find out how smart your partner here is?" I step closer. "I'm kinda thinkin' we're about to find out how much of your brain is white pudding. What do you say? Shall we take a look? Check on your intellectual capacity, Germaine?"

His eyes are wide, face taught and tense.

"Now, let's see if you can lift that gun out with two fingers.

Thumb and little finger. Drop it. If you can't, well, Clarence and me... we're about to discover the color of your intellect."

The gun drops to the pavement with a thud. Germaine pulls his buddy up by the arm.

"Hey," Clarence whines. "Watcha doin' this for, chica?"

I cock the hammer. The unmistakable click is obvious to the two stink bugs.

"Hey, hey, hey," Clarence cries. "No need. Come on, cariño; we don't mean nothin' bad to ya. Entiendes?"

My hand is steady, but mentally I'm out of control. Blood running hot. Trigger finger slowly, ever so slowly, tightening.

Stop, Natalie. Stop.

Too late. "On your knees, boys. Say hello to whatever God you guys pray to."

The alley goes blurry in my head—rain, the buildings, lights, two cracks of thunder, their bodies stretch and twist like slithering snakes. They look up at me in deformed masses of swirling color and anguish and pleadings, screechings in my head, bitter taste in my mouth. Then things go calm when I see headlights coming down the alley.

Get out of here. Run.

The wet alley pavement glistens as the car approach. I glare at the two goons on the ground.

Don't panic. Don't run. Just walk.

I tuck the .38 into my waistband and turn, feigning a casual stroll, moving aside to let it pass. A muddy red sedan with windshield wipers swishing rhythmically. I glance at the driver's window but can't see through the fogged glass. A cop, perhaps? My breath catches as it slows to match my pace. I draw the .38, holding it visibly at my side as a warning. The car crawls past.

Up the alley, I look back to see the sedan make a U-turn and stop where I left Clarence and Germaine. Moments later, two flashes of light, two muffled thunderclaps echo off the buildings. Wind-driven rain stings my eyes.

Shit.

I pick up the walking pace. Then lean into a jog until I suddenly stop. Realization.

The tote.

I turn to look back. That car is still there, with the door open. The driver is outside. I don't see Clarence or Germain.

Go back for the tote?

I wipe water from my face. The urge is strong. But... also stupid. It's only money.

Avril, Avril. Where are you, girl?

CHAPTER FORTY-SIX

Jimmy sits in his car at the back, far end of the lot. The rain pounds on the roof filling him with an unusual sense of pride in his ability to control people. He stares at the Majestic Theatre, amused at how smarter he is than everyone around him until he frowns.

Except maybe that girl, Runner. She's a crackerjack.

A call comes in from Vance Oakes, breaking his subconscious spell.

"We got trouble, Barone."

"Trouble?"

Vance sounds irate. "Runner just stole forty grand from me."

"Calm down. What happened?"

"Calm down. You tell me to calm down?" Vance can't believe what he just heard. "Forty fucking grand, and you tell me to calm down. Maybe you didn't hear me correctly. Forty goddamned grand, brother?"

"Yeah. I did. But just cool off, Vance. Now listen. Do you remember that detective that came asking about Runner?"

"Yeah. I guess so."

"Well, Cicero called him, gave him my name, and told him Runner works for me. Why would Cicero tell him anything about her at all? All he had to do was just shut the fuck up." Hesitation. "Jimmy, I think Cicero's got cold feet and wants out. He's gonna rat on us. You got to do something before he gives us up."

"Calm down, Vance. I've got it covered. I made a call to someone who knows how to take care of those types."

"What do you mean, 'take care of,?"

"Think about it. What do you think?"

"Violence?"

"I prefer the term, 'taking care of.'"

"I thought you said there'd be no violence in this operation."

"Yes, I did. But. But sometimes a plan needs some mid-course correction."

"But..."

"I said don't worry, Vance."

"Gezus Christ, Jimmy. I don't know." Vance pauses. "So who is this guy you've hired?"

"A guy Henry has used before. A strong arm. For when things need to be corrected."

"You're hiring Henry's own strong arm to take him down. Is that what you're saying?"

Jimmy lights a cigarette. "Yeah."

Vance grunts at Jimmy's explanation. "What about Cicero? He's part of your plan."

"Not anymore. This guy will explain the change of plans to him."

"Are you saying what I think you are?"

"We need to neutralize objections to what we need to do."

"Quieted? Neutralized? You're talking about murder, Jimmy."

"Let's watch Cicero before we make any rash decisions on him. I hope it doesn't get to that."

"What's this guy you hired like?"

"He's efficient. A pro."

"I don't like this. Who is he?"

"Mauldin."

"You trust him?"

"As much as you can trust any man who kills for a living. The only drawback with him are his methods."

"Methods?"

"He's a cruel son-of-a bitch. Sees no shame in killing men, women, or kids if they get in the way. Rumor has it he likes to torture women. Cut their tongues out before killing them. Apparently a woman once testified against him. Put him in prison for a while. I guess this is his crazy way to get back at all women."

"You've met him?"

"Years ago. When I was with the bureau, we got intelligence on cartel activity from him. He's a Bulgarian. Former Marine sniper. International mercenary. Lives on a houseboat trawler on the eastern seaboard somewhere. He's slippery."

"So he's working for you now."

"Yeah."

"Doesn't sound good, Jimmy. Not what I signed up for."

"I've got things under control, Vance. Relax. Sit tight."

"Jimmy."

"What?"

"Why is this girl so important in all of this?"

"I'll tell you why. It's because Denny is reckless in his hatred for her. She knocked him off his ivory tower in public. Nobody does that to him. Especially a snot-nosed girl. If Henry gets his hands on her, he'll kill her. So, if and when he does, he'll be arrested. I got that all figured out. My job will be complete. I'll get the blessing of the big man to run the operation. You and I will be rewarded handsomely."

"Back to the girl. How are you gonna get to her?"

"I've baited the hook to lure her in with her best friend. She's being held here."

"Who is that?"

"Her roommate. Avril."

"Christ, Jimmy. I know Avril. She bartends for me. She's innocent in all of this. I don't want her hurt."

"I'm just using her as bait. I had her call Runner. Made her think she's in trouble in the Majestic Theatre. She pleaded to Runner to come get her. Our girl will show. I know she will. It's just who she is."

"Runner is smart. Why will she walk into an obvious trap if she knows Avril is bait?"

"Because she's audacious, stubborn, and reckless. She thinks she can do anything. She'll come up with some plan. And I believe she may have a gun. Unfortunately, it will probably get her killed."

"Okay. So you're sure Runner is going to show up. And someone is going to die. Is that what you're saying?"

"Yep. If Runner doesn't show up, it's plan B."

"What's plan B?"

"Mauldin kills Denny. And Mauldin will then find Runner and kill her."

Vance pauses. "As much as I don't like Runner, I see her as nothing but an immature kid. Going up against an operation like Denny's is suicide."

"Look. Denny acts big and important. But he's a pussy when it comes to strong-willed women who don't fall for his bullshit. He's a wimp, a coward when quick-thinking women confront him. Strangely, those types of females are the ones he wants to get in bed. Break them. Feel victorious."

"You think Runner actually has a chance to save Avril?"

"She's fearless enough to think she can. That's all that counts."

"What do you think, Jimmy?"

Jimmy lights another cigarette. "If she comes face-to-face with him alone, he'll shrink like a wet piece of toilet paper. Give him a few drinks, and he'll turn crazy. Who knows what he'll do?" He takes a long drag and exhales. "I hope she gets through this okay."

"You really mean that, Barone?"

"Yeah. Yeah, I do. Don't get me wrong. I hate her smart-ass spirit. But at the same time, she's entertaining. Fun to watch. She's put me in my place a few times. The world needs more like her."

Jimmy flips his cigarette out the window. "Gotta go."

Minutes later a call comes in. He answers.

"It's Mauldin. You said you needed a job filled?"

Jimmy is just as brief. "Yeah. Two hits."

"Oh, yeah?"

"Cicero LeBlanc and Vance Oakes. I need them done now. Can you handle it?"

"Details?"

Jimmy gives details and where they can be found. "Make it quick. I'll probably have others after you finish with them."

A hour later, he sees thinks he someone creeping through the rain in the alley, close to the back of the buildings, toward the theatre.

Is that you, Runner?

CHAPTER FORTY-SEVEN

I squeeze into a bit of shelter between the building next to the Majestic, kneeling in search for any sign of activity. I'm soaked, freezing, and out of breath. Three cars sit in the lot at the back door. Another one is a muddy red sedan idling exhaust in the weeds out next to the perimeter fence. I pull the rain-soaked Red Sox cap down low, water dripping from the bill. The door to the theatre is just as Cicero said it would be. It looks all boarded up and covered with graffiti. Is this where he told me I'd be safe for a night?

Humm.

And this is the building where Avril called from, scared and crying out for help.

You'd be stupid to go in there, Nat. Think this over.

Bobby must be confused by now with the location changes. What are his chances of finding me? I bury my face in my cold hands, groaning in despair. Winds swirl, rain slants in sideways, water streams off the bill of my cap as a blue Jeep pulls into the parking lot. I lurch up.

Yes. Yes.

Bobby sees me, drives up close, and rolls down the window.

"Oh God, Bobby. You made it. Thank you."

He nods. "Get in."

"Hang on for a few minutes. I've got to go inside. Not sure how long it will be. But don't leave me."

"Well, hurry. I can't wait forever."

I run to the door, pry it open, and slip inside, shivering, wet and cold, into a small, dark, low-ceilinged entranceway. I have two ways to go. To the left is an aisle leading up into the audience seating area. To the right is a low, wide concrete tunnel behind the stage completely dark except for a small lantern at the far end of the dusky, curving passageway.

It's quiet and musty in here. A deathlike stillness rolls over me.

Decision time. Go right.

I stumble through trash, looking for a place to stay for the night if I don't get to the boat. It's so dark and cluttered with trash and old theater equipment that I turn back to the aisle leading up to the audience seating area. A dim red haze bathes the auditorium from a single red bulb high overhead. Hardly enough light to see much. Just a cavernous room with rows of seats, many broken or missing. I try to focus and get my bearings. All of a sudden, I see people. Hundreds sitting, eerily quiet, not a sound. Expressionless. Somber. No reaction to my presence. I creep down a row of seats about ten rows up from the stage and kneel next to a man. Or is it a woman? I lean in.

"Hey," I whisper.

No answer.

I squint, looking closer. "Hey."

No wonder—it's a mannequin. Dozens of them fill in the rows. I take a seat.

No sign of the one-eyed caretaker. Or Avril.

Let's go, Natalie. Avril must be upstairs somewhere. That boat's not going to wait for you.

Before I can move, voices come from the top of the aisle near the lobby. Men in bitter conversation following the light of a cell phone down the aisle. I scoot lower, holding my breath. They stop at the stage, quarreling. One of their phones lights up, revealing Henry Denny and Barlow with four men following. One of them is Tank, Henry's bodyguard—the thug whose head I broke a wine bottle over at the Grand Plaza. I think I recognize one other guy standing off to the side. The spitting image of Jonathan. I shake my head to clear the idea of him being alive. His death still gives me chills and even brings on visions I'm not sure are real.

Denny and Barlow argue. It heats up about what to do with me when they find me. Barlow sounds intense. "Listen to me, Henry. We're only after who's behind the blackmail scheme. We'd be stupid to do something to her before we get to who was behind the blackmail setup."

"Don't try to defend her, Barlow. She deserves what's coming to her. No one treats me like she did. She'll pay. And it will be sweet pleasure to do what I want with her. Do you understand that I won't be satisfied until I have her up there?" He nods up at windows overlooking the audience seating. "And I want her untouched. No one puts a finger on her. She's mine. Got it? Mine."

I scoot lower.

"Good," says Denny, satisfied with his command of them. "I'm staying up there tonight." He nods upstairs. "Now go. Go. Go. Find her. I can't have the thought of that little tramp on the loose while I'm dealing with my business. One of our cargo ships is landing in the morning. I have to be there to see to the loading of our shipment."

Barlow ignores Denny's whining about his business. "Listen. This girl we're looking for is just a kid. We should concentrate on who put her up to what she did. She shouldn't be hurt. We're not villains, are we? We should agree on that, shouldn't we?"

Denny steps chest to chest with Barlow. "She's mine, Orin. I'll do whatever I want with her." He straightens his jacket. "Now I have to go home for a few minutes and check in with the wife and kids. I won't be long. Call me at home if anything comes up before I get back. Don't call my mobile. Use the home number. I won't be long."

Barlow calls out, "I don't have your home number."

Denny shouts it out before he disappears through the door.

I'm trembling as low on the floor as I can be, shaking from the cold and hearing how obsessed Henry is to get his hands on me. Barlow is the only rational voice of those guys.

Avey, I hope you know what I'm going through to get to you.

I get up off the floor with Jonathan on my mind. Seeing that hallucination had me for a few seconds. Like he was real, standing there not taking my side in the argument.

Oh, man, the mind can be so cruel sometime, playing tricks.

And what Denny said about a cargo boat tomorrow morning.

Coincidence? Yes, yes. Pure coincidence.

I sit with arms wrapped around my knees to my chin wondering how to go about finding her. I'm so tired. I close my eyes for just a few seconds.

CHAPTER FORTY-EIGHT

It's been two hours since Mauldin's call. Jimmy sits smoking, one after the other, listening to the end of a Dodgers game on the radio. He's more nervous and jittery now since he lost sight of whoever or whatever it was he saw moving in the alley. He'll wait a little longer.

Headlights appear in the parking lot coming his way. A Ford Bronco splashing through potholes approaching. He turns off the ball game and grabs his gun. It's total darkness inside the Bronco as it pulls up, window to window. The burning end of a cigarette is all he sees. The driver's window comes down partially. Jimmy lowers his window halfway to avoid as much rain as possible. "That you in there? Mauldin?"

A gravelly voice answers. "Who else would meet you here on a night like this?"

"Right." Jimmy gets right to the point. "You get it done?"

A cigarette butt flips out the Bronco window and fizzles in a puddle. "Yep, all done."

"Both of 'em?"

"Yeah."

"How did it go?"

"What do you think?"

"Cicero and Vance? Both?"

"Isn't that what you wanted?"

"How?"

"Does it matter?"

"Yeah. I'd like to know."

"They died in a fire. Both."

A cigarette lighter flares inside the Bronco briefly, revealing fearsome eyes for a second.

"Anything else, Barone?"

"Yeah. It's kinda complicated."

"What do you mean?"

"Henry Denny."

"Denny? Ha. I know him. Worked with him before. He wants to hire me again."

"Well, I'm hiring you instead. I'll beat his offer."

"I'm not married to Denny. What do you need?"

"Well, there's this girl, Runner. She's gonna meet up with Henry. She wants him dead. And he wants *her* dead. One will kill the other. I need you to make sure that happens. I prefer it's her who wins. In other words, I want Henry Denny dead. I want it to look like she killed him. But if he kills her, you take him out." He pauses. "I'll say it again. You go up there and wait somewhere where you can listen and see who wins. If it's her, you leave and fly home. If Henry kills her, you shoot him. How easy can that be? Got it?"

"How sure are you that she's gonna show up?"

"Pretty sure. We have her girlfriend up there as bait."

"Girlfriend?" Mauldin grunts. "What girlfriend?"

"Runner's roommate. I recruited her to work with us. She

thinks there's a big payoff coming for my plan to unseat a mob boss. She has no idea what I intend to do to Runner. When Henry saw her... well, she's a damned pretty girl so, he had to do his thing with her. He's a sexual predator. She had to withstand Denny's sick lust for any young woman he has control over."

"So, this Runner girl is playing superhero to save her bestie? What a soap opera this is."

"It's not the only reason Runner is going up there. She has a score to settle with Denny."

"Score?"

"I provided her as a prostitute for him. The hookup went bad. She embarrassed him in public. I set up the meeting to blackmail him. Denny turned into a lunatic wanting revenge on her. He got rough in his efforts to find her. Ruined her love life with a guy. Now she might be out to make it right. She's not your ordinary twenty-year-old. This is one heads-up bitch."

"So this Runner girl is a prostitute."

"No. No, hell no, just the opposite. She's anything but. And she's smart. Cagy, sharp and fearless. If she gets up there, and Denny is his same arrogant, self-absorbed, hostile jerk, sparks will fly."

"What do you mean *if* she gets up there?"

"Well, she wants to board a ship to Tahiti. She has a decision to make. Board that ship or save her friend."

"Would she do that? Knowing the risk of coming here tonight?"

"It's just her way."

"So, you say she's twenty. Nice. What's her name?"

"Runner."

"Where is this Runner now?"

"Pretty sure she's on her way to find Denny upstairs there in that theatre."

"How do you know?"

"Friends of cops. A while ago, she was seen at a diner down the road. She wouldn't be here if she's gonna catch that ship tomorrow."

"She up there now?"

"Haven't seen her yet."

"What did she do to be on your shit list?"

"I'd rather not say. But..."

"You are a chicken shit, aren't you? You can't even handle some twenty-year-old girl. Fuckin' pussy."

"I don't care what you think, Mauldin."

"Is she that tough, Barone?"

"You'll find out when you meet her."

Mauldin puts the Bronco in gear to leave. "You think your little girl has what it takes to do this?"

"I'm betting on it. One way or the other. He's not violent unless he's been drinking. Normally he pays people like you to do his dirty work."

Mauldin laughs. "Denny called me to come in and find this girl already. So, he thinks I'm coming in to finish her off. But he doesn't know I'm now working for you. And he's the target."

"Yep. Brilliant, isn't it?"

"Barone, you think this girl is gonna do this? Does she have the nerve to pull the trigger?"

"Yes. Now, go up there, stay out of sight, listen, and find out what happens. If she shows up and gets the job done, fine. I'm done, you get paid, and off you go. And let's suppose she doesn't finish Denny off. Well then you kill him."

"What about her?"

"You can do whatever you want with her."

"What about the girlfriend?"

"Might as well do her too. I don't want any extra people hanging around as witnesses. Got it?"

Mauldin takes a deep breath. "So after I'm finished with this girl, am I done?"

"Yeah."

"This is gonna get expensive, Barone. I charge by the body count. You know that."

"I don't care."

"One last question." Mauldin leans on the steering wheel and asks, "What makes you think this kid can really kill someone?"

Jimmy scratches the back of his neck. "Because she murdered a federal marshall."

"Wow." The Bronco spins out across the lot and parks at the back door of the theatre.

A half-hour later, Jimmy fidgets, on edge, chain-smoking. He's waited long enough for something to happen. Patience isn't a strength of his. He lights another cigarette, feeling uneasy about Mauldin. How easy it was to buy him away from Denny. Could it be just as easy for Mauldin to come after Jimmy?

You don't have the cash to pay him. You'll have to neutralize the fucker when this is over.

CHAPTER FORTY-NINE

I don't know how long I've been out when a voice wakens me.

Natalie.

Out of the shadows comes a man on stage. He steps to the front and stares down at me. I grip Barlow's gun tighter when he jumps from the stage and comes at me. I swallow hard, ready to shoot.

Would you actually shoot someone?

My eyes widen. "Daddy?"

You okay, Nat?

"I'm fine."

It doesn't look like it.

"Well, I am."

He rubs his chin. *Really? You really think you're fine? You know you can't lie worth a damn, especially to me.*

"Okay. Maybe I'm in a bit of a situation."

Situation. Is that what you call it?

"I've got it figured out."

Do you now?

"Well…"

So I see you have that gun. What do you intend to do with it?

"I might need it."

What for?

"What do you think?"

All of a sudden, a bright light shines in my eyes from the stage. It comes at me. Then a squeaky voice. "Who are you talking to, young lady?"

I shield my eyes and squint. "Daddy?"

"I'm not your daddy, kid. Now get out of this building."

I jump up. "Who are you?"

"Is that a gun you have there?"

"Yes, it is."

"You ain't supposed to be in here. You ain't supposed to have no gun neither. I don't tolerate that kinda thing. So leave right now. Go. Get."

"Look. I'm not hurting anyone. I just came in to get out of the rain. I'm wet and cold."

"Like I said, you ain't supposed to be in here. Specially with that there gun. Go. Now."

In a shiver and teeth rattling desperate voice, I ask, "Who are you?"

He moves closer for a better look. Close enough to see a dark hole where an eye used to be. It's nothing more than a black, dried socket.

"I take care a this place."

"So, you're Norman?"

"Yeah. How d' you know my name?"

"Cicero told me."

"Don't know no Cicero."

"I'm here to find a girl. Kidnapped."

He inches closer. "Kidnapped, you say? A girl?"

"Yeah."

"Why'd she be here?"

"I got a call from her. Said this is where she is. I want to find her and take her away."

"Did ya call the poleece?"

"No."

"Why not?"

"Long story."

His one eye stares at me like it's thinking. "You're shakin'. You're cold."

"Yes, I am. Freezing."

He nods up at the windows on the second floor. "It's nice an' warm up there. But you don't wanna go up there right now."

I turn back and look up at a row of windows. A hint of light slips through heavy curtains.

Bet that's where Avril is.

"Listen, Norman. That's where she might be. I want to get her out."

"By yerself?"

"No other choice."

"Truss me. You don't wanna go up there now. Specially now."

"Can't wait." I start to move.

"Nope." He moves to block me. "Can't let ya. That body-guard fella, Tank, he's... he's still up there."

I start again.

Again, another block. "I said sit down."

I think of Bobby outside, waiting.

Can't keep him there much longer. And there's still time to catch that boat if you go now.

So I lift the gun showing determination. "Norman. I'm going up there now. Don't try to stop me."

"Wait," he says, tipping his ear to something. Then the outside door squeaks open and slams shut.

Norman pushes me down on the floor. I raise up just enough to see Denny coming in, pulling a small suitcase, Tank following.

Oh, God.

I'm ready to get up and follow them. Norman shushes me and pushes me down again. "Tank will be leavin' pretty soon. Denny will be all alone. If you're intendin' to go up there, then's the time."

I check my phone battery.

Just enough to make one fast call.

I dial Bobby outside.

"Runner," he answers. "What's going on?"

"Bobby, no time to explain. Please believe me. I'll be down as soon as I can. But I have to do this first. Please stay just a little longer. I'll give you some juicy information about Henry Denny and his father for your story. So just stay there. Wait for me."

"Okay. But…"

"Gotta go."

Click.

I check my phone.

Enough battery for one more call.

I dial a number from memory. A woman's sleepy voice answers. "Hello?"

"I'm sorry to bother you at this late hour, but I think you'll be interested in what I have to say."

"Who is this?"

In a whisper, I say, "Just listen. Please." I tell her something she doesn't seem to understand. She goes silent. I give a clear message and directions from where I'm calling from. "Don't delay."

She asks, "What…"

The phone screen goes black.

Coming down from the lobby is Tank. Norman crouches low with me until we hear the outside door open and slam shut.

Norman stands and starts his way along the seats to the aisle. "Denny's up there alone now. If you're gonna go, now's the time. Go."

It's eerily serene except for the occasional creaks and groans of the wind buffeting the old building. Faint noises of something going on outside? I hear the faint sounds of sirens.

Sit tight, Bobby. Please don't leave.

I creep up the aisle, holding the gun with both hands. It's so dark I need to feel the seats to make my way. Something runs over my foot, squealing as it scurries away through trash. Two squatters jump up and scamper from the shadows, run down the aisle, and out.

I make it to the lobby. Plywood covers the big front doors and windows. Small lights lead upstairs to where a bare bulb illuminates a green door. I try the door. Unlocked. I push it open slightly. A TV plays inside. My heart races, mouth dry. A man sits with his back to me while he watches the news. I slide the gun into the back of my waistband. Without a sound I step one foot inside.

CHAPTER FIFTY

Jimmy checks the time again. Has Runner already made it there without him seeing her? How could he have missed her? Has she found Avril?

He calls Norman backstage to find out. "How is our guest?"

"She's okay."

Jimmy frowns at the brevity of the one-eyed caretaker known to be a blabby talking nuisance. "Something wrong, Norman?"

"Nope."

"You sound different. Is she all right?"

"She's…" Pause. "Not in very good spirits."

"Okay. She's fine then."

"Whatever you say, boss."

"Just keep her calm."

"Wait," Norman says. "She wants to talk to you."

"Put her on."

"Jimmy," Avril moans. "Get me out of here. That Denny guy, he—"

A gravelly, harsh voice interrupts and comes on the line. "Just met the girlfriend, the bestie. "Wow. Fine. Everything's okay here. Just go back to sleep, Jimmy." Then comes a blast. The phone goes dead.

Jimmy stares at his phone.

Oh no. Shit, shit, shit.

He pulls on his hooded rain jacket. "Fucking Mauldin. What have you done, you lousy, low-life dog?"

He needs to see for himself and leaves the car running to keep it warm and have it ready for a quick escape if needed.

In the storm, he's hunched over, braving the rain and the stinging wind against his face. There are red and blue lights flashing in the alley. A floodlight suddenly comes on. He hopes it's what he thinks it is and heads toward the commotion. Yellow perimeter tape surrounds the crime scene. Overhead floodlights create a surreal effect over the scene. He stands with a few bystanders curious enough to brave the cold stormy night. He comes to a young police officer.

Name badge—Hogan. "Sir, you need to stand back."

"Oh. Sure. Sorry." Jimmy steps back.

A sergeant comes up to Hogan. Name badge—Battaglia. They discuss findings. Hard to hear because of the wind. But he catches one thing in their conversation. "The head wounds look like they were from a .22."

Jimmy turns away, thinking of the .22 pistol in his pocket.

Get rid of it as soon as possible.

Walking away, he glances back at the police activity. Plenty of them to arrest Denny after he kills Runner. Or take out Mauldin in a shootout. Or catch Runner and send her back to a mental ward where she belongs. They'll come running when they hear the shots. The noise of the wind and rain is a problem, though. Will they hear shots coming from the theatre so far away?

Nearing the theatre, he comes up on a new vehicle parked. A blue Jeep with the engine running, a man behind the wheel.

He knocks on the window. The driver jumps and cracks the window. "Yes?"

"Excuse me, sir. What are you doing here?"

"Sorry. Can't hear you."

Jimmy shouts, "I said, what are you doing here?"

"Waiting on someone."

"Who?"

The driver asks back, "Who are you?"

"I'm security here."

"Well, I'm a reporter. Working on a story. So, I can be here."

"What story, sir?"

"I can't say right now."

"Well, who are you waiting for?"

"I hope you don't take this wrong. But it's none of your business."

"I'm gonna have to ask you to leave."

"I will as soon as she comes back."

"She? Who is she?"

"I'd rather not say."

Jimmy nods back toward the alley and the flashing lights. "Don't you think that's a better story down there?"

"Not my type of story. So if you don't mind, I'll just sit here and wait for her." He rolls up his window and returns to writing.

Jimmy bites his lip in frustration. Not good. And now another car pulls in two vehicles away.

Jimmy ducks. *Who the hell is this?*

He leaves the Jeep driver and crouches over to see Barlow and a blonde girl in neon-colored leggings follow him inside. That's Runner's friend. Holly.

What's she doing here?

CHAPTER FIFTY-ONE

I catch Henry Denny surprised at my appearance in the doorway. He jumps up, wide-eyed, looking ridiculous in striped boxer shorts and a white dress shirt opened neck to belly with unbuttoned sleeves. Not the picture of respectability he's put over on the public.

"Am I interrupting something, Mister Denny?"

"No, no. Not at all. Come in." It's obvious he's in shock. He instinctively takes a drink of whatever he's drinking with a feeble smile.

I take one step in. "Since our last meeting didn't end so well, I thought we might try it again."

He motions me in. "You look cold."

The room is warm. Feeling is returning to my fingers. "So what is this place?"

He watches me as might a sinful preacher caught with his zipper down. "It's the old projection room when this was a movie house. It's now a VIP party room. I've refurbished it. What do you think? You like it?"

I enter and walk around, touching the impressive furnishings, appliances, and all the conveniences of a modern apartment. A rich man's hideaway. "Yeah, nice," I say, all the time wondering...

Where are you, Avril?

"Sorry for my attire," he says, buttoning his shirt but forgetting he's still in boxer shorts. "I wasn't expecting guests."

"You look like shit, Henry. Or should I say, Mikey?"

"Why would you call me Mikey?"

"That's how you introduced yourself at the Grand Plaza. Remember?"

"Oh, Yeah. I remember." He finishes off his drink and stares at me, sorta dumbstruck at my sudden appearance.

I nod at the TV. "What you watching, Henry?"

He waves at the TV. "There's been a shooting. Only a couple blocks away." Now, he's lost for words and changes the subject. "You look terrible. You're all wet? And what happened to your lip?"

I ignore his question and stare at the TV clips of bodies being loaded into ambulances. Germain and Clarence. Dead. But how?

It wasn't you, Natalie. Who killed them?

I jerk out of it and glance around. "You alone, Henry?"

"Yeah, yeah. Why do you ask?"

"I have a friend who called me a little while ago. She said she's here."

He wipes his mouth with the back of his hand. "How did you find this place?"

"Google. It knows everything." I wander around acting nonchalant. "So she's here somewhere. Mind if I have a look around?" Not waiting for an answer, I meander toward a door at the back of the long room.

Locked.

"Is this where you bring your girls? The ones you don't take to a fancy hotel room?"

"It's my bedroom."

"Is Avril in there?"

"No one is in there." He nods at his bar setup. "Get you something to drink?"

He's setting you up. Two can play at this game.

"Well, you know, Henry, I'm a bartender. How about I make us something special?"

He leans over to touch to me. He hesitates but gets up the courage. I draw back at his touch. The urge to pull the gun and finish him off is intense.

You're here for Avril. Nothing else. Jonathan is dead—nothing you can do about that now. But she's alive. At least, you think she is. Go find her before you do something you'll regret.

But hurry. The boat is waiting. So is Bobby. Neither will wait for long.

CHAPTER FIFTY-TWO

I slip behind the bar, avoiding his touch. "So you say my girlfriend isn't here."

"No." He takes a stool, faking innocence.

I nod and look over the liquor cabinet options. On the back shelf, there's a bottle of 190-proof Everclear. I've seen what it can do from my time at Oakes where I served it to guys to loosen up their uptight dates. On the bar top, there is an open bottle of vodka.

"Can I mix us up something special?"

"Sure."

While he takes a call on his phone, I make his drink extra strong. He doesn't notice I make mine very light. He takes a long drink, wipes his mouth, and excuses himself, leaving his drink on the bar to go back to the bedroom to finish his call. While he's away, I grab the Everclear to refresh his drink.

He returns with a cat-who-ate-the-canary grin, no longer the mild-mannered, fraidy-cat he was a few minutes ago. "Well, here's to tonight. Let's have some fun." He downs half his drink, ice and all. "Phew," he blows out. "You really know how to mix 'em, girl." He finishes the rest of the drink in another long swallow with new courage to deal with me. It's in his eyes.

"You got a cute ass, Runner."

Okay, off come the gloves.

I push a fresh drink over and pander to his ego. He's eating it up until he smirks, realizing the obvious phony coddling.

"Let's talk about you, Runner."

"What do you want to know, Henry?"

"Who used you to set me up with those photos?"

I chuckle and take a sip. "That'll cost you."

His turn to chuckle. "How did you get to be so brazen?"

I lower a stare to invade his subconscious, to unnerve him. "Is that what I am?"

It works. He stumbles with meaningless mumbles. With amusement, I watch him struggle.

You've got him, Natalie. Don't let him go.

"Let's talk about you, Henry. What do you want to do with me?"

He searches for how to compose the thoughts running through his head into words.

"Is it sex, Henry? Is that what you want?" I wait. "Is that what itches you? Makes you want to scratch that itch?"

"I..."

"You know, Henry. It's nothing to be ashamed of. You're not alone. It's an overactive biological compulsion. I, myself, struggle with it. As did my mother."

"Are you a prostitute, Runner?"

"Oh, heck no. Why do you ask?"

"Because Jimmy said you were. That's why I—"

"Forget it. Jimmy is a moron. And, oh, by the way, Jimmy was the one who arranged the photo shoot in the Grand Plaza. Does that surprise you?" I push another drink over to him. Stronger yet. Denny downs half of it again.

"Is that why you have Avril captive in this place? Is that what you want? A young girl to satisfy that itch? Is that what you do with the girls you lure in? Use them once or twice and then find another?"

"What are you talking about?"

"What do you do with the girls after you're finished with them?"

"I pay them, and they walk out the door with a hand full of money."

"Even the fifteen-year-olds?"

He frowns, finishes the rest of his drink, and slams the glass down. "I have never been with a fifteen-year-old. How did you get that idea? I have standards. Like you."

I laugh and push over another, even stronger. "Your reputation precedes you, Henry."

"You're making me out to be a pedophile. I am no such thing."

"How about we talk about that girl you have back there?"

The bloom is off the rose. He drinks, frowns, and pushes over his empty glass for more.

Sure thing, mister.

His nostrils flare, and he bares his teeth. "You think you're clever, don't you? What a fucking brat. Think you can come in here and, and..."

"And what, Henry?"

"Embarrass me like you did at the Grand Plaza." He glares. "I'll crush you."

"Because you're rich, you mean? Well, your wealth can't compensate for the intellectual void between your ears, buddy."

Denny is in a rage now. He pushes his glass over for another and leers at my body while I pour. He's getting so drunk he stumbles around the bar to put his hand between my legs. I lean into him and do the dreamy-eyed look up at his red, unfocused eyes. "Who do you think I am, Henry?"

He's handsy and slurring. "You're a whore, Runner. You set me up to be bl... black...mailed, an... I'm gonna get even with... you... you..."

"Is that what you think, Henry?"

"Yup..."

His filthy-smelling body lies against me. His fingers slip up under my t-shirt. I twist and push away to avoid his hands finding the gun.

"What's a madder, Runner? Are you gonna run again? Like, like lass time? Where's that photographer for more photos?"

I'm up in his red, puffy face. "Give me the keys to that door."

"Huh."

He grabs me and pulls me in. He's a big man. Liquid courage has primed him ready for his payoff. He rips at my clothes.

I squirm free. "Where is Avril?" I yell.

"Probly dead by now."

"Where is she?"

He lunges at me. His heavy body pins me to the wall with a hand under my shirt, fondling. I bite his neck. He screams and pulls back to hit me, but a voice from the door stops him.

"Hello, Henry," says a woman at the open door—a revolver in hand.

Seeing her, Denny freezes. Goon-faced, he pushes me away.

She walks in with a swagger. "It's just me, honey, your loving wife. Mother of your children."

"Teresa," he blurts out, stumbling into the side of the bar. "What you doin' here?"

"I got a call from some young-sounding woman telling me I

should come over and see what my husband does in his free time." She pushes back wet bangs from her eyes, swinging the gun around. She frowns at the pretentious display of flashy furnishings. "So this is your little hideaway."

Denny pitches and leans in drunken insensibility, watching her walk through the room.

"I got the call a wife never wants to get in the middle of the night. So I just had to come and see for myself." She nods at me. "It was you. Wasn't it?"

I back away, shoving hands in my back pockets.

Teresa stands in front of her husband. Then she gives him one hell of an articulate verbal whipping, cudgeling him with guarantees of financial torture and laying emasculation squarely on the table, stripping him of everything he's ever accomplished, professionally, socially, and in his relationship with his family. Her performance is the result of money well spent on an Ivy League education. It's one of the best castigations I've ever witnessed. Then she raises the gun and pulls the trigger twice. The big caliber gun bucks twice—*boom, boom*. Both shots pass by his head, close. She tosses the gun on the bar and leans her chin at him. "Don't. You. Ever. Step foot in my house again. If you do, I'll not miss. Do you understand?"

Denny teeters, looking down at the floor.

She turns to the door. Looks back. "What a pathetic piece of rot you are, Henry Denny." With that said, she leaves.

I'm jealous. Wish I could be as cold-hearted and ruthless with words as Teresa was. Textbook on how to dispose of a cheating husband.

But you have your own methods for dealing with appalling men, Natalie.

CHAPTER FIFTY-THREE

Flashing red and blue lights illuminate the shiny, wet alley of the murder scene. A uniformed young cop looks over at his sergeant. "Did you hear that, Frank? Was that what I think it was?"

"What?" Sergeant Battaglia frowns at Hayden. "I didn't hear anything."

"I thought I heard something. Like gunshots."

They cock heads, listening for anything unusual. Frank shrugs. "Didn't hear it. Just the storm. Thunder, maybe."

They return to search the crime scene. Both bodies have been taken away.

The coroner drones on, briefing the cops on what he knows and what he suspects. "Drug dealers."

Another cop tells him, "One of them is also a known pimp, Clarence Espino. The other, Germaine Gordon. We found a soggy cigarette butt, an unfiltered Camel."

Hayden searches around in the light from the mobile light tower. He doesn't like these night crime scenes. Another of the reasons he's leaving the force. This work is too dangerous. He doesn't have the mentality other gung-ho cops have. No aggressive instincts. But for now, he's a cop, and he's loyal to his duties. He prowls the murder scene with his flashlight, looking for anything that might mean something to the case. He squints through the rain at a few spectators braving the weather, curious about what's going on. One guy has crept closer than he should be. Hayden approaches the redheaded man. "Sir, you need to stand back."

"Oh. Sure. Sorry." The man turns away without another word.

Two flashes of lightning followed by two cracks of thunder make Hayden jump.

"Hayden," Battaglia calls out.

"Yeah, Sarge?"

"What's that big building up there at the end of the block?"

"That's the old Majestic Theatre."

Another flash overhead, followed by a sharp clap and then thunder rolling in the distance.

Hayden shudders.

Christ, I hate this work.

CHAPTER FIFTY-FOUR

With Teresa gone, Denny stumbles to the bar, knocks his drink over and demands another.

I ask, "Where are the keys to the door, Henry?"

He shakes his head. "I said get me another drink."

I grab Teresa's gun and stick it under his nose. "Where are the keys?"

He laughs and flops into an easy chair, looking me up and down. "You're a brave little turd, aren't ya? Gotta give ya that. But stupid, comin' in here like this. And calling my wife. You're gonna be sorry for that."

"Where is the key, Henry?"

He giggles and nods at a drawer. "Sooo... you wanna go in there with... with me in this con... condishun?" He hiccups. "Okay, if... if thas what you want. I'll do my bess."

I grab the key from the drawer and then yank the door open to an empty room. "Where is she?"

"Where's who?"

"Avril. Where is she?"

His head bobs, mouth hanging open, and stares at his feet.

I grab his chin and pull his face up. "Where is she?"

His unfocused eyes are not with me.

"Where is Avril?"

"You're all wet. You know that?"

I throw the gun down, fold my arms, turn away, and sit staring at the clock. It's three forty-five. Less than three hours to make it to the docks on time.

Next I know, Denny is standing over me with a gleaming kitchen knife coming at me. I roll off the chair, avoiding the knife by inches. I sidestep the next slashing blade. On the next attempt, I catch his hand with both of mine. He's strong but teetering, confused, and blubbering. We stumble and fall, him on top of me, pressing the knife at my throat.

"You're shus a dirty lil bitch. All I wanted was a good fuck an... an... that redheaded pimp brings you to me. Why you, for fuck's sake? Why?"

Our faces inches apart, the blade shaking at my throat, I force out a last-ditch attempt to save my life. I purr. "Don't you understand, Mister Denny?"

He frowns, curiosity etched on his sweaty face, puzzled at what I said. He relaxes slightly.

Now, Natalie. Do it.

With a trembling finger, I gradually inch the cold blade away from my throat. When it's to the side, I stare into his confused, blurry eyes, and then... then... then I lunge with a head-butt into his nose. There's a sickening crunch.

He screams and crumples backward, both hands clutching his bleeding nose. The knife clatters to the floor. I struggle to my knees. He swings a glancing fist off the side of my head, sending me reeling.

He snatches up the knife. Our eyes lock on the gun. I dive

for it, but he beats me to it. Staggering to his feet, he presses the barrel into my forehead. He's wild, pressing the back of his knife hand against the pain in his nose. "You lil' cunt." His wild eyes try to focus, and his gun hand wavers.

I steady my voice into an alluring drawl. "Henry, look, I'm on my knees, trying to make you understand that you're the man I'm in love with. You don't need your wife. You don't need anyone. Come on, Henry. You're the man. You need someone like me at your side to support you. To help glorify your contribution to the world."

He wavers, eyes half-lidded. "Huh?"

Slowly, I reach out, my hand trembling slightly. "Here, let me help you."

Confusion clouds his face as he struggles to process my words. "What? Wha, wha do ya mean?"

"This has been all a big mistake. Jimmy's fault," I whisper, my voice dripping like honey.

"Huh?"

"When he told me I was to meet a rich, handsome man at the hotel, I got hot. You were what I've been waiting for. But Jimmy was all about the blackmail. I was just following orders. I was hoping to feel your strong body against mine when that camera guy ran in and messed everything up. It's Jimmy's fault."

He's frozen in thought.

You've got his drunken attention, Nat.

Gently, I peel back his fingers on the knife, one at a time, while I continue to sweet-talk him. But his bloated, bloody face contorts into a scowl. He jerks the knife back so hard the gun in the other hand goes off, exploding over his shoulder, shattering a clerestory window. The noise shocks him so badly that he drops the gun; his hands clench into fists and press to his temples. But he still has the knife.

"It's okay, Henry. It's okay, fella." My voice is soft and baby-bottom smooth. I take the trembling knife from his weakened grasp. Sweat pours down his face; his breathing is ragged.

But the moment he realizes I have the knife, his expression shifts from pathetic to vicious. "You bitch." He lunges at my face.

I dodge with the blade gripped tightly in both hands, poised above my head as he falls to his knees.

There's a movement out of the corner of my eye. Father with his pipe.

Go ahead, girl. Let's see you do it.

The blade shakes, sweat runs into my eyes. I look over at Father, expecting to see him proud of me. Excited to see his daughter kill this bastard.

What's wrong, Natalie? Can't do it?

Denny is crying. I look back at Father for a nod to proceed.

You're not as strong as you think you are. Are you?

I mumble to him smoking his pipe. "Do you know what this man is like, Father? What he does to women? He needs to be out of business. He needs to go to Hell."

What if you're wrong, Nat?

My upper lip twitches, the knife shakes. "What do you mean?"

How do you know what he's like?

"I was told what he's like."

By who?

"A friend."

You mean that pimp? So now you're friends with pimps?

"I don't want to hear this, Dad."

What else do you know about this man you want to kill?

"He killed a friend of mine. A boyfriend. A man I might have married."

Oh, really? Is this that Jonathan fellow?

I grip and regrip the sweaty knife. "Yeah. I loved him. They beat him and drowned him."

So you say.

"Uh-huh. I saw him killed with my own two eyes."

Does he know you love him?

I blink hard, sweat stinging my eyes. "He's dead, Dad." I squeeze the knife handle hard.

Is this the Jonathan you're talking about? Right over there?

A new voice from the open door. *Hello, Natalie. Glad to finally hear you love me.*

Denny cries, harboring his ill will like a child nursing a grudge. "I have to go home to my wife and kids. So I'll go now."

My upper lip twitches, the knife quivering in my grasp. A scream tears from my throat as I fall to my knees, bringing the knife down with all my might. But not into his neck. No, I drive it deep down into the top of his bare foot, plunging into the ancient hardwood oak floor.

An inhuman howl rips from him. Then obscenities.

"Ha!" I scream. "Now, tell me where Avril is."

He yells and growls, desperately trying to free the knife. When he fails, his cries fade into a whimpering whine. "I don't know what you're talking about."

Liar.

CHAPTER FIFTY-FIVE

Under a temporary canopy, Police Officer Hayden Hogan is about finished going over the alley's crime scene. Nothing more for him to do. It's up to the lab technicians to finish up in the driving rain.

Sergeant Battaglia comes in under the tarp out of the rain. He approaches Hogan. "Is what I hear about you wanting to leave the department true? Or is it just a rumor?"

"Yeah, thinking about it, Sarge."

"Almost finished with law school, then?"

"Pretty much finished. Now I gotta get ready to take the bar exam."

"Well, I guess you've already made up your mind then."

"Yeah. These kinda nights make me want it more than ever. I'll stay dry as an attorney."

"Ha," chuckles Batagglia. "What a pussy."

Hogan grins. "Speaking of rumors, Sarge, I heard you let an APB suspect get away from right under your nose."

"News travels fast. Yeah."

"Heard she called herself Runner."

"That's right." Then a call comes in on Batagglia's phone. He walks away talking.

Hayden shakes his head, walking to his car. No way it's a coincidence that there are two girls who call themselves Runner. But can it really be the same girl who wanted him to run away with her? He stops and looks up instinctively when he thinks he hears something.

"Sarge, did you hear that?"

"What?"

"I heard a pop. Like a gunshot."

"No. Didn't hear anything."

"Pretty sure of it, Sarge."

"From where?"

"Up the alley."

"Better take a look."

They start random checks at the backsides of buildings in the alley. With guns drawn, they carefully check into pitch-black shadows around dumpsters, doors, and windows. Grumpy cop joins in the search. It's cold arduous work in the relentless wind and rain of the powerful storm.

CHAPTER FIFTY-SIX

Henry Denny's opulent hideaway is quiet but foul-smelling of alcohol, blood and urine. Denny has pissed himself. Barlow, who just walked in, leans over Henry on the floor. He's sobbing and trying to pull out the knife which runs through his foot and is stuck in the floor.

I yell at Henry, "Where the hell is Avril?"

"Wha?" Saliva drooling from his mouth.

"Where is Avril?"

"Who?"

"Avril. She's here somewhere."

Barlow looks puzzled. That's when I realize he doesn't understand what's going on and has no idea about Avril being here. I'm getting panicked.

You have to find her fast and then get to that boat. And if Bobby is still outside waiting, won't wait much longer.

I'm leaving to search for her when I meet a man coming in with fierce eyes. He pushes past me in a snarl, pulls the bill of my cap down over my face and knocks me out of his way. My head slams back against the wall. I fall dazed, dizzy, ringing in my ears.

"Stay put, bitch." Then a boot comes at me.

The lights go out—

Dad and I are fishing in the creek again, Mother with us, but it's bedtime, me with teddy bear. Someone yells, "You didn't have to do that."

Then Dad is pulling me out of bed but...

I stare up. It's not Dad. It's Barlow lifting me to sit with my back against the wall. "Runner? You okay?"

Wake up, Natalie. Get with it. I look around. The brute that knocked me out sits in a chair across the room.

He points at me. "What's your real name, girl? It can't be Runner?"

"What?"

"I said, what's your real name?"

I ask, "What's *your* name?"

"I'm Mauldin," he says. "Now, I'll ask again. What's your real name?"

I think about answering for a few seconds, not knowing what he's asking or who I'm answering to. My head hurts from his boot hitting my head. I squint, trying to make out who he is. "Screw you, Mauldin, or whatever your real name is."

"I hear you're what all the fuss is about. Is that right, Runner?"

I nod. "Yeah, I'm what all the fuss is about, all right."

"You've been a bother to a lot of people, you know."

"Really? How would you know?"

"I've got friends."

"I doubt you have any friends."

"You're a smart ass, you know that?"

Barlow intervenes, "Leave her alone."

Mauldin waves his gun at Barlow. "Fuck off."

"Hey," I shout. "Who do you think you are?"

"Someone who's going to shoot you now."

"Why? I haven't done anything to you. Any money on my head? I'm worthless."

"That's for sure."

"Well then, why shoot me? No reason to kill me."

"I just got a contract from Jimmy Barone with your name on it."

"Why?"

"Ask him."

I laugh. "Ha, Jimmy doesn't have any money to kill anyone. He's a loser. Or do you kill just for the pleasure of it?"

Bam. His gun jerks up. The bullet penetrates deep into my chest.

Ugh.

I hold my breath. No pain. Just pressure. *Presssssure, presssuu-uure* breathing. I swallow. *But this isn't so bad.*

Bam, the second plows into my shoulder. I spin and fall face first and roll to my side and onto my back. Mauldin just grins. Denny stares at me drunk like. Barlow, off to the side, standing helpless.

I see the next bullet coming right out of the barrel, spinning in slow motion as it slams into my belly.

Oh, shit. Oh God, that one hurts. Really hurts. *Oh. Ooooh, damn.*

Innards ooze out in my hands. The smell of the excretion mixed with cigarette smoke and gunsmoke is horrible.

God.

Can't move. Can't breathe. Blood's pooling around my face on the floor.

Lights going out as Father bends down, running fingers through my hair. He whispers. *It's not so bad here, girl. No more worries. Easy peasy.*

CHAPTER FIFTY-SEVEN

Jimmy walks into the hideaway, breathing hard and wet, unprepared for what he sees. Denny is in deplorable condition, blubbering to himself, and Natalie is crumpled and bloody on the floor next to the wall. Barlow looks confused, standing over Denny. In an armchair, sitting quietly in a trancelike stare is his lowlife hitman, Mauldin, who doesn't acknowledge Jimmy's entrance. A gun is in his lap.

And there's Holly. Yes, Holly standing in the corner like a schoolgirl, avoiding eye contact with anyone, staring at the floor.

Jimmy lights a cigarette to calm down and to think straight. "What are you doing here, Barlow?"

"Got a call. Heard Runner had been found. I came to see her and found this mess."

Jimmy leans over a sobbing Denny and nudges him. He nods over at Natalie on the floor. "Well, junior, there's your girl. Is this what you wanted for her?" He pats him on the head and turns to Barlow.

"Okay, this is what's going to happen. The cops are going to come in and find Henry dead, the victim of female revenge. They'll suspect Runner, dead on the floor, was the killer."

"How are they gonna figure Runner's death then?" asks Barlow.

Jimmy looks over at Mauldin, who hasn't moved or said a word. He's just frowning at Runner on the floor.

Barlow takes a deep breath and looks down at Henry. He eyes Mauldin and then Jimmy with uncertainty. He runs his tongue around in his mouth, ready with a warning. "This is a Denny. Do you guys know what his father's gonna do when he finds out his son is dead? Murdered. Well, I do. He won't let this go without retaliation. He'll have everyone's head who was remotely associated with his death."

Jimmy corrects Barlow. "But Henry's not dead. Is he?"

"By the looks of that blood, he will be soon. And I'm not shitting you guys. When it comes to family, Mister Denny won't fuck around. I know him well. Believe what I say."

Jimmy hisses. "Listen. For the record, I didn't have anything to do with this."

Mauldin jumps up. "What a crock. This whole fucking plan was your stupid idea, Barone. You've started somethin' you can't finish. You're way outta your league."

Mauldin is on a roll, waving the gun around. "This is the most fucked-up operation I've ever been on." He raises a finger to Jimmy. "First, I get a call about killing two guys. Then you need me to bring in some girl so you can watch me kill her in front of you. Now, here we are. You hired me to kill the kid of some billionaire. Crazy, right? But it looks like someone has already started the process. The way this guy's bleeding, he's gonna be dead soon." He points at Jimmy again. "Like I said, this is one odd operation. So don't look at me. I've had nothing to do with killing Junior there. Nothing to be afraid of from the old man." Then Mauldin gets all cocky. "And you," he says, pointing at Barlow. "I bet you'll squeal to the old man about us. Rat me out as the killer. I don't think leaving you hanging around is a good idea. Maybe you should be put out to pasture."

Barlow ignores him and goes over to see about Runner.

CHAPTER FIFTY-EIGHT

I hear...

Natalie, wake up. Get up out of bed, dear.

But Father, I can't, I'm dead. Can't you see?

"Runner. Let's get you up."

"What?"

"Come on, girl. Get up."

What's he talking about?

"I'm dead."

"No, you're not," the odd voice says. "Come on, sit up, Runner."

Hands on you. What's he doing? You shouldn't feel anything when you're dead.

"Death... ha!" I mumble to Dad. "Death has no currency, does it? No. Nothing of value to force on anyone anymore. Death can't be influenced or controlled by life's values. Like now. I feel myself breathing. Therefore, logic says... I'm not dead," I whisper to him. Then I blurt out, "I am not dead."

"That's right, you're not. So open your eyes."

Things slowly come into focus. Bleary-eyed, I stare up at the face.

Barlow.

He lifts me to sit against the wall. Out of the blood I was lying in.

"You busted your nose when you fell face first."

"Huh? I fell?"

"Yeah. You fainted. Come on, Runner. Get up."

With his help, I stand up wobbly and lean against the wall seeing three bullet holes where I had been standing before everything went black. I glance around listlessly. There's a girl standing in the corner. On the floor is a man crying. Henry. And that girl in the corner, that's Holly I think.

Barlow goes over to the man with the gun and begins yelling at him. The confrontation is fierce. Mauldin glances over at Jimmy once then points his gun at Barlow.

Barlow lunges at him; the gun goes off into the ceiling. They fight for control, slugging, kicking, gouging with the gun clutched in both of their hands.

There's Jimmy. He ducks behind furniture for cover.

Holly strolls over and picks up the vodka bottle off the bar. She wades into the middle of the fight and with both hands slams it into the back of Mauldin's head, knocking him over, landing on the coffee table, and dragging Barlow with him.

I'm alert now. Barlow's getting the best of Mauldin. The hit man rolls on the floor like a drunken salamander. What men will do to each other in battle. The instinctive need to send each other to hell. That's where I'm going if I don't get to... to...

That boat. Damn.

I yell, "I've got to go."

Jimmy stands out of reach of the fight. He looks dumbstruck, not knowing what to do.

Barlow wipes his bloody nose and yells for us to get out. "Now."

I shout back, "I have to find Avril."

"Avril? What? Why is she here?"

"No time to explain. I have a boat to catch. Where would they hold a girl around here?"

Jimmy asks, "What boat?"

We ignore him. Barlow yells, "We gotta go, Runner. Denny's men will be back any minute." He nods at Mauldin. "This guy will come out of it soon enough."

Denny grunts and moves, sobbing with his foot pinned to the floor, pouring blood. I can only stare at the tattered, degraded schmuck. "Should we do something for him or leave him like this?"

Barlow waves his gun like a toy. "You're crazy, Runner. C'mon, let's get out of here."

Mauldin coughs as his eyes open unfocused.

I leap down the stairs to the lobby, calling out for Avril. Barlow makes quick checks of all the rooms and restrooms where she might be.

She's nowhere. Holly, too. We've lost her.

I follow Barlow down the dark auditorium aisle, feeling our way in the dark toward the exit door. Halfway down, we bump into someone. Avril, just standing there, visibly shaken, with her duffle bag.

"Christ, where have you been?" I grab her hand. "C'mon. Let's go."

Barlow stops at the exit door, waits for us and watches out for Jimmy or Mauldin behind us. "Where's Holly?"

"I didn't see her leave the room." We three stare at each other for a second before he pushes us to the door. "Can't worry about her now. Go, go," he yells.

I force Avril out and follow her into the roaring storm. No sooner than we're out in the glow of the overhead door light are three police officers with guns drawn, yelling and squinting through the heavy rain not thirty yards away. Two I recognize: Frank Battaglia and his grumpy partner. The third cop is farther out. They yell for us to stop. We hold back with hands up. Busting out through the door with a gun in hand comes Barlow.

In a flash, wild-eyed Grumpy yells, "Stop, drop it," and fires before the words are out of his mouth. Barlow goes down hard. Frank and Grumpy cautiously come toward Barlow on the ground, guns extended. The door flies open, and Mauldin runs out firing. Frank goes down. Grumpy is hit. Avril follows me on hands and knees crawling away as muzzle blasts flash through the dark.

We reach Bobby's Jeep.

"Oh, no. Oh, my God."

Bobby lies over the steering wheel. Dead. We leave him and take off across the lot when I see Jimmy.

He's running toward the far side of the parking lot to a parked car next to the fence.

Out of the dark comes a big black vehicle sliding to a stop, blocking him. He changes direction. Two guys jump out and chase after him.

"Look, Avey." I point at the dirty red car's idling exhaust. "Let's go." Holly comes running fast, past us. She jumps in behind the wheel. "Hurry, hurry." We pile in before she spins out. She calmly puts the car through its paces. "I assume you want to catch that boat."

"How do you know about the boat, Holly"

"I just do."

We're on Main Street headed west when I look back and see a brown Bronco pulling out and after us.

"Mauldin," I yell. "Go, go, go."

From the unassuming little trollop I thought Holly was when I first met her, I now realize she's nothing like that. She's unpretentious, oddly thoughtful and cautious. And geez, she really knows how to drive a getaway car. Within minutes, she's lost the Bronco.

"Good Christ, Holly," I shout. "Where did you learn to drive like this?"

"Google."

CHAPTER FIFTY-NINE

Jimmy sits squeezed between two big men in the back seat of a Suburban, in jeans, work shirts, and ball caps. A woman wearing a vest and a tattered ball cap drives. It's been thirty minutes since being picked up in the Majestic parking lot and not a word spoken between them.

Are these FBI? Military ops? Or Denny's thugs?

Up front is a blond guy in a suit jacket and an open-collared shirt. He tosses Jimmy a phone, "Make a call."

Jimmy frowns. "What call?"

"To your hit man. Mauldin."

"I don't know what you're talking about."

"We know who you are, Barone. We know who he is. I want to hear you say his name." He sets his phone on record and holds it in front of Jimmy.

Jimmy swallows hard. "His name is Mauldin."

"Whole name, please."

"Anton Mauldin."

"Okay. Now, call him."

"What... what do you want me to say?"

"Tell him there's real cash to make if he takes on one more hit."

Jimmy frowns.

"And when he accepts, let him know you'll be around to see that the job is completed. So, go ahead, make the call."

"And what's real money? And what's the job?"

"Make up some number that gets him to accept the job. All he has to do is kill the girl."

"Girl?"

"You know who we're talking about. She's on her way to board that ship."

"What ship?"

"You know what ship, Barone. We're wasting time here."

"Okay. Okay." Jimmy hesitates. "Who are you guys? You don't look like FBI."

"We're not. But we work closely with them. If you're smart you'll work with us. Now, make the call, Barone."

"What if I can't convince him?"

"You're a con man. Isn't that what you con men do?"

Jimmy holds the phone, studying the blond guy.

"Make the fucking call on speaker, Barone."

Jimmy connects.

Mauldin answers. "What?"

"Where are you?"

"Just escaped those cops at that old theatre. Chased them girls. But they gave me the slip. I have a flight to catch. Why?"

Jimmy stumbles with a response. "Where are you now?"

"On my way to Hayward Airport."

"How'd you like to double your money?"

Silence. "I've done well on this trip. Getting greedy will get you killed."

"Okay. But what if the cash you can make is enough to set you up for the rest of your life?"

"I'm listening."

"That girl, Runner. She's a witness we don't want showing up later as a witness. We need her gone."

"This place is crawling with heat, Barone. And she's a hot commodity."

"I have big-time backing enough to offer whatever it takes to get rid of her."

"How much?"

"How does a half a million sound?"

"How much?"

"Five hundred thousand."

Mauldin whistles. "Half a million? Are you serious?"

"Not a penny less. I can have it waiting for you at the airport when you're finished."

"You know what I'll do to you if you're lying about this?"

"I'd be stupid to screw with you, Anton."

"Tell me more."

"She's about to board a cargo ship. That's where you take her out."

"What ship and where and when will she be boarding?"

"She's about to board a cargo ship, the Bonnie Lynne. Oakland." Jimmy gives the berth number. "After you take her down, the cash will be waiting for you at your plane."

Mauldin hesitates. "This better be on the up and up for your sake, pimp."

"Mauldin," Jimmy says.

"What?"

"Why didn't you kill her back there when you had a chance?"

Mauldin snickers. "Every job has to have a little fun to it. Call it foreplay. Loosen her up. I wanted to see the fear in her eyes before I cut her tongue out. But she fainted. I was about to finish the job when Barlow butted in. Everything turned to shit. I had to get out a there.”

“Don’t fuck around with your torture habits, Mauldin. Just get it over with, get your money, and get on that plane.”

“Don’t tell me how to do my job, carrot top. This will be my second chance at her. For that kind of cash, I won’t miss.”

“I’ll be at the ship to see that things go according to plan.” Then he tosses the phone back, up front. “What’s your name, anyway? Have we met?”

“No. But you called an FBI agent in New York, an old friend of mine, asking about a federal marshal killing in Vermont.”

“So you know about this girl, Runner.”

“I know who she is.”

“How do you know about Mauldin?”

CHAPTER SIXTY

Holly gets us through the driving rain to the docks in one piece. We sit speechless after the helter-skelter ride and stare at an orange and white ship docked where the Almarani ETA notice said it would be.

I whisper, "It's smaller than I expected. But what do I know?"

Holly says, "It looks like a general cargo merchant ship."

"What do they carry?"

"General cargo like different packaged stuff—chemicals, food, furniture, machinery, clothing, you name it. The occasional container."

"Is that an apartment on the back? And a flagpole in the middle?" asks Avril.

"That's the bridge where they operate and steer the ship. Below it is the living space for passengers and crews with all the living amenities—galley, cabins, and engines. That's a crane in the middle, not a flag pole."

"How do you know so much about a ship?"

"When I was in Houston, Denny's men had me driving, running errands, and moving stuff on and off ships."

Avril isn't impressed. "Nothing romantic about it. Just an ordinary-looking ship to me. It looks a little dirty."

"I don't care what it looks like, Avey."

"You sure you want to get on that thing?"

"If I don't get on that boat, I'll be dead by the end of the week. Or worse, in handcuffs headed back to jail or a mental ward."

"How did you get passage on that ship? Couldn't you have found a better-looking boat?"

"Shut up, Avey. I didn't choose it. I had to take what I got."

"How'd you get it booked? What'd you pay for it?"

"Nothing. A friend set it up. I won't be listed on any manifest. I'll be under the radar while on board."

"Then go," Holly says, grabbing a rain jacket and my ball cap. "You'll need these. Go. It's almost 6:30. Get out of here."

Crestfallen, I think of Father, all the good times with him in the good old USA, as he called it.

Avril interrupts the memories. "You gonna get on the bucket?"

I tug my cap down and pull on the rain jacket, zipping it tight to the neck.

You have no money, no papers, no passport. No idea where that boat's going. Blind faith, Natalie. Friggin' blind faith that it's going to Tahiti, and that it's paid for.

"Better get going," Holly says.

I climb out into the rain, confused, despondent, and guilty for the mess I've created for myself and everyone around me. After a few feet, I stop, turn back to the car, open the door and grab Avril. "You're coming with me."

"What?" Avril's eyes are big.

"You too, Holly."

Holly is composed and cool-headed. She shakes her head. "I'll be okay. You guys go."

I squeeze her shoulder. "Take care of yourself."

She shrugs and nods, looking straight ahead out the windshield. "I'll be okay."

Avril lugs her big duffle, walking behind me. A long wooden bench is at the gate from the road to the seafront and the dock. A black man sits hunched over at the end of the bench in a pea coat with a collar turned up against the rain, smoking. With a duffle bag at his feet, he's involved with his phone.

I stop. "Wait a minute, Avey. I gotta think this through." We sit on the other side of the bench opposite him. I'm sick to my stomach, whispering, mumbling insignificant claptrap concerns. The man notices. His face is friendly with gentle blue eyes. We share a nod. I glance back down at the boat and begin to shake visibly, teeth chattering.

"You okay, miss?"

"Yeah."

Seconds pass before he asks again. "You sure? You've got blood on your face."

I wipe it away with a sleeve and sit up straight to gather myself and look over at him. "So what are you doing out on such a miserable morning like this?"

"Going to work."

"Where?"

"I'm part of the crew on that freighter down there. The Bonnie Lynne."

"Oh," I say. "We're passengers on that boat."

"Yeah. I heard we had passengers this trip."

"What's it carrying? Where's it going?"

"Bunch a shit headed to French Polynesia."

A minute passes. "I'm going to Tahiti?"

He nods.

"Can I ask where you're from, sir?"

"Nigeria." He gets up. "I gotta go." He hauls his duffel over his shoulder.

"What's your name, sir?"

"Zacharie. Maybe see you on board."

Zacharie moseys down the long landing to the dock. Avril has yet to say a word, letting me decide if I should actually go ahead without her opinions.

I finally decide. "Let's do it, Avey." As we get up, there's a big black car slowly coming down the street. "Come on. Let's go, now."

CHAPTER SIXTY-ONE

I hunch over and walk with Avey under jacket hoods, looking back at the big car passing by with several men inside. One is easy to pick out: the guy with the yellow hair and mustache—FBI Agent Ray Waters. As it goes by I think my eyes are playing tricks on me. It looks like Jimmy's red head in the back seat.

Avril takes my arm. "Come on," she says, hustling me along faster. "Let's get down there."

We hurry, leaning into the wet wind toward a gangplank a few hundred yards away. Halfway there, Avril stops. Fear in her eyes. A tall man is approaching. Not leisurely. He's in a trot.

Oh, God.

I pull the cap down, turn my back, ignoring him and frantically search for which direction to run. I take off in a sprint.

"Stop," he yells. "It's me."

I slow, look back at him standing next to Avril.

Poor Avril. She can't run like you. And you can't just turn your back on her. You've come too far with her now.

It's my way when I'm caught at something bad without

knowing what to do. I get angry and come back to face the man taller than me.

"Hey," he says with a poke in my chest.

My hands ball into fists to hit back. Avril steps between us. She knows what I'm capable of.

"Hey." He puts a hand on my shoulder.

I lean back about to let go with a roundhouse when... when... when I do a double take. I frown at the face under the brim of an oilskin outback hat. I almost recognize it. But don't. Something meaningful in those eyes slowly emerges. My hand instinctively covers my mouth with an, "Oh, my God. I know you."

He smiles and tweaks my nose. "Yes, you do."

"Peter." I punch him in the chest. "God damn you, Peter Longer." I glance around at who might be watching before going up on my toes and hugging him tight around his sopping-wet neck. "What the hell are you doing here?"

"I came to see you off."

I can't tell if it's tears or rainwater in my eyes. But I have trouble talking because of my sobbing.

"You paid for this boat, didn't you? How did you know?"

"It was obvious you were in some trouble. Redd and I discussed it. So what was I to do but figure a way to get you out of it? It took some doing, but nothing a little money and intimidation couldn't fix."

"God, how I miss you."

"Who's this?" he says, eyeing Avril.

I pull her over. "This is who I told you about, Avey, the guy I met in Denver. Pete Longer. He took me under his wing and gave me money to get out here. And now here he is again to pull my ass out of a jam."

I take his hands and stare at him through the wind and rain. "So many things I want to ask you."

"Not now. No time." He pulls a manila envelope from his trench coat. "Here. Bon voyage, kid." He shoves it under my jacket. "It's been a real treat knowing you, kid."

"Is this what I think it is? Some of your handiwork?"

"Travel documents?" He nods at the duffel by Avril's feet. "Is that your stuff there, Natalie?"

"No, I have nothing. That's her stuff. She's coming with me."

He frowns. "Really? Do you have papers? Paid passage?"

Avril shakes her head.

"We're gonna use our charm and clever repartee to schmooze her way on."

"Think so?" He rubs his chin. "There's a thousand dollars in that envelope. Maybe you guys can use that to bribe her on board. This ship's owner group seems to be open for cash negotiations." He addresses Avril. "I'll get you a set of documents like Runner has. They'll be waiting for you when you get there."

"He's a master document forger, Avey. Been at it for years."

He pulls four hundred-dollar bills from his wallet. "Maybe this will help." He stuffs them in Avril's hand, then nods at the big car parked on the street. "Now get out of here, both of you."

He gives me a peck on the forehead. "These people don't know who they're dealing with, do they, sport?" He winks. "Gotta go." He walks away without turning back.

CHAPTER SIXTY-TWO

I watch Peter disappear into the mist.

Will you ever see him again?

Then I look over at the big black Suburban. Avril pushes me ahead toward the boat's gangplank. "Okay, let's see how this is going to turn out, Avey."

A ship's officer stands under a canopy at a podium inspecting passengers' boarding papers. Two couples ahead of us have trouble finding their papers. I have my new passport, driver's license, and other travel papers out and ready to show and begin the negotiations to get Avey on board. The disorganized couple search through bag after bag. And there are many and just as many questions.

I'm getting frantic. Avril holds my arm. While they search, I look for any sign of the Bronco.

C'mon, folks. Move it.

A big Cadillac limousine drives through the street gate where we met Zacharie, down the landing and stops near the boarding officer working the passenger line. Two men in black trench coats step out to a back door window coming down. Then, one of them signals the boarding officer to come over.

"Just a moment, please," the officer tells us in line. "I be right back."

Oh, God.

Then I notice the Bronco sitting at the street gate.

"For Christ's sake, folks, come on," I whisper under my breath to the couple in disarray ahead of us. "Let's go, folks. C'mon."

Avril murmurs out of the side of her mouth, watching the limousine, "What the hell's going on, Natalie?"

I whisper back. "I'm dead meat, Avey."

"Shut up. Let's just see."

The boarding officer returns and quickly passes the unorganized couple through and the next couple after them.

Alright, we're next.

The officer snaps a quick look back at the limo before holding out his hand to me. "I'm Ship's Officer Alfred Luen. Papers, please."

I'm afraid to move.

"Please, madam. Your papers."

I'm frozen, holding my papers, having second thoughts.

Two more antsy couples lined up behind us begin to snort their dissatisfaction with my stalling as the high wet wind hits the canopy, blowing its fabric and flapping hard.

"Please, ladies and gentlemen," Officer Luen interrupts the boarding process. "Make room for crew members to pass through to board."

We move to the side. Zacharie and three other crew members in heavy sea clothing pass us and walk up the gangplank. One more of them comes running to catch up, hustling by with an upturned collar and knit cap pulled low.

Luen returns to our boarding. "Madam, please, your papers."

He's irritated at my hesitation.

The limo's back door opens for a short, stubby man in a black leather double-breasted overcoat to step out. He has a round, fleshy face and adjusts a black wide-brimmed hat. He walks with a slight limp. A long cigar bobs in his thick lips. What looks to be the ship's captain trots down the gangway, says something to the deck officer, and then goes down and shakes hands with the man in black standing under an umbrella held by one of his men.

This is somebody's boss man.

Hands gesturing, they discuss something with a few outbursts. Both men look over at us and nod. The boss man summons one of his men over to give the captain documents. The captain shakes his head vigorously and hands them back. I'm close to panic now. Where to run?

No sign of the Bronco. Where is Mauldin now? My nerves speed up. I ask the officer, "What's wrong?"

"No problem, miss. Uno momento." Then he signals the growing number of couples behind us to come forward. He quickly passes them through. Now it's just me and Avril. I blurt out, "It's cold out here. This is frustrating. Let us on that boat. Now."

"Momentito, por favor." He turns back to the conversation with his captain and the boss man.

Avril leans into me, whispering, "Natalie."

"What?"

"I know who that man is."

"Who? Which one."

"Him, with the cigar."

"Who is he?"

"That's Mister Denny. Henry Denny's father. Gerald Denny himself."

CHAPTER SIXTY-THREE

I stare at Avril, astonished. "You're telling me I'm about to meet the father of the man I probably killed. And he knows it by now."

The rain softens to a slight drizzle mist.

Officer Luen asks again. "Papers, please, miss."

A police car comes rolling down the street, turning through the gate and down the landing. I swallow hard and hold my breath. I offer papers to Luen.

He takes them straight to the captain. I'm close enough to overhear Captain Costa tell Mister Denny, "She is not getting on my ship."

A gentlemanly disagreement ensues for a few minutes. Apparently Mister Denny owns the Bonnie Lynne.

Oh, God.

"Ms. Grace will be traveling to Tahiti," Denny tells Costa. "With her two companions."

Costa looks surprised. As am I.

Costa snaps, "Who else besides Miss Avril?"

Denny steps aside. Holly steps forward, staring at the ground like an innocent doe.

"Do these young ladies have papers, Señor Denny?"

"They will when you dock in Tahiti."

Costa, objects. "But..."

"Enough of this," Denny snaps. He coaxes Holly to join us in line. "Their papers will be waiting for them when you get there. I'll check in with the girls when you clear the bridge. I want to hear how you're taking good care of them."

I'm listening to this with an open mouth when I realize who's standing behind Mister Denny—Jimmy Barone.

Good, God.

Two police officers in rain jackets are approaching the group of men.

Captain Costa turns to us with a forced reception greeting. "Welcome aboard the Bonnie Lynne, ladies."

The officers signal Luen to stop. One of the cops engages Costa and Mister Denny. The group steps away, out of earshot, their voices raised with hands gesturing with emotion.

I wait patiently and notice a crew member leaning over the railing, looking down on the confrontation. My paranoia rages with a neurotic fixation of Mauldin watching me from behind every rock and tree, every window and door. I can't be sure of anything I see anymore.

That can't be him. You're seeing things, Natalie.

The confrontation ends with Luen waving us aboard. Mister Denny shuffles over to us as we pass close to him onto the gangplank. "You girls never come back. You hear what I'm telling you?"

I nod, knowing what he means and walk up the gangplank. One of the cops points for me to stay where I am on deck.

Oh no.

I stop while Avril and Holly continue following a crew member. The cop walks up the gangplank, onto the deck and approaches me. "Hello, Runner."

I go cold when I see his face clearly. "Hayden!"

He removes his cap and wipes water from his face. "Well, now I see what kind of trouble you were in. When you do things, you do them in style, don't you?"

I'm sheepish with no good response.

"Take care of yourself, girl. Maybe we'll meet up in Costa Rica, like we talked about."

I grab his arm. "I didn't know you were a cop. How? When... Why didn't you..."

"Had no reason to mention it."

We speak for only a few minutes, exchanging apologies and genuine niceties.

"Today is my last day in this uniform."

"That lawyer thing got its hooks in you, then?"

He nods.

"Before we say goodbye, I have one question, cowboy?"

"What?"

"What does Denny know?"

Hayden gives a short version of what the law knows about Jimmy. "We've been aware of his plan ever since the blackmail scheme. How quickly the plan got to what happened at the Majestic Theatre took us by surprise. And we didn't know about a hitman being involved. We're looking for him now."

I grab his arm. "Hayden. There's a hitman on board. His name is Mauldin. He's here to kill me."

Hayden pats my arm. "We know he's headed to Hayward to catch a plane. We'll grab him there."

"Hayden, he's here. On board. I know what I'm talking about."

"Believe me, Runner. We have eyes on him. We'll get him. Don't worry."

"Hayden, I didn't know anything about a blackmail. I just..."

He puts a finger over his lips. "Shush. Don't say a thing. Just get on this ship and sail away."

"But..."

"Ah, ah, ah. Not a word, understand? Get out of here before they want to bring you in for questioning. And Denny's seen enough of you girls. The captain knows what's at stake for him if you guys don't get to the islands safe and sound."

I drag a hand down over mouth to chin. *Shut up, Natalie. Do what he says.*

I touch his face gently. "Look, Hayden. I gotta go. Take care of yourself." I give him a quick hug. "Maybe see you around."

Hayden walks to his cruiser. I wave; he returns the wave.

I quickly pull my cap bill down shielding my face and walk away but not before seeing that crew member who was watching the brouhaha of the boarding issue earlier. I hurry off to catch up with Avril and Holly.

CHAPTER SIXTY-FOUR

I'm lost in the boat's corridors, hallways, and steel doors until I'm rescued by one of the ship's officers who escorts me to a smallish, nicely appointed cabin. Avril or Holly aren't there.

"Where are my friends?"

He looks at me confused. "What friends?" Then he leaves.

I stick my head out the door when he's gone. Down the hall crewmen are discussing the three young women on board. I close the door and wonder if I'm mistaken about Mauldin being on board. I step out in the hallway and make my way out to the upper deck. It's an early misty evening. Zacharie is smoking, leisurely hanging over the railing, taking in the hazy harbor lights. He sees me, flicks the cigarette butt over the railing. "I see you made it."

"Yeah." I hug myself from the cold.

"And your friend?"

"Yeah. She and another came on board. But I can't find them."

Zacharie frowns. "Not in your cabin?"

"No."

"That is strange. I don't know what to tell you."

"I'm also looking for someone who might be on board." I give Mauldin's description. "Any chance you might have seen some guy like this?"

He thinks for a second. "Yeah. Maybe. New guy, just today." He nods, lighting another cigarette. "Sounds like Anton."

I squeal, "Anton. Yes, that's him. Anton Mauldin. He's here to kill me." I crawl up on the railing and start to jump.

Zacharie grabs me and eases me down. "What the fuck you doin', lady?"

I touch his face to know that he's real. Then I back away, stumble, fall, get up, and race back to the cabin. Avril and Holly are eating from a fruit tray in the room.

"I'm getting off this boat as fast as I can, guys. Where's my jacket?"

Avril nods at the closet.

I grab the rain jacket from the top shelf. With it comes Avril's big oversized duffle falling to the floor. I stare in disbelief at the scattered clothes, toiletries, running shoes. Stuff from my tote bag lying on the floor. I glare at her as I grab the plastic bag off the floor with the forty thousand. "Where'd you find my tote, Avey? How long have you had it?"

She's just as surprised to see the money as I am. She sees the look in my eyes and grabs my arm. I peel her hand off me. "What were you thinking, Avey?"

"It's not what it looks like."

"Well, what could it be that I don't understand?"

She's reticent, standing with her hands at her side like a schoolgirl explaining how she got duped into Denny's bullshit about taking care of her, changing her life. "It was all a lie." She sniffs. "The man he introduced me to is a psycho vulgar sicko. What he did to me..." her voice trails off in thought.

"So you've been with Denny and Jimmy all the time I was so worried about you?"

"I couldn't get away or call. I was a prisoner. And that's not all until..."

"Until what?"

"Until that Mauldin guy shot that caretaker. Then Jimmy showed up with your tote bag. Said he found it in the alley. He threw it at me and went upstairs with that murderer. Then all hell broke loose when you bumped into me. I never looked inside the tote. I didn't know you had that kind of money until now."

Holly picks up Barlow's blue .38 gun that had fallen from the tote. "What's this pretty little thing?" Hefting it, she asks, "Is it yours, Runner?"

"No. Long story. Not mine. I don't want it."

She aims it around the cabin, and then holds it pointed at me. "Where did you get the fucking money, Runner?" The questions come with a reckless smile. For a second, just a millisecond, I feel fear, awful terror until I push the barrel aside, saying the money came from Oakes. "His office safe. I stole it."

She grins. "Just joshin'."

The ship's engines groan with a tiny bump.

"We need to get off this boat before it leave the dock. Anyone coming with me?"

The boat bumps slightly. I stick my head out the door to check the hall. What I see stuns me. Jonathan walking away. I recognize the back of his head, his walk. For just a second, he turns back and smiles. I blink. He disappears up the stairs.

I inch back in the cabin coldly, robotically afraid of what I just saw.

"What is it, Runner?"

"Nothing. Not a thing."

Then we all decide to rush out and jump over the side. We're ready. I go to open the door when there's a knock.

A ship's officer. "Sorry to bother you. But there's a delay in departing. An engine issue. We're waiting for a piece of equipment. So sorry for the delay." He touches his hat and leaves.

We wait for minutes before deciding to go. Holly leads to the door. It's locked. We pound on it. We try the ships phone. Dead. Our phones have no cell connection. No one hears us.

Avril begins to cry.

CHAPTER SIXTY-FIVE

Hours pass. It must be getting late in the day. The cabin is stuffy. We sit around with no idea of when we'll be moving. Two officers bring a spread of sandwiches, chips, and drinks. On their departure Holly sees them to the door and without their notice she sticks a folded piece of paper in the strike plate to prevent the latch from fully locking in place.

We eat and wait for our chance to escape. Hours pass before it's quiet in the hallway.

I finally decide.

"Time to go."

But they've lost their nerve. So I bid them farewell and take off running with my tote. By now, I'm so tired the more I run, the more confused I become. I'm physically giving out. My throat is dry. I'm sweating, and my heart is racing. This is a dreamland with no way out. Far down the hall, a fog bank appears. I squint at the idea of fog inside the boat. But it is and it's rolling at me. There's something alive inside it. A living, breathing thing stomping after me.

Jezus.

I turn back and find an emergency escape route with a ladder going up into a long, dark chute. Up I climb, losing count of how many floors I pass. It seems to go on forever, with no end in sight. I reach a landing for a breather. Seconds later, sounds of footsteps clang on the metal stairs below, climbing up. Exhausted, pulse-pounding, I find a small enclave with fire hoses where I squeeze into the dark, cramped space. Clang, clang after clang, whoever it is, coming up for me. On the landing, a few feet away from where I'm crouched, the clanging stops.

"Runner, where are you?"

Oh, God.

"Where are you? I know you're here somewhere."

"Why are you hiding from me? Where are you? Come out so I can see you."

I hold my breath and try to push back deeper into the darkness.

"There's a guy looking for you," he mumbles. "A bad guy. Did you know that?"

I want to yell, *Yeah, for Christ's sake. He wants to kill me.* But I hold my tongue.

"Come out. He wants to fertilize you again. So come out. Let's go find him. He says he's a federal marshal. Did you have a child with him, Runner? Huh? Did you?"

Good, god.

"Come on, Runner. Let's get this cleared up and over with."

I get to my knees and lunge, swinging the tote with everything I have, knocking him down the ladder shaft.

The boat bumps, engines rumble. Clanging, and clanging on the ladder. Hands appear pulling up a man out of the chute.

He frowns. "Why did you do that?" Zacharie says, crawling out onto the landing and rubbing the back of his head.

"Oh, God. It's you."

"Who did you think it was?"

"I... I thought..."

"Who?"

"I thought you were someone else. Sorry. Can't chat now. I need to get off this boat. How? Which way?"

"Don't call it a boat. This is a ship. And the way out is that way."

I run down a long narrow hallway. My cap scrapes the ceiling, which slants lower and lower as I crawl. The sides and the ceiling push against my body the farther I go.

Oh God. Ceiling and walls are closing in behind me.

I'm stuck, can't move forward, can't push back.

Voices! Chatter, laughing, plates and tableware plinking.

A dining room.

I suck in my breath, grab the end of the shaft and squeeze, and squeeze out into an empty room. The only light is from a small bulb over a long table littered with dirty glasses and plates. It's deathly quiet. Out of the shadows walk two men. But no noise from their footsteps. One man is a barefoot skeletal dwarf-like thing in jeans and a plaid work shirt. His eyes are deep-set and black as coal. The other, a friendly-faced one, wears jeans, a flannel shirt and work boots.

Goosebumps break over me. "Father."

There you are, Natalie. Been looking for you.

"Who's your friend, Dad?"

This is Grim. You might a heard about him. He doesn't carry that long, curved blade anymore. And he's ditched the cloaked hoodie for Carhartts and Wranglers. Things have changed, my dear.

"Why is he here? Why are you here?"

Grim has a quota to fill. Thought I'd help.

Dad introduces me. *Mister Reaper, this is my daughter, Natalie Grace... isn't she beautiful?*

"Oh, Dad. Do you really think this is it for me? Is my time up?"

His eyes twinkle as he clicks his pipe on his front teeth and snickers.

I turn and run. Up the stairs, out into the night, into the rain and into the waiting arms of Ray Waters. He grabs my wrist. "Why did you knock me down the ladder chute back there?"

CHAPTER SIXTY-SIX

Waters pulls me stumbling along. "Come on. Let's find a place to talk." He finds a crew's utility locker room mid-deck and pulls me inside. He takes a towel from a bin, removes my cap, and rubs my wet face and hair like a parent drying a child after a bath.

I grab the towel and toss it in his face and fold my arms.

"Now." He pushes me to sit on a bench. "Calm down."

"You know what happened in Vermont, don't you? You're taking me in?"

"I'm not here to take you in. You are a byproduct of another case I'm working. You are a different matter for me."

"So if the FBI knows about what I did in Vermont, why aren't you taking me in?"

"Calm down, I'm not with the FBI."

"I don't want to calm down, Ray." I jump up.

He pushes me back down. "Will you just shut up and listen?"

I slam my cap back on, yank the bill down low and hug the tote to my chest in a pout.

"How do you get away with being such a brat?"

"You're a brat. You shut up."

"God you sound like a first grader. Everything you do, you do with anger, attitude, and arrogance."

I lift off my cap with an idiotic grin. "Wow. The master of alliteration. How long did it take you to put that one together?"

"You think you're so smart."

"It's just my way, Ray."

"You are the most stubborn person I've ever met."

"Is that right? Well, you must not get out much then." I fold my arms and return to a long-face pout.

He sits down and leans forward, clasping his hands. "Why do you think I've been following you?"

"Cuz you're lost. Can't find your ass from a ham sandwich? Need someone to take care of your lousy tush." I pause. "But to better answer your question, I guess you want to take me in. Put me away in a rubber room. That's what you get paid for, isn't it?"

He loses his sermonizing adult attitude. His body posture slouches. He stares at the floor, clasping and rubbing hands in his lap like he's trying to tell me something important.

I frown at his down-dog demeanor. It's almost touching. "Hey," I whisper. "What is it?"

He looks up. "You didn't kill your father, Natalie."

Oxygen escapes me at the mention of my Father. Time stands still. I drop the tote and clutch my hands together at my mouth, thinking of that morning, the fire, the marshal, the gun. The worst nightmare of my life. I stare at him trying to show composure. But the snot filling my nose, my eyes blurring, and struggling to breathe makes composure hard to pull off.

He sees my distress and calmly bends me forward, and tells me to breathe. "Breathe in through your nose and out through your mouth. Slowly." He rubs the back of my neck.

I'm breathing normally again.

He describes how the lab work proved my innocence that morning. "Gunpowder residue on your father's hands. None on yours. The gas can from the garage with his fingerprints. None of yours. A witness saw your father take the gun from you. He described the shooting. A suicide. It seems your father was dying of cancer. He must have decided to go with his wife, your mother, that day."

Tears run down my cheek. "I don't believe it. He wouldn't do something like that."

"Well, believe it."

"You came all this way to tell me this?"

"No. I belong to a civilian force. Some call us a militia. Some see us as self-righteous rednecks. We're a small but highly efficient group of relentless watchdogs sniffing out underhanded, dirty lawmen and politicians who use their power to enrich their lives with money, power, and immoral gratification. We mostly concentrate on the justice community—lawyers, judges, and law enforcement. We work off the books with the FBI. That federal marshal killed in that fire... We were building a case on him before he died. The girl who ran away that day thought she was to blame. I needed to find her. Set her straight. Get the case against her dismissed. That's why I've been after you."

I wipe my eyes and pick up the tote. "Anything else, Mister Waters?"

"No, not from me. Local law probably will want to talk with you, though. We have no intention of turning you over to them."

I start to leave but linger for a few seconds. "Sorry, I've been so mean to you."

He nods. "No worries. Glad I got you off my to-do list. Best of luck to you in your life, Natalie. Now I'm working on this other case, so I got a call to make." He turns away and listens to his phone contact without looking back.

CHAPTER SIXTY-SEVEN

Jimmy stands on the landing, looking up at the ship, rain pelting him, thinking he's done what those gun-toting vigilantes asked him to do. At the same time he's frustrated at having his operation breached. And Lord only knows who else knows about it. So is his aspiration of taking over Henry's operation dead? Should he take off and get out of Dodge? Those guys didn't ask or say anything about what he's doing.

And they probably don't care. Maybe things are still a go?

"Oh, come on, Jimmy," he mumbles into the rain. "Anyone would be crazy to continue on with an operation that got screwed up like this one. God, you really misjudged her. She screwed this all up."

Runner, Runner. Oh, you little shit.

His phone rings. It's Captain Costa.

"Mister Barone. We have little problem. Mister Denny just call. He on his way back to Bonnie Lynne. He wants to come aboard. I don't like this. What should I do?"

"What do you mean? Why would Gerald Denny want to come to your ship?"

"But he is."

"But my man's not going to board your ship."

"You tole me to let your man come aboard to make an arrest to some young lady. That's why you pay me. Okay?"

"Yeah. But she's not getting on your ship."

"Well, that what you think. She on board now. And she have two other women with her. Mister Denny tole me to let them passage to Tahiti. He very clear we take care of them. I think his words, not a hair on their heads to find trouble. You hear it all. I saw you there. So you know. So, tell me. What should I do?"

"You welcome him with a smile."

"I about to get underway, Barone."

"Just wait. Wait for him. Do whatever he says. Don't act any different. He'll have men with him. There is nothing you can do except to welcome him. Just make sure those girls are safe and happy."

"But why he come?"

"Hell, I don't know. It's probably nothing of significance. Don't worry."

"I not comfortable with this."

"Captain, listen to me. He probably just wants to have one last word with the girls."

Costa snorts disapproval of Jimmy's opinion.

"Hear me out, Captain. Don't let Mauldin on board. Do you hear?"

"You told me to accept him. He may already be on board."

Jimmy pulls over to think. "Captain, stay calm. I'll be there soon."

Jimmy shoves his hands in his pockets. Decision time.

CHAPTER SIXTY-EIGHT

Heading down the hallway, crew members are chatting around a corner. I duck into an unlocked storage room to wait them out. Perched on a stack of boxes and casually eating a banana, is Father. He speaks with his mouth full.

Where are you off to now, Nat?

I close the door and lean back against it. I want to ignore him. But after hearing what Waters had to say, I have to ask, "Is it true, Dad? What Waters said about you?"

Father nods. *Yeah, he got most of it right.*

"So you started the fire. You shot the marshal, not me. And then you turned the gun on yourself?"

He sighs. *A man can only take so much, Nat. You women are so much stronger than us men. When I saw that roof collapse, my heart snapped and I crumbled with it. Your mother was my destiny, my everything. I saw no reason to live with the little time I had left. The—*

Voices outside the door interrupt us. *Poof.* He's gone. I wipe a tear.

What a dream.

. . .

I wait for the voices to leave then pull myself together and run back to the cabin to convince Avril and Holly to come with me. I push in, close the door and I see in the middle of the floor, a body in a pool of blood, throat slashed, eyes open but vacant. I fall to my knees hoping this is a dream. One of my hallucinations

I crawl over and gently touch her. "Avril. Avril, my God, Avey, is it you?"

Oh, good Lord. No, no. Oh, no.

From a voice in the dark. "What now?"

I flinch at the voice. It's Holly.

I settle against Avril's side, mumbling apologies and regrets and how I loved her. After minutes of soft regrets, rage and despair begin to boil up in me. I've never felt such evil inside me as the hatred stirring in me right now.

Holly pulls a blanket from the bed. We lay it over her and see that it's spread nice and neat.

"We need to get the hell out of here, Holly. Off boat."

She rubs her hands together. "You go. I've got unfinished business to deal with."

I plead with her to come with me but to no avail. I hug her tight, unsure if I'll ever see her again. I grab the tote and tear out of the cabin to find a way off this death trap. I'm crushed. Avey is dead. My father committed suicide, I killed my Mother. I almost gave myself to a pimp. I have to sit down to catch my breath. But no time to process all this now. And there's a killer after me. I gotta, just gotta get off this boat. Go find Holly. Don't take no for an answer. Convince her to go overboard with me.

I run up the stairs and to the dock-side railing and hang over, wondering about leaving through the gangplank. But it's being attended by the boarding officer and another crew member checking papers for a few people coming and going. Can't leave that way.

I stare down at the dark ocean beckoning me. My legs shake. I'm fatigued. The distance to the black water below figures to be about forty feet. You've jumped from higher than this back home from cliffs over the lake. Clutching the tote, I feel ashamed but justified that I'm running out on Holly. I climb up on the railing and teeter in the blowing rain, holding on to a rope running down from a crane. Gauging the long drop into the cold Pacific, I chew on a fingernail with indecision. Running away without Holly is wrong. But... I hold my breath and pinch my nose. A battle rages in my head. Escape, or stay to find Holly and avenge Avril's murder with her?

I jump down to the deck, sling the tote over my shoulder, and head to find Waters. Hopefully, he's near the utility room where I left him. He's armed. Ray is the one to take Mauldin out.

Yes, yes.

CHAPTER SIXTY-NINE

On the bridge, Captain Costa paces the floor as uptight as a coiled spring and full of questions when Jimmy walks in. He needs to calm the Captain down. Project confidence. But self-confidence is something Jimmy himself isn't totally full of at the moment.

Costa snaps, "What's going on, Barone? What am I in for? Why is Mister Denny coming back?"

"Nothing to worry about, Captain."

Costa shakes his head. "Dios, necesito este trabajo." He stares at me. "I need this job. The wife's expecting our third kid, and we just buy new house. I cannot get fired over what you talk me into!"

Jimmy fires back. "Talked you into? Is that what you said? Talked you into? I didn't talk you into anything, Captain. I paid you. Remember? You were all too anxious to get that little bonus for just a few hours of looking the other way. So don't give me that shit about talking you into something." Then he turns away to cool off and return to his calmer self. "I'm sure Denny just forgot something with the girls. That's all." Even though Jimmy knows it's wishful thinking. He's worried himself.

Why is a billionaire mogul rushing back here at this hour?

From the bridge, a high perch on the ship, Jimmy and Costa can see far down the road. Headlights approaching. No other vehicles. Just that one car headed their way. They share an anxious look. Jimmy squares his shoulders. "I'll find the girls, make sure they're all right. And I'll call off Mauldin. What cabin are they in, Captain?"

"Cabin one."

"Okay. Just sit tight." Even though he doesn't know the ship and has no idea where to find his hired hit man, he heads out to try the cabin first. The door is ajar. Inside, a chair lies overturned, surrounded by a shattered lamp lying on its side. A blanket covers a lump on the floor.

Oh no.

He crouches to it, draws back the cover, and recoils. Avril's stony face and lifeless eyes stare up at eternity. Blood pooled around her body. Her severed tongue on the floor. "Oh God. Oh shit!" He jumps up, mind reeling, mumbling, "Should've never hired that crazy fuck." He paces. "And Mister Denny's... oh shit, what've I got on my hands now?"

Think, Jimmy. Think.

"Run or make something up?" He runs fingers through his hair. "Running... not a good idea. He'll hire men like Mauldin to find me. Can't hide."

He bites a fingernail.

He's confident that with a sophisticated story of lies and calculated pretense, he can pull off an excuse for Denny to believe. He's a con man. It's what he does. Blame it on Mauldin.

Tie Henry's death to Avril's murder. Both are Mauldin's doings. Tell him Henry hired Mauldin. Something happened between them. But now he has to find Runner. She's just as guilty in Henry's death as Jimmy. Getting her story to match up with his is critical. She better still be alive.

Christ! Where are you, girl? And where are you, Mauldin?

There's movement in the room. He slowly stands up, gun ready. In the corner partially hidden behind curtains is a silhouette. "Who's there?"

CHAPTER SEVENTY

Ray Waters is my only hope. I must find the utility room where I left him earlier.

Christ! I jump, shaken, and stop. Someone is coming through the fog. Mauldin hunched over like a mad bull in a pea jacket. I brace for his attack, ready to fight with bare fists.

A muffled voice. "Good evenin', Miss. Better get out of this rain or catch your death of cold," says a crewman as he passes by. I regain my composure and press on to find that utility room.

Why isn't this boat moving? It should have left hours ago.

After a few wrong turns I find the room. Waters is there. I find him all right. But he's on the floor with a gunshot wound to the back of the head. He lies on his side in a slick of blood and gray matter. I stumble back against a wall and slide to the floor. My only chance to get out of this mess.

His gun! Get his gun.

I feel around him. His jacket is open; the holster inside is empty. Mauldin took it. Now what? Who else can I turn to?

I race back out, through the storm to the bridge. Captain
Costa may be my only hope now.

CHAPTER SEVENTY-ONE

In the dark cabin, Jimmy's neck hair stands on end, seeing the curtain move. He pulls his gun. "Who's there?"

A finger inches the curtain aside.

"Holly!" She has a gun.

"What are you doing here?"

She shrugs.

He slowly approaches. She's sullen, subdued, arms hanging loosely at her side with a blue-tinted .38 revolver in hand. He nods at her and then at the gun. He gestures at the body on the floor. "Did you see what happened?"

"Nope."

"When did you get here?"

"Just now."

"Is this Mauldin's doings?"

"Who else?"

"Did he see you?"

"I said I wasn't here."

He cautiously steps closer and whispers, "You okay?"

"I'm fine."

"Can I have that?" he says, reaching for the gun.

No reaction from her.

"Holly?"

Indifference.

He carefully and gently takes the gun from her hand.

She clasps her hands together without emotion.

He tucks the .38 in his belt and paces, going over the story he's made up for Mister Denny. He whispers to Holly, "I'm going to go find Runner. Mister Denny is on his way back to see about something. I'll need to tell him what happened here." He paces for a few more seconds. "Yeah. I'll tell him his son hired a killer who did this." He looks over at Holly for her reaction. "You'll agree. Right?"

She's silent. Hands still clasped.

Jimmy frowns but continues. "His son is dead, so he can't deny it. I can pull it off. We'll be okay." He stuffs his hands in his pockets. "What do you think a that?"

She shrugs.

Jimmy rubs his temples, thinking out loud. "I hope Runner is okay. She needs to cooperate in this plan. But that might be wishful thinking." How many men will Mister Denny have with him? Let this play out. Whoever survives, just use them in your story to sell to Mister Denny. He'll deal with them. Not you. Yeah. That's it."

You're a genius, Jimmy Barone. A fucking genius.

He points to Holly. "You stay put. I'll be back as soon as I find Mauldin." He frowns at her indifference. "Are you okay?"

She shrugs.

"Okay. Just stay here. Don't leave. I'll be right back."

CHAPTER SEVENTY-TWO

I run the length of the deck and charge up onto the bridge. Costa looks edgy, staring out into the evening abyss. He frowns at my approach. "Señor Barone is looking for you."

"There's been a murder, Captain. My friend, Avril. She's dead in the cabin. And a man is dead in your mid-ship locker room. And I'm next."

Costa is stunned.

"I heard what Mister Denny demanded of you before we boarded at the gangplank. Safe passage to Tahiti. Isn't that what you promised him, Captain?"

"Yes, I did."

"Well now, look what's happened even before this ship has pushed off. What's he going to think when he learns about this?"

His jaw clenches. He falls back into his tall Captain's perch, staring out into the stormy night.

"Did you hear me, Captain?"

He rubs his forehead and nods. "Mauldin. The man Mister Barone paid me to let come aboard. He's the one responsible, isn't he?" He folds his arms with an ugly stare at me. "Who are you? Why are so many people interested in you?"

Father appears, smirking at me from behind the Captain's shoulder.

Good question, daughter. How you gonna answer that one? Who are you, Natalie? Have you decided yet?

"Captain Costa." I grab him by his lapels. "Do you have a family?"

"Yes. Yes, I do."

I yank him close. "Well, I'm the one who's going to make sure you see them again. That's a promise I intend to keep."

Costa pulls my hands away, presses the lapels flat and looks away back into the black of night.

"You think I'm incapable of getting us out of this. Well, think again, Captain."

"I am incapable of understanding anything right now." He pats me on the shoulder. "What would you have me do?"

I feel alert. Audacity is my hallmark. Let's take one step at a time. Right or wrong. Then adjust as needed.

Father smiles.

Atta girl.

"Captain, why aren't we leaving? What's the holdup?"

"Young lady, this vessel is not to leave because the owner of this ship is Señor Gerald Denny. He just call. He's on his way back here. Deus ajuda a todos nós. So, I do not move until he tells me so."

"Why is he coming back?"

"I do not know why."

"Where is Jimmy?"

"He looking for that Mauldin man to stop him from doing any harm to you girls."

"Well, that Mauldin man is on board to kill me and my

friends. We know too much about him. He killed one of us. Two more to go.”

Costa’s hands ball into fists. “Oh, my God.” He nods at a car coming in the distance. “That’s him. Señor Denny.”

“Costa, if you want to see your family again, you’ll get this ship on its way. Don’t wait. Get it going. Now.”

“I just can not pull out like a car from a garage. It takes time.”

“Well, you better get this thing on the road as fast as possible.” I drop the tote bag and nod at it. “That’s all I have in the world. I’ll be back for it.”

Back at the cabin I find Holly gone. I search around for a weapon. Nothing of any significance.

The ship’s kitchen has knives.

Minutes later, the cooks stop what they’re doing and watch me bust in, grab a chef’s knife, and race out into the dining room. No sooner than I do, two loud blasts shatter the quiet of the empty room; two bullets whiz past my ear. Mauldin is coming through another door across the room. Another blast whizzes by. I duck and lunge through a door into the hall and run past Jimmy, standing there with a gun in his hand, making no effort to stop me. I make it to the stairs leading up to the outside deck. Two blasts and two bullets slam into the wall behind me. I leap up the stairs. The next shot misses wide. I glance back to see Mauldin throw his gun away, grab Jimmy’s gun, then slip and fall. The blue .38 spins on the floor.

Out on deck I have a bit of lead. Just enough time to escape over the side. I climb up on the railing. After taking a big breath,

I let go of the rope, teetering, holding my nose. The wind whip-ping harder now, pushing me. Eyes blurry from the wind and rain. A crack of thunder. Shame and remorse rip at my sense of integrity. I bend to jump, and blow my cheeks out. A grunting guttural *hmmm* comes from deep in my throat. A strong gale almost tosses me over before I can let go. I snatch back at the rope and hug for dear life. I can't leave without Holly. Or the damn tote. I jump down.

Now go find Holly, get that tote.

I suck in a big breath and launch into a run to put an end to this nightmare.

CHAPTER SEVENTY-THREE

In a panic after jumping from the railing, I wipe stinging eyes. Tall shore lights cast a misty halo over the ship with eerie shadows. A gusting wind fans salt water spray over the deck.

But I can see enough to catch sight of a swaggering creature coming at me. Mauldin, with a shit-eating grin. I turn and run. But it's just minutes before I slide to a stop at the front of the ship. Trapped. I turn with the knife held cocked, threatening.

"Well, well. Now look what we have here," he whispers, inching closer and dodging the wild swing I take at him. He pushes me in the chest after my slash misses again. With my back at the railing I hack and rip at him. He's agile, avoids the blade, catches my hand and throws me to the deck. I swing the knife at his legs, ripping through a pant leg. He drops on me, pinning my legs. I slash furiously but he catches my hand, peels the knife away and drops it on the deck. Now I'm staring into the barrel of the blue .38.

"What is it that men see in you, anyway? Are you that good in bed?"

"You'll never know, will you?"

"I'll be the judge of that."

"Meaning what? You going to rape me first before you kill me?"

"I'll do whatever I want with you. You're mine now."

"What's it like killing people, Mister Mauldin?"

"Just a job."

"So, you don't mind killing women?"

"If her name is on the hit list, she's just like anyone else."

"I hear you have fun with us girls. Sick fun."

"Where'd you hear that?"

"Your reputation precedes you."

"What I do with them is my own business. Call it a bonus."

"Torture, rape. You call that a bonus?"

"Call it a perk."

"Well, I call it cowardice. You're a weak child."

He studies me under him like I'm some kind of lab experiment. He reaches to unbutton my jeans. I slap his hand away. He slaps me back and returns to the buttons. I throw a fist, a glancing blow. Then his fist catches me high on the forehead, slamming my head on the deck.

Ugh, damn.

I yell, "Stop it. Just stop hitting me. Okay?"

He's in his own world now, concentrating on hard-to-open buttons on the tight, wet jeans.

"Mauldin," I scream. "Let me up. You don't want to do this."

"Why not?"

"Because of your buddy, Jimmy Barone."

"Ha. He's not my friend. But I'm getting a half million from him to kill you. It's waiting for me on a plane as soon as I finish with you."

I laugh. "He doesn't have a half million to pay you. Hell, he doesn't have a pot to pee in, much less have that kind of money. He's conned you, you stupid jackass."

Mauldin leans over and whispers in my ear. "You're soft and wet, and you're mine." He sticks his tongue in my ear. I jerk away. He tries again. I yank my head around and sink teeth into his cheek. He howls. "You little shit." He wipes blood from his cheek and sends a punch to my face.

I cower and almost start to cry.

"You ready for this now," he whispers. "Huh?"

I spit blood in his face. "You know that money waiting for you at the airport?"

He wipes the spit from his cheek. "Yeah, what about it?"

"You'll never get there."

"Yeah? Why's that?"

"Cuz Mister Denny's men will cut you up into fish bait."

"What are you talking about?" He mumbles while working on opening the last button.

"You saw all the fuss when we were boarding, didn't you? With Mister Denny and the cops."

"What if I did?"

"Well, I'm here because of Denny. He wants me in Tahiti for his own purposes. You figure it out."

"I don't care about him. I want what I want, and that's this right now."

I struggle, pushing at his hands to stop. "Denny ordered the Captain to get us to Tahiti safe and sound. What's he gonna do when he finds me dead?"

"I'll be long gone when he hears about you."

"Nope. Wrong. He's on his way back here right now. Should be showing up any minute."

"You're a crazy, lying bitch." He unbuckles his belt and unzips.

Out of the corner of my eye, I see Jimmy in the fog that's rolled in. He steps into the halo of the overhead light. "She's telling the truth, Anton. Denny just called the Captain to hold the ship until he gets here."

Mauldin frowns, picks up his gun and aims it at Jimmy.

I hit Mauldin upside the head.

He retaliates with a fist to my eye.

Oh, ow, ow, ow.

"Next time, it'll be harder. You understand?"

"Anton." Jimmy comes closer. "I'm telling the truth. Shoot if you want, but it won't change anything."

"Shut up, Barone." He returns to arranging my body, lifting my hips to force down the troublesome wet jeans.

I scream and hit him hard in the mouth.

He drops the gun and grabs my jaw in a viselike grip. His other hand grabs the knife off the deck and teases. Slowly he runs the back of the blade up and down, over my t-shirt, throat to belly. He's ready to satisfy the sick perversion running through his veins.

CHAPTER SEVENTY-FOUR

I look away from the savagery in Mauldin's eyes and wait for it. I see Jimmy, with fear in his eyes come over and tug at Mauldin's shoulder to stop. Mauldin flinches, grabs the .38, yanks around and sticks it in Jimmy's face.

Do something, Natalie. Say something.

"Mauldin. You still think Jimmy's got that half million waiting for you in Heyward?"

Mauldin shakes with rage and cocks the gun.

I ask cooly, "What about that half million?"

Mauldin turns back to me, drops the gun, and lays the knife against my neck. "I'm going to cut you now. And I'm gonna start here." He squeezes my cheeks and lays the blade to my lips. "You scared now? Huh? Goddamn, this is what I live for. The fear. The crying." He frowns. "Why aren't you crying?"

"You know if you finish me off, you're going to be top dog on Old Man Denny's shit list. You're public enemy number one. His assassins will track you down and cut you up. Those guys don't play nice. You know that, don't you?"

"Stop right there," says Holly, leaning over for the .38 at Mauldin's side. But he sees her in time, rolls off me, gets to the gun and jumps up, aiming at her. "Welcome to the party, little girl."

I jump up, yanking the jeans up. He grabs my arm. "I'm not finished with you."

"You better shoot me now or let me go. But if you kill me, you don't stand a chance."

He grips and regrips the gun. He wipes his nose in frustration. He turns to Jimmy and Holly. "Denny will have no issue with me killing you two." Points the blue .38 at them. Jimmy's hands go up, pleading for his life. Holly just shrugs.

Mauldin turns the gun on me. "You believe in God?"

"I do."

"Well, good. Cuz you're gonna get your chance to meet him." I hold my breath, thinking and wishing I knew prayers. With all my advanced homeschooling, the Bible or prayers were never part of it.

Mauldin smirks.

I've run out of providence. My eyes slowly close, waiting for it.

A gull screams overhead. The Bonnie Lynne's horn blasts once, twice; engines rumble; she bumps slightly. My eyes fly open in time to see the flash. Again and again and again, four shots flashing before me. Mauldin frowns. One more blast and flash. Then *click, click, click*. Our stares collide. The next blast comes not from the little blue .38. No. It comes from a big black gun, much louder.

Mauldin buckles and falls over staring up at me confusion etched in his face. Holly walks over and puts one more into his head. "Compliments of Ray Waters."

It's the first time I've ever really seen a genuine smile from her.

She grins. "Ray Waters' gun. He didn't need it no more." Then she breaks out in song. "Ding-dong, the witch is dead, the wicked witch is dead."

So uncharacteristic of her.

The night is calm now, cool, fog-bound. We stand, staring at Mauldin's body without a word. Jimmy picks up the little blue .38 and gives it a look. "Blanks." He smiles at me. "Did you know?"

I shake my head.

"I did," Holly says. "When you gave it to me, I recognized them in the cylinder."

My jaw drops, remembering when Barlow showed up in my kitchen. Didn't trust giving me a loaded gun. He wasn't stupid. Giving a scared naked girl a loaded gun? "He left it on the counter that morning. I just dropped it in my tote bag without giving it much thought."

CHAPTER SEVENTY-FIVE

A strange calm comes over us, ethereal and ghostly. The end of an awful dream. We exchange silent glances when the ship jostles. A distant clang and the sound of water lapping against its side. A weak sound of thumping.

Jimmy runs fingers through his hair, smiles, lights a cigarette and stares at the body for a minute before leaving. "See you around, kid."

"Jimmy." I grab his arm. "You did this. This is all your fault. Look what your stupid, selfish greed did. People are dead because of you."

"My plan was solid. It was you, Runner. You screwed everything up. This is all on you."

"God, you really know how to spin bullshit, don't you?"

"I'm a lightweight compared to you, honey."

"How will you explain this to Henry's father when he gets here? Any idea how you're going to handle his son being dead?"

The thumping, closer.

"I can handle the old man. What do you care, anyway?"

"He got me on this boat with my friends. He's a good man who had a bad son."

"Why?"

"Why what?"

"How is he indebted to you?"

"I don't know why."

"You got his son killed, Runner. If it hadn't been for you driving him crazy for revenge, he'd still be alive."

"Ha. That's going to be a hard sell, Jimbo."

We stand silent, listening to harbor sounds through the fog. The heady, damp smell of brine carried in on the ocean breeze is invigorating. The soft thumping moves closer.

Jimmy lights up.

"I don't know what to do, Jimmy. I don't know where I fit into this mess."

He can only stare into the night, flicking ash. Holly folds her arms and leans back on a ladder.

The ship moves. We're actually pulling away.

The thumping emerges slowly out of the gray mist. Two figures, barely visible.

Jimmy and I share a glance at the thumping, more definite now.

Gotta be Mister Gerald Denny.

They materialize, the two men. I squint. One a deranged-looking mess of a man, wild-eyed, hate-filled, hobbling on a crutch—*thump, thump*—struggling with each step. The other is in a trench coat with gun in hand.

Jimmy and I straighten up. Holly has no such concern. She lounges on the ladder.

The man on the crutch grabs the gun from his associate and thumps forward, clearly visible now. Sopping wet, his foot wrapped in bloody bandages. In the same wine-stained white shirt from the hideaway.

Henry Denny.

Jimmy steps forward. "Henry, we were expecting your father. But it's good to see you."

Henry's fierce, angry stare is fury on display. He studies us intently. Then, shifts focus on me.

"Henry," I whisper. "Good to see you're okay. Sorry about the foot."

Jimmy steps over next to me. "We were worried about you. It's good to see you're okay."

No emotion as he raises the gun with a shaking hand. He's delirious and in poor shape.

"Don't do this, Henry," Jimmy says. "You don't have to do this. Your foot will heal. You don't want to go to prison if you do this."

Henry sees Mauldin dead on the deck. Then he turns the gun on Jimmy and fires. "I'm killing all of you." His next shot misses Holly who was caught off guard but launched off the ladder just in time. Her gun falls to the deck as she leaps for cover.

I'm next.

He hops forward. Stares me in the face, teetering and grinning. He wipes drool from his mouth. "So, who wins, Runner?"

I give the gun a long hard look. How to answer? I go for what I feel. "He who forgives first wins, Henry."

The stare-down is interrupted by running feet—Zacharie and friends. "FBI," he yells, grabbing the gun from Henry's hand. Two other agents are with him, one disarming trench coat man and the other searching for Jimmy.

Holly and I scatter.

. . .

I make it to the bridge to retrieve the tote. Captain Costa is with a tall, broad-shouldered man who is looking down over the ship, concerned about the sounds of gunshots. They both turn when I run bust in.

I go light-headed. My heart flutters when the tall man comes at me with his hands out. I back up, bumping against the wall. He looks into my eyes as if I mean something to him. His big hands pull my hips to his. I touch his face to see if it's really him. He runs fingers through my hair and touches my swollen face. The blood and bruises don't seem to bother him.

"No. No. This can't be true."

"I see you're still doing things your way, Ruckus."

I push away with the tote and run as fast as I can.

CHAPTER SEVENTY-SIX

Gasping for breath, coughing, and dragging myself out of the water with the sodden heavy tote bag, I crawl up onto dry land and roll over on my back, shaking. "I made it. Oh, my God, I made it."

Twenty feet ahead on a sandy rise, staring down at me, sits Holly.

"Damn, girl. How long you been here?"

"Bout a half hour. Waitin' on you to show up."

I cough and chuckle. "Well, I'm happy to see you made it. I figured those gawd-awful neon leggings would attract some big fish thinking he'd found dinner."

She laughs and throws a glob of sand at me. "You surprise me, Runner. Thought you might not make it. You ought to see yourself. You're going to be hard-pressed to get a date looking like that. You're a perfect lead for a horror movie."

"Shut up." I touch a lip. "I don't care about men right now. I think I just saw one I should have wrapped up and taken home long ago. Not sure he was real though."

"What do you mean?"

I lie back and look up into the clearing sky. "Never mind, Holly. You wouldn't believe me if I told you."

"You must be in love with that tote to drag it through the water like you did."

"You understand why, don't you?"

"Yeah. I know."

After catching my breath, my teeth chatter, and I tremble. "I'm so tired of being c-c-cold."

Holly bends for a closer look at my face. "That nose looks broken. How's your teeth?"

I run my tongue around and shake my head. "So far, none broken. Oh. Maybe one." I feel my nose. It hurts.

With the storm's passing, a slight breeze lies over us. We huddle together for warmth, sitting on the buoy rings we used to get to shore.

"Tell me what happened back there, Holly. How are we sitting here alive like this? Did you see Jimmy? Think he made it? Or is he on his way to Tahiti?"

"He's a con man. They're like cockroaches. They know where to hide. And when to come out."

We sit quietly, too tired to say much, just watching the lights of the Bonnie Lynne fade in the distance.

"What now, Runner?"

"Well. Let's start by calling me Natalie."

She laughs. "But you're so good at running."

I sigh and punch her in the arm. "What are you gonna do, Holly?"

"Tahiti, I think sounds good."

"Really?"

"You got the islands in my head."

"How you gonna get there?"

"I'll figure it out."

Minutes pass. With Tahiti on my mind, I look over at her and push the tote bag over. "Here, take this."

Her look is deadpan. "I don't need it."

"I don't care if you need it or not. I want you to do me a favor. We're going to split up. Right?"

"Yeah. So?"

"You know where The Coffee Bean is in Danfield?

She nods.

"Take it there. Lorraine is the owner. Give it to her. Tell her it's from me. Natalie Grace. Don't take any guff from her. Tell her I insist. She'll understand."

Without questions, she takes the tote with a nod. After a few minutes and short goodbyes, she's gone. Watching her walk away, I laugh at the memory of first meeting her. "Holly Hangloose."

We'll girl, what have you got to say for yourself?

"Dad!"

I'm proud of you, girl. This was a real test. You've grown. Done things your own way.

I stare at him in his jeans and plaid flannel shirt, the breeze in his hair. "Dad, you started to say something about Mother when we were interrupted in the storage room."

Oh yeah, about my cancer. Yeah, I knew you were going to leave me after the fire. So, what did I have to live for?

"Oh, Dad."

Three losses of loved ones are more than anyone should have to tolerate. I couldn't take another one. You leaving. So, I decided my time was up.

"Three losses? What do you mean, three?"

Lorraine was my first love. We met at Berkley, long before your mother. A heavenly whirlwind relationship it was. We planned on sharing our souls for eternity.

"What happened?"

Fate is what happened. We had a child. It broke us up.

"What?"

Yeah, I moved to Vermont, found your mother after that. She was new destiny. I vowed to never lose her in spite of her frailties.

"Child? What child? Where is she or him now?"

Pediatric cancer at two months.

"Oh, Dad. You guys lived with that for the rest of your lives. I never knew. God, why didn't you tell me?"

Because of what your mother told you one drunken night. Told you you were an unwelcome pregnancy. You were only five. You've struggled with thinking you were an unloved child ever since. We didn't want you to suffer with more news family tragedy.

"So you lost Lorraine, a baby, and then Mother. But you kept in touch with Lorraine through letters while you were with Mother."

Yes, but not for any romantic lingering.

But Sunshine wrote letters also.

Sunshine took up writing the letters later on. The one you found was the last letter written. Sunshine's.

I nod. "Did you ever meet her, Dad? Sunshine."

He taps his pipe against his teeth in deep contemplation. Hesitation. *Never face-to-face, Natalie. But, yeah. You could say I had something to do with her.*

Poof. He's gone.

I get up, brush myself off and walk into a new life.

CHAPTER SEVENTY-SEVEN

Vaitape, Bora Bora. Five years later.

As the sun dips into the warm, peaceful waters of the Pacific, a vacationing tour group unloads from a sunset cruise boat and marches in for dinner.

Tahiti something less than I thought it would be. So after a year of working in Papeete, I discovered Bora Bora. The laid-back pure island paradise I've always longed for.

The maître d' shows the party of six to their table with his scripted lines. "Welcome to Mary's Beach Bar, the crown jewel of French Polynesia entertainment, wine, and cuisine. We sincerely desire to serve your every dining wish."

After polishing wine glasses I lean over at the end of the bar and chuckle to my friend. "Don't you love Charles trying to make this tiki bar sound first-class?"

The server comes back and lays the drink order on the bar for me to fill. Minutes later, he does his flamboyant strut back to their table with Polynesian cocktails and Shirley Temples.

I wipe my hands and slip down the bar across from her sitting with a rum punch. She's thumbing over her phone and chewing on the stir stick. Her silky blonde hair falls over a fashionably tattered Laguna Beach t-shirt. The gaudy-colored leggings are contrary to her subdued personality.

"Hungry?" I ask.

"Yeah. But I'll wait for Hayden."

I chew on a cherry. "Can you believe it's been five years, Holly?"

"Seems like only yesterday."

Think back to those years, I wipe at the bar and throw the towel over my shoulder. "Since Hayden got here, time has flown, hasn't it?"

She nods. "What made you change your mind about him, Natalie?"

"That lawyer business, I guess. But once he got it out of his system, he turned into a decent guy. But too late for us. He's a better match for you anyway."

She plays with her glass in thought. "And here we are, married. Who'd a thunk it? Me and Hayden sittin' in a tree..."

We watch the big vacation family laughing and enjoying the warm evening breeze. Holly gives me a wondering gaze. "You really headed back to the States, Nat?"

"Think so. I've had enough of this pure blue-water paradise and beautiful sunsets for a while."

"Where to?"

"Not sure yet. Somewhere with some action. Not quiet and serene every day like it is here."

"What about Jonathan? Made up your mind about him?"

"Oh, I think he died in that pool that day. He just keeps showing up, though. It seems so real when he does."

"Well, you seem fine now after you got that schizophrenia nonsense out of your system."

"Well, maybe I'll go back and meet up with Lorraine. She and Sunshine are the only family I have." I think about them in their little coffee cafe in Danfield. "But I don't know about California, Holly. I'd also like to find that redheaded pimp though. I hope he's still alive so I can kill him. Then I'll find a place to settle down. Maybe look for Peter."

"Peter?"

"Uh huh, yeah. Pete Longer. The guy who helped us board the Bonnie Lynne that rainy day. Remember?

She nods and sips her drink.

"I'd love to see him again and his little girl. But he's no doubt found a comfortable life under the radar where he won't be found unless he wants to. Looking him up wouldn't be good."

A sunburned young tourist comes sauntering in looking full of himself. The surfer type. A knockout and he knows it. I catch his eye. He settles on a stool two down from Holly; his deep blue eyes studying us. He's certain his looks and charm make girls like us a sure thing for the evening. Which one of us will he take to bed tonight?

But he finally notices the ring on Holly's finger and turns and concentrates on me like I'm the entrée for the evening. Holly and I exchange a knowing glance. She slides off the stool and leans over in my ear. "Good night, Nat. Make sure his gun is loaded with blanks."

I nod and touch my temple. "Let's thank Barlow for the memory." We share knowing grins as she walks away.

He notices the exchange, flips his long blonde hair back and grins with the cutest dimples. "What was that all about?"

"Inside joke. My way of stirring things up."

"Are you good at stirring things up?"

"Oh, yeah. You could say that. It's just my way."

"Your way?"

I chew on the stir stick and give him my best flirty smile. "I just want you to know what you're getting into tonight, mister."

"I know what I'm getting into, Ruckus."

ACKNOWLEDGMENTS

I want to thank the following for their valuable knowledge, care, and expertise in making this book a success.

Doug Kurtz, Development editing

Judy Roth, Copy editing

Rosie Walker, Proofing

Damonza, Cover design

Dana Kaye, Marketing

And special thanks go out to my readers. You know who you are.

ALSO BY CHET BAKER

BLOODLINE RUN 2022

Kirkus Reviews —"The faint of heart should probably stay away, but fans of dark, cerebral horror tales will likely enjoy unraveling this one. A gripping, fast-pace, devious psychological thriller Jekyll-and-Hyde–inspired mystery chock full of reversals and complications." with delusion, fear, and desperation. A hunt for redemption.

www.ingramcontent.com/pod-product-compliance
Lightning Source LLC
Chambersburg PA
CBHW072051190726
48294CB00005B/1465